In the Devil's Territory

in the
devil's
territory
stories

Kyle Minor

DZANC
BOOKS

**DZANC
BOOKS**

1334 Woodbourne Street
Westland, MI 48186

www.dzancbooks.org

Earlier versions of some of these stories originally appeared in *The Southern Review*, *The Gettysburg Review*, and *Best American Mystery Stories 2008*. "goodbye Hills, hello night" won the 2005 Tara M. Kroger Prize for Short Fiction.

Published 2008 by Dzanc Books
Book design by Steven Seighman

06 07 08 09 10 11 5 4 3 2 1
First Edition June 2008

ISBN – 13: 978-0-9793123-6-6
ISBN – 10: 0-9793123-6-1

Printed in the United States of America

Contents

to Deborah Jayne

"It seemed to him that this dark quarter of death and assignation would go on and on whispering to him secrets he did not want to hear as long as he had the strength to listen."
—William Gay

The San Diego County Credit Union Poinsettia Bowl Party

I hate Christmas, but this year is different because there is a small chance my wife will die and take our unborn child with her. It's hard, this December 19th, to imagine that this could be so. Bed rest has become routine, as had last week's hospitalization, at least by the third day. I bring her food. We eat, we talk, we watch television, all as though we were not only days removed from early morning bleeding, 911, the orange ambulance, triage, the high-risk ward of Labor & Delivery, our growing acquaintance with the vast, blocks-long labyrinth of the Ohio State University Medical Center. Then wheelchairs, steroids to promote fetal lung development, then doctor's orders: fifteen weeks home bed rest.

"What I want," she says, "is some ice cream. Vanilla, on top of a brownie, with hot fudge microwaved and melted over top, and some crushed almonds on top of that."

What I object to is the specificity of the request. "The over-specificity," I say. "Ice cream I can do. Brownies I can do." I don't like to prepare food.

"If it was you," she says, "I would do whatever you wanted. Anything."

"If it was me I wouldn't tell you how to prepare the food."

"But I would," she says. "I would buy avocados and make sure they were just firm enough, and I would chop up onions and tomatoes and squeeze lemons and hand-agitate everything, bring you up trays of chips and guacamole and Coca Cola and apple sauce with cinnamon sprinkled on top."

I believe all this to be true, and though it is no good excuse, I am worn out, and I am starting to resent the many trips up and down the stairs to bring her things. "It's true you would do all those things," I say, "but I wouldn't ask you to do them. And if I was going to send you downstairs to get something, I would give you a list, so you could go downstairs and get everything I needed all at once. I wouldn't wait until you came back up the stairs and then say, 'Oh, but there's one more thing,' or, 'thank you for the rice and gravy but now could you bring me some salt?'"

She goes silent, and I know that I have hurt her and that she is rightfully angry and wonder what kind of connection there might be between her emotions and her body, and then I wonder if I am right now killing our baby, killing her.

There is so much to wonder, and my mind is full of the talk the doctors have been talking—placenta previa, foreshortened cervix, cervical funneling, uterine tearing, uterine contractions, uterine bleeding, the mucus plug—and there she is, lying on the bed in my black sleep pants, the only pants in the house that do not irritate her belly, and she is steaming angry.

"What if," I say, "I make you some ice cream and put it over the brownie and crush some almonds and sprinkle them on top." Because despite all, I can't bring myself to open the refrigerator and take the glass bottle with the cold and near-hardened fudge and fight out the fudge with a spoon and take a second glass bowl from the cupboard and dump the fudge in the bowl and microwave it and try to figure out how to microwave it just long enough that it is warm and nearly hot but not runny or watery. Not when I have to at the same time cut and warm the brownie, then take the ice cream from the freezer and make two shapely scoops and crush the almonds.

"Don't bother," she says. "Forget it." But then she says, "How hard is it to just take the extra effort and make the ice cream the way I like the ice cream? If I could go downstairs and do it, I would do it, and I would make you some, too, but I can't, and it's eating me up inside, and it just seems like I need it."

"But just you need it one certain way?"

"Some pregnant women," she says, "need pickles." Her first pregnancy, what she needed was she-crab soup, and the only place to get it was one particular restaurant in Georgetown, South Carolina, where she had once lived with her brother, which was all well and good, except that then we lived in Florida. That year we found a reason to go to Georgetown, South Carolina—a bodybuilding show on the marine base at Parris Island, where her brother was the emcee, where I was going to do some immersion journalism—and we brought home enough she-crab soup to last the winter and then the spring.

So I say all right, I'll do it, but then coming down the stairs I see my parents watching with my three-year-old son Owen, and they look tired, too. When I called my mother two weeks ago to say that we had rushed Brenda to the hospital, she was in Florida, recovering from major surgery—removal of a massive fibroid uterine cyst and then hysterectomy—and my father was in Arizona, overseeing construction of a retail pet store. It was six o'clock in the morning when I called her, and by midnight she and my father were at the Port Columbus airport, renting a car, driving it to our house. By then, Owen had been in and out of the first floor emergency room—flu, vomiting, diarrhea, dehydration—and I had spent most of the afternoon there with him, there on the first floor, all the while wondering about Brenda, alone on the sixth floor, and whether they would take the 23-week fetus—no, the baby, our son—by

C-section, and whether he would survive, and then that flood of words: retinopathy, lung damage, brain damage . . .

My father is helping Owen put together a Winnie the Pooh puzzle, though it seems as though my father is doing all the work. The television is on, and it has been on nearly every waking hour since my parents arrived. Owen wants the television tuned to the cable channel Noggin at all times, a steady diet of brain candy I fear will rot his synapses, though, for now, my mother has prevailed by way of Food TV. Owen is three years old and can read already, but he prefers TV, even Food TV. My mother is leaned back in the recliner, reading her Betty Crocker CookBook, and I say, "Mom, if you're reading, could we just turn the TV off for awhile?" and she doesn't say anything, which I take— wrongly—for consent. I turn off the television, and then she says, "It's easy for you to say there's too much TV when I'm the one watching him all day."

She has been complaining that Owen has been a child less calm and manageable than he usually is. "He's just overstimulated, Mom," I say. "We've seen this before. If the TV's on all the time, he gets all wired."

"He's been watching his cartoons all day," she says. "I can't just sit here in silence. I need my TV, too."

My father is not saying anything. He wants all this to blow over. He wants us to stop talking. We've been here before, under less stressful circumstances.

"I can turn it back on," I say. "It's not anything personal to you."

She holds up her hand. "I don't want to talk about it," she says.

"Yeah, but you did talk about it," I say, and though I know I shouldn't: "You always talk about it. You say your say, throw your sucker punch, then don't let me have mine."

By now her head is buried deep in her Betty Crocker cookbook, and if she is listening to what I am saying, she is giving no indication. What happens now, if experience is any indication, is I keep talking and trying to get her to talk, and she responds with silence or leaves the room. Her silence is a balloon of finite elasticity filling rapidly with my anger.

My father is not looking at me, either. The way this has always worked is: In any dispute, anytime, anywhere in the world, my father will take my side, unless my mother is involved, in which case the only solution will be that I modify my behavior to her pleasure.

The television off, my son has turned his attention to the puzzle, which he is happily piecing together. I have won the battle of the television, and I have given my mother what I thought she wanted, which was a quiet grandchild to watch, but that's not what she seems to have wanted at all. She wanted to watch television, and she did not want me to tell her what to do. I resolve to know that she is a deeply selfish person and that, even at thirty, I am a child too open to wounding.

I go into the kitchen and take the ice cream from the freezer and make three scoops, fully round, into the bowl. Then I cut a brownie from the pan my mother has made and put it in a second bowl and take the glass bottle of fudge from the refrigerator and open it and try to pour some from the bottle onto the brownie, but it is hardened in the bottle. I tap it with my fingers and then my fist, trying to loosen the fudge as one would loosen ketchup from the Heinz 57 bottle, but it will not loosen.

There is nothing any glass bottle of fudge has done to anger anyone, so far as I can tell. Not throughout all time. But what I want to do is take that glass bottle of fudge and smash it against the linoleum of the kitchen floor, or throw it through the kitchen window. Instead I set it down too hard against the tile counter, and it does not break or even make a sound loud enough to satisfy whatever it is inside me that needs satisfied.

My father is standing behind me, now, in the kitchen, and he says, "She is hurting."

I turn to face him, and the look on his face is a familiar look of disappointment, the kind I believe myself capable of bringing. "Brenda?" I say.

"Your mom," he says.

"I didn't mean to hurt her," I say, but what I really mean is that I didn't want to hurt him, or bring him again into the ongoing conflict between my mother and myself, a conflict that has brought him pain for the last twenty years, a conflict that everyone pretends does not exist, and which sometimes, thanks to our pretending, seems not to exist, until something small happens, like the turning off of a television, or a wisecrack about the Cherry Road Baptist Church, or about the relative immaculacy of the conception of Mary or the Christ child, or a tongue loosened by some false comfort to saying one of the marginally blue words—suck, crap, hell, and so on—that take on varying levels of gravity depending upon whether they reach my ears or my mother's.

"I don't mean you hurt her," my father says. "I mean she's hurting. Down there." Her hysterectomy.

"Oh," I say. The bottle of fudge is in my hand, and I begin to catalogue my selfishnesses, and the list is long and unyielding.

"Cut her some slack," he says.

I want to tell him to tell her to cut me some slack, except that my philosophy teachers trained me in logic, which requires a dispassionate sort of sorting-out, and my writing teachers have trained me in empathy, which requires some attempt at figuring out what grievances, needs, wants, desires, fears, and habits of mind cause other people to do and think and say the things and ways they do.

So here's the scorecard. My wife: bored; scared; in danger of bleeding to death; lying as still as she can in the hope that she can keep our child in her womb long enough to keep him alive. My mother: angry from years-old grievances I can't help but continue to inflame despite the fact that she has traveled eighteen-hundred miles to take care of my child and my household in the aftermath of surgery to remove her childbearing organs and a fibroid cyst larger than the child my wife is carrying. Me: nursing perceived wounds from childhood; resentful of overly specific ice cream requests.

I tell my father okay, I'll cut her some slack. I go into the living room and tell my mother I am sorry, that I have been unreasonable, and I leave out all the parts about how unreasonable I know her to have been. Back in the kitchen I consider that part of my motivation for apologizing and not entirely articulating the grievances I fully and truly want to articulate is that I don't want my parents to leave. If they leave, how will I manage the house? If they leave, will my wife's elderly and altogether more difficult parents come and try to help me manage the house?

By now, the ice cream is getting soft, so I put it back in the freezer and go to work again on the fudge, which has not and will not, it seems, go soft enough to pour. The spoon works better. I spoon some chunks of hardened fudge onto the brownie and then put the whole thing in the microwave for fifteen seconds. I'm not pleased with the results, but now I suddenly have to go to the bathroom with great urgency, and the bathroom is upstairs, so I pull the still soft ice cream from the freezer and dump it on top of the brownies and the not-warm fudge, and then I crush some almonds and throw them on top and rush upstairs the ugly mess I've made in the brownie bowl upstairs and hand it to my wife in her sickbed and rush to the bathroom and shut the door and stay longer than I know I should, because it is quiet in there, and if you turn on the fan you can no longer hear any of the sounds or voices from the rest of the house, and because there is a biography of the abstract impressionist painter Willem de Kooning on top of the water tank, and it has pictures, and they are complicated and lovely.

When I am finished, I wash my hands and splash some cold water onto my eyes. In the bedroom, Brenda is finishing her ice cream. There are tears in her eyes.

I sit down beside her. "The ice cream's not *that* good, I'd say. I know because I did a half-assed job making it."

"I don't know if I'm going to make it to Christmas," she says. She doesn't say it in any kind of over-emotional way, despite the tears. It's matter-of-fact. She's saying what's likely.

I don't contradict her.

"It's December 19," she says, "and we haven't even decorated the tree."

"That's fine by me," I say, because I don't like Christmas, and most of all I don't like Christmas decorations, because when I was growing up, my mother started thinking about hers around June 1, amid a red, white, and blue house already announcing our nation's independence a full month early, and around which time she was also preparing fall decorations—a leaves-changing theme despite the fact that the leaves in Florida did not ever change—and Halloween decorations and Thanksgiving decorations. Around the first of every month, my father put a ladder underneath the trapdoor leading to the attic and brought down a new set of cardboard boxes full of lights and front porch flags and handmade and overly bright wooden knickknacks bought at craft fairs, and then hauled up the old set.

"Owen," she says, "is three and a half years old. This is the first time he'll understand what's going on. This might be the first Christmas he remembers."

"But tonight," I say, "is the San Diego County Credit Union Poinsettia Bowl," the first college football bowl game in a season in which I have resolved to watch every one, and she has agreed to this plan, too, because I have only learned to love college football because she loved it first, because it was something we could enjoy together.

"But tonight," she says, "might be all the Christmas we're going to get."

"But, Brenda," I say. "It's Texas Christian against Northern Illinois," and now she's laughing, out of courtesy, maybe, but also because she likes me, even though or maybe because I am a person who cannot get excited about Christmas but who can get excited about Texas Christian and Northern Illinois and a sham of a bowl game, sponsored by the bank for county employees in a city neither of us has ever visited.

"Never mind, then," she says, "about the Christmas decorations," and I say, "Yes, forget Christmas. Tonight we celebrate the San Diego County Credit Union."

Then I go downstairs and announce it to my parents. Tonight we celebrate the San Diego County Credit Union. Then I go to the basement and sort through the boxes and find the artificial Christmas tree, in its boxes, and the strings of white lights, and the red ornaments, and the stockings with our names on them, and the red Santa Claus hat we've always used as a tree-topper rather than a star.

By time I reach the top of the basement stairs, my father says, "You serious about this?" and I say, yes, we're doing it up big-time, and I send him to the store with a list of things Brenda likes to eat, and he buys things my mother likes, too.

The game starts at eight o'clock, and at seven I go upstairs and tell her what he's bought—the Tostitos and all the ingredients for the cream cheese and salsa dip she likes—and she says, joking, "What about the crab legs?" and I know that she is joking because she really wants them and knows she will not have them, and I also know that the Giant Eagle supermarket across the street will steam crab legs on the spot—ten minutes, max—so I go across the street and order the snow crabs she likes, and extra sticks of butter to make the dipping sauce she likes. Then I see them: in rows, by the checkout line, miniature poinsettias in pots wrapped in red foil. Beautiful poinsettias, their leaves of deepest red, a color hardly imaginable on a living thing in Columbus, Ohio, in winter. I buy two of them.

Quarter to eight, I walk in the back door, see my father standing in the kitchen, mixing the cream cheese and the salsa and putting the chips out on a serving tray. I set the bucket of crab legs down on the tile counter and set out a glass bowl and drop in a stick of butter and start it melting in the microwave. In the living room my mother is dozing on one side of the couch. From the kitchen, my father yells, "I'll wake her."

"No, don't."

"No, she wants me to. Trust me."

Upstairs, Owen is chattering at Brenda. When he sees me, he holds out something he has made of his Legos. "A tower," I say. "Air traffic control tower," Brenda says. "Airplanes," Owen says.

"You want to come downstairs?" She hasn't been downstairs for a week.

She doesn't hesitate. "Yes." I help her up, and we tell Owen we're going to build a Christmas tree, and he runs down the stairs ahead of us.

We make it in time for kickoff, and I help her settle in the couch recliner, beside my mother, and soon they are both draped in blankets. The poinsettias rest above the television. My father and I bring out the trays of chips and dip, and both of them are dipping their crab legs into the butter sauce by time Texas Christian scores their first touchdown.

Owen helps me sort the plastic branches of the artificial tree. They are coded by colored tape wrapped around the twisted aluminum base of each bough, and he takes pleasure in the sorting, and even more, perhaps, in the new knowledge that he is a person who can sort. He looks up at my wife, my mother, my father, me, and says, "Look at me," and there is pleasure for each of us in looking at him, and in letting him know we are looking at him, and somehow, for me, at least, there is a pleasure in our doing it together. For the first time in my life, I am enjoying putting together the Christmas tree, and then, stringing the lights, I am caught. My father says, "You're enjoying this," and my first impulse is to say that I am not, but this, whatever it is, is good enough that I don't want to ruin it, and it strikes me that the impulse to ruin it at all is childish, wrong.

"I am enjoying it," I say, and my son is handing me the red ornaments, and I wonder in that moment why my mother and father aren't guiding the experience—*put this one here, that one there*—the way they always have, and it's not a stretch to chalk their restraint up to a kind of generosity.

This high doesn't last long. Before the end of the first quarter, Brenda is doubled over with pain. Contractions again, and I help her upstairs and into bed, and she sets again to drinking the water that seems to have helped her ease them nights previous, and she stares again at no fixed point near the ceiling and tries to clear her mind of any distraction so that she might again fool her body into the quiet necessary to keep the baby inside her.

My mother's pain, too, moves her upstairs, to our guest bedroom, and by the start of the second quarter they are settled, and it is my father, my son, and me, left with a football game that does not seem half so sweet in their absence. My son is too young to understand, and my father and I are too proud to articulate, how fragile life itself has come to seem, and there is no way I can imagine to keep this awareness front and center where it belongs. There is recycling to separate from trash, and orange trash stickers to affix to trash cans, and dishes to wash, and laundry to dry and fold, and, somehow, we must find a way to air the smell of crab legs from the living room and kitchen. For now, we sit on the couch and watch the young men throw their bodies against one another and watch my son crash his toy trucks into each other, and whistle low when one hits another the wrong way and causes the kind of damage no one could have foreseen.

A Day Meant to Do Less

Reverend Jack Wenderoth carried his mother into the bathroom and sat her on the closed toilet lid, and then he began to undress her. She was wearing her threadbare old housedress, the red one that she had worn when he was a child and which had now faded to pink. He had bought her gowns, bathrobes, cotton pajamas, other housedresses, but she would not wear them. She said no by making sounds in the back of her throat. The sounds were terrible, the sounds someone made when she was dying. Which she was.

He knelt at her feet. Her body slumped and her shoulders tilted to the left, toward the sink and the table that held it and the sharp Formica edgework. He raised himself from his knees and reached up and righted her. Her eyes were alert but not bright. He noticed that he was avoiding them. He noticed that he was noticing himself quite a bit and her not so much. It took effort not to notice her, but it was hard on him to notice her. It required him to acquaint himself with the droop of her face's left side, the gurgling sound her throat made involuntarily, and worst of all the foul smell of her body. He had noticed the smell a few minutes earlier and that's why he was undressing her.

He did not want to undress her. It was the first time he had undressed her. His wife Julie usually undressed her. His mother used to say, when they were young and courting, *Jack and Julie, like the song*. It was not a song he knew. He knew Jack and Jill, the nursery rhyme she had sung to him when

he was a boy, to the tune of "The Yellow Rose of Texas."
His hands were on her shoulders, righting her, and yet he
was touching her with as little of himself as he could. His
own body was so far from hers that righting her with his
hands made his back and shoulders ache.

He thought he should maybe hold her for a minute.
She was watching him with those eyes. He thought maybe
she did not want him to hold her. He did not know if she
wanted him to wash her. She was not making the noises,
and she knew why they were in the bathroom. He had told
her. To hold her he would have to straddle her with his legs.
He was very aware of the proximity, already, of his parts to
hers. When he was small he would lay his head in her lap
and she would stroke his hair, and when he turned twelve
he tried to lay his head in her lap so she would stroke his
hair and she said there would be no more of that. When he
asked her why she said, "Because you're too old now."

So he stood for another moment, righting her but
not holding her. He said, "Mother, I'm going to take off
your shoes and socks now, all right?"

Her lips moved but not to form a word. He thought
what she was giving was permission. He couldn't be sure,
but the smell of her was all over him. He took his hands
from her shoulders. She did not topple. He knelt again and
though he did not want to, he wanted to: he put his fingers
to his nose and smelled them. They smelled like her body.
She was not looking down at him. He did not want her to
see that he was smelling his fingers. He was ashamed of the
act and he did not know why. No one had seen except him.

"Your shoes, mother," he said. He had never called
her mother, not in his whole life. He called her mama, or,
later, mom. When he was very young he called her mommy,
but he had not for a long time. His father had called her
Francine, and everyone else called her Franny. She was

wearing house slippers, fairly new ones he had bought for her. They were rubber soled, but they were lined with furry cotton. She could not wear them in the winter because they built up a charge and she gave and received a shock whenever she was touched.

He took the slippers from her feet. Then he began to pull at the toe of the black sock on her right foot. She made the gurgling sound. No. He let go of the sock.

"Does it hurt, mother?" he said.

She did not say anything.

"Does it hurt?"

Nothing.

He stood again and looked at her in the eyes. Mother. "Mom," he said, more kindly. "Does it hurt?"

She winked her right eyelid, twice. Slowly. That was something new.

"I saw that, Mom," he said. "Can you do it again? I want to be sure."

She winked the eyelid again, twice, slow. Then she lost control of it and it began to twitch.

"Well, that's something," he said, but mostly to himself. "Okay," he said, to himself, but then, louder, for her: "Okay."

She did it a third time, the eyelid, maybe to affirm her yes, maybe to stop the twitching. "I see it," he said. "I don't want to hurt you," he said. "I'm going to wash you now. I'm going to do it, but not if you don't want me to. I'm going to take that sock off by unrolling it from the top, all right?"

A fourth time she blinked twice. A regular conversation.

He knelt again. This time he began at the top of the sock, and unrolled it slowly down her calf. When he touched her there, he could feel the muscle contract a little. Her skin was cold. He unrolled the sock to her heel. Then he put his other hand beneath her foot and lifted it. He was careful around the heel to stretch the fabric, but when he reached the arch of her foot she made the gurgling sound again, and he stopped. She inhaled sharply. He was hurting his mother.

The sock had to come off. He tried again, this time stretching the fabric as carefully around the arch as he had around the heel. When sock cleared skin, he saw something like a rash, a reddish-purple blemish that covered most of the arch, surrounded by a deep yellowish-purple ring, a deep, deep bruise.

"Mom," he said, "you've got a nasty sore down here. On the arch of your foot. It's bruised. It's a bad one."

He patted her calf to reassure her, but she tensed at his touch, so he stopped. He said, "The other one now, Mom," and began to work on the other shoe and sock.

Her silence bothered him almost as much as the throat noises had. When he was young her voice was a constant, a drone that must have been the same kind of comfort for her that the television had been for him, in college, when he was lonely and could not sleep without the sound of it. When he was young she chattered and what mattered to her—he could see it now, for the first time— what mattered to her was not the content of her talk, but just its continuation. He remembered something his sister Millie had often said about her, uncharitably—*she just talks to hear the sound of her own voice*—but that wasn't true, not entirely. Her voice, which had irritated him so often, especially in his adolescence, when he began to think of her as being more and more ignorant the more books he read, was now, in his memory, taking on some kind of a musical quality, a soft companionable drone.

He took off her right shoe, then began to unroll her sock, and thought that if she could talk now, about nothing—no, that was uncharitable—about, say, the shower curtains, how they were starting to yellow, and how that was the problem with translucent shower curtains, the way they yellowed so quickly and needed to be replaced so often, unlike shower curtains patterned in mostly solid colors . . . if she could talk now, and say things like this, she would be bringing comfort not only to herself, but also to him.

So he said, "Mom, have you noticed the shower curtains?" It felt forced, but he pushed on. "They're starting to yellow, and that's the problem, I think, with translucent shower curtains . . ."

The shoes and the socks were off now, and—this was most remarkable—her breathing had become less labored. Maybe he was imagining it. It was barely discernible, this change in her breathing, but it meant something to him. He heard himself saying, "Julie was thinking of buying some shower curtains to match the hand towels. Maybe something forest green, like the towels, with some purple accents," and it was automatic, this talk. It was not the talk he talked, not usually, but it was the talk that was coming from his mouth. It was received talk, like telephone hellos and goodbyes, or how are you doings and see you laters passing between half-courteous strangers on the street. He found that it comforted him the way he imagined the same kind of talk had comforted his mother. It made him uneasy even as it comforted him. He kept it up because it seemed to comfort her.

The shoes and socks were off, but that meant he would soon have to take off the housedress. He had been moving so slowly, and he knew this was why. He was about to confront his mother's nakedness. To, in a sense, be the cause of it. He considered what other tasks he might perform to delay unbuttoning the front of the housedress and sliding it from her body. He was still talking—". . . the Formica is so out of date, and Julie thinks it might be nice to refinish all the countertops in the house with tile, but that kind of work takes so much time, so I was thinking about maybe vinyl laminate . . ."—but mostly he was thinking of what else he could do, and then—of course!—he remembered the bathwater.

Julie had given him instructions before she left to pick up a few things they had left the night before at the house of their friends, the Marinos. She had said maybe two inches of water, like a bath drawn for a baby. Make the water warm, but not lukewarm, but not too hot either. Test it by dipping two fingers in the bathwater near the faucet and splashing a little on the tender skin on the inside of the arm, just below the wrist, where the crossing blue veins could be seen beneath the skin.

Or at least beneath his pale skin. He was still talking automatically, at his mother but not necessarily to her, but his mind was on his skin. He straightened and folded the black socks so he could turn his palms toward his face and get a good look at his own arms, how pale they were, how he had always hated their color. It was a color he had inherited from her. He could look beyond his arms and see the pale skin of his mother's legs. They were the same color, his arms and her legs. He wondered if she had ever hated the color of her skin and almost asked her, then thought better of it.

He was always thinking better of it, had always been thinking better of it his whole life. On Sundays he preached sermons that revealed, say, how love hurt at four o'clock in the morning when Julie was still asleep, her hair piled up on the pillow, and him knowing he had to be off to accompany the out-of-town family of an indigent killed beneath a bridge to identify the body at the morgue, and that he might not be home again until after she had awakened and gone about her day and gone back to sleep again. In those sermons he gave away parts of himself more intimate than those he was willing to share with his mother, except in that public space. He looked at his arms and her legs and wanted to tell her a closely held secret, which was that when he drove the interstates on the way to hospital visits and minister's meetings and church softball games, he often as not would play cassette tapes of black singers like Al Green or Marvin Gaye or, hell, James Brown. He'd drive down the road and let himself imagine he was himself some famous maestro of soul, be transported to what he imagined must be some run-down bar in Detroit or, who knows, Watts, some place he had never been and would never go and which for all he knew was nothing like whatever it was he was trying to imagine. But he'd be there, in the car, singing for an audience of twelve or twenty, an appreciative audience to be sure, except maybe a few drunks. And here was the centerpiece of the fantasy. The skin, his skin, would have somehow darkened to a deep brown, a skin tone he imagined would give him access to whole worlds he could never know, and one that would not embarrass him under the lights of that dirty club the way it had always embarrassed him at the beach or on the sandlots or anytime he had to wear shorts to play some ballgame or to feign comfort at some overly casual social function.

He was looking at his mother's legs, and talking about kitchen remodeling, and then without even finishing his sentence he stopped talking and began humming. At first he was not aware of what he was humming, and then he realized that what he was humming was "Sexual Healing" by Marvin Gaye. It was not a song his mother would have approved of his singing or even knowing. At once he was aware of the, oh, three dozen ironies that wrapped themselves around his choice of song to hum, of all things Freudian and Jungian, all those blowhards, that his seemingly subconscious choice of that tune might imply. The Oedipal and the—good great hell, what was he doing?

What he was doing was undressing his mother. What he was doing was *not* undressing his mother, he could see that well enough. So could she probably. He had been in the bathroom for probably fifteen minutes and had only managed to take off her socks and shoes. He had not even begun to run the bathwater.

He finished folding the socks and placed them neatly on top of the shoes and kept humming Marvin Gaye since no other tune came readily to mind and since he knew, really, it didn't mean anything, and because it was a fine tune, and because, strangely enough, his mother was starting to relax a little. He could see it in her posture and he could see it in her face.

He turned the hot and the cold knobs and tried to find the right temperature. The phone rang. He let it ring but turned off the water and stopped humming and kicked open the bathroom door with his foot so he could hear the answering machine when it picked up. Technically, he was working. But, technically, he was always working. Always on call, at least. He heard Julie's voice on the machine— . . . *we'll get back with you as soon as we can, and God bless* . . . —that last part, *God bless*, always irritating him because it was a cliché so well-worn that it didn't mean anything anymore, except it did mean something to Julie, which irritated him, too, but not so much that he would say anything to her about it.

The machine beeped, and he heard Lindsay Marino, a parishioner for whom both he and Julie had some affection. Lindsay and her husband Tom, too, a fine couple. She was saying, ". . . Art Miller, Room 319, Good Samaritan

Hospital . . ." Art was Lindsay's husband's uncle, and a real curmudgeon, the kind of guy who would invite you over to pray for his, say, lack of appetite, then get cranky when you said, "Art, buddy, I'm pretty thirsty. Would you mind if I got a glass of water from your tap?"

Art Miller, Lindsay was saying, had collapsed this morning. Right away they had thought heart attack, but it turned out to be a false alarm, some sort of panic attack that anyway felt like a heart attack, and Art wasn't himself so convinced that it wasn't. "He's asking for you," Lindsay was saying. "This is rich, really rich, Jack, but he says my prayers aren't quite enough to get him through the night. He needs the *man of God*. He keeps saying that. 'Bring me the man of God!' I thought you'd get a kick out of that. So, for serious, Jack, can you come over to Good Sam? He's driving me nuts and I need to get out of here by three so I can take Mike Junior to baseball practice."

The machine beeped again, and he looked at his mother sitting on the toilet lid and could not discern any response coming from her. He wanted to say, *Come on, momma, say something disapproving*, but of course he would not. Instead, he said it himself. "Art Miller," he said. "Now there's one guy who can wait."

Still, she did not respond, but he thought maybe it gave her some satisfaction. It gave *him* some satisfaction. And was his mother any less a member of his congregation than Art Miller? A man who was in the hospital, sure, but who was, in any case, in better health, even on this panic attack day, than she was on this or any other day. Jack could not be sure how much she was or was not engaged with all that surrounded her. Already her eyes seemed to be less alert than they had seemed when he had brought her into the bathroom, but how can a person tell, anyway, exactly what another person's eyes reveal about them? Perhaps she was growing tired, or maybe he was growing tired and looking at her eyes differently.

He turned the hot and cold knobs again and tested the water. When he had regulated the temperature to his liking, he put the stopper in the tub. Then he tested the water again with his hands, adjusted the water some more. Checked the stopper. Measured the depth of the water with his index finger. Tested the temperature again. Made a tiny adjustment to the cold knob. Just a little more cold, so it wouldn't be too hot. In defiance of the words of God as reported by the crazy exiled and starved apostle John, in the Book of Revelation, Jack's least favorite book of the Bible because it so defied anything like rational meaning: "Because thou art lukewarm, and neither hot nor cold, I will spew thee out of my mouth." No. What he was *after* was something like lukewarm, just a little warmer than lukewarm and two inches deep.

The water had risen to one inch. He had run out of things to do with his hands. He noticed that his back was turned to her. He knew how intentional it was, his back being turned to her. It was turned, he realized, because he was still trying to avoid looking at her.

He forced himself to turn and look at her. There she was. She was sitting on the toilet seat, half-slumped, or at least not nearly as upright as he had left her, resting her weight against the back of the toilet. She was looking at him.

He looked down at her feet and saw that they were bare. Of course they were bare; he had taken off her shoes and socks. But were they cold? Should he cover them?

Then he knew that he was looking at her feet because she was not her feet. She was her face and eyes. She was not her body—God no—not this body, not his mother. But if she was not this body, what was she? What had she become? And if the mother he had known—the mom, the momma, the mommy—had vacated this body, who was it then who sat before him?

Then he knew that he was letting himself be drawn deeper and deeper into these abstractions because it was another way of not looking at her. It was a way of looking but not looking. Of seeing but letting sight lead him to a place not present.

The tub was filling with water behind him, and he turned to see how high he had let the water get. It was four inches, probably. He turned off the faucets, then reached down and pulled the stopper. It wasn't the act of pulling the stopper that got him, that made his throat catch in the same way he had seen hundreds of other throats catch in ways so predictable it had long since ceased to move him. It was the sound of that stopper. The *plop* and the soft sucking that followed.

He turned again and saw her. She had not moved. His own eyes had not filled with tears, and he knew they would not because he had long since trained himself to do a duty when a duty was called for, and now was the time. The time was now. "Now, Mom," he said. "After I stop the tub, okay?"

She winked her eye twice.

He plugged the tub, and it was about two inches, just right. Then he moved toward her and smelled her stink and put his face near hers, his eyes at the level of hers. He couldn't help but think that the only thing like what he was about to do, what he was in fact doing . . . the only that he could recall from his whole experience of life was a certain kind of lovemaking he had once known with Julie, a lovemaking of the most intimate kind, a lovemaking that all but precludes knowledge of the body in favor of a different kind of lostness. A lovemaking punctuated only by the involuntary blinking that for brief but too-long moments breaks the illusion, the spell, of complete connection, two sets of eyes locking upon one another in near-inviolate attention while bodies perform their lesser task. The pleasure of that deepest kind of intimacy, sure, but the terror, too. The complete giving and undoing of self.

He said, "I'm going to put you in the bath now, momma," but what he meant was harder: *I'm going to take off your clothes now.*

He began to unbutton the big white fake pearl buttons that ran the length of her housedress, starting with the top button, near her neck. He looked into her eyes as he did it. She looked back into his, too. She did not make a sound or wink her eye. She did not do anything but breathe shallowly and watch his eyes.

He worked his way down the front of her, button by button. He was sure to keep a tension on the fabric with his fingers. He did not want to touch the skin on the front of her, only button, fabric, button, fabric. He did not know what he was so afraid of. He had been at so many bedsides, seen so many frail bodies uncovered. He did not know what he was so afraid of.

But then he did know. What he was afraid of was his mother's body. He reached the button near her waist, and then his arms could go no farther without his body moving down with them. He crouched down and tried to keep his eyes locked upon hers, but of course his eyes were at the level of her wrecked, sagging breasts. He was struck by something his father had told him, once, when they had gone on a fishing trip and talked once, only once, about things they never otherwise discussed. His mother's family had been poor, themselves the children of day laborers in rural Kentucky, escaped to better lives in Florida, where his father was a wellpoint foreman. They had tried to convince his mother not to nurse him. They had taken up with a circle of friends who found the practice disturbing and who were weaning their children at two months and offering instead bottles of Karo syrup and cow's milk. "Your mother didn't take to that talk," his father had said. "Two years she got the silent treatment, but she said, 'No baby of mine.'"

Now, eye-level with his own mother's breasts, he could not ignore his own speculations about what might have passed between them before he was old enough to know. He continued to unbutton, now the waist, now the lap, now the knees.

The housedress came apart then. The flaps of it flanked his mother on either side. She was sitting with her legs uncrossed. He was almost kneeling now, and his eyes continued to seek hers. The next thing he had to do was lift her and put her in the tub. As he stood he lost her eyes and found himself—for a moment, for less than a moment—staring between her legs. She was almost hairless there, but for some stray white wisps and one large alarming black one.

He did not back away. He reached up, toward her, and pulled her arms free of the sleeves. Then he placed his left arm beneath both her legs. With his right arm he encircled her, lifting carefully so he was holding most of her weight under both her armpits. He lifted her and carried her to the bathtub and lowered her into the bathwater and took the washcloth and reached down to touch her body with it. She began to tremble as he moved it toward her, and he said, "Shh, shh." What word could he say to help her be okay? He said, "Mommy, Mommy. It's all right Mommy."

Then her body began to convulse in the water.

Franny Wenderoth had a secret she kept from everyone: the memory of a tobacco field in summer in Kentucky, she running, and a boy, her cousin, giving chase. It started as a game she called house. They played in the kitchen, her mother's kitchen in the house on John Claremont Hollow Road, a hundred feet from the tobacco field where her father sometimes worked as a day laborer. She said, "You be the Mommy, I'll be the Daddy."

Her cousin blanched at this. His name was Roy. He said, "I'm not being no Mommy." So it was agreed. He would be the Daddy, she the Mommy. He was eleven years old, she nine. It did not occur to her that they were too old to be playing such a child's game because it did not occur to her that she was anything but a child, or that he was, or that there was anything but a child to be.

They were in the kitchen, and she put wood in the stove and lit it and he stoked the flames until they were burning. Her mother was somewhere; she couldn't remember where. Her mother was often enough somewhere. Her mother and her father were gone most of the time, but then so was everyone's mother and father. Roy's mother was laid up and was around all the time. His mother made him fetch her things, and more and more Roy did like his seventeen-year-old brother Donny—*a bad seed, that Donny Prather,* her father would say—and found someplace else to be.

"Put the eggs on," she said. He did like she said and cracked the imaginary eggs over the griddle. "Now the bacon," she said, and he did likewise.

Her father would beat her with a switch, and probably Roy, too, if he knew they were burning the wood after all it took to keep it cut and stacked and get the pile high enough for all they would need for winter. Roy stoked the fire some more, and she got nervous and said, "Bacon's done, Roy, and eggs are starting to burn."

It was getting hot in the kitchen. She was starting to panic about the wood. Roy noticed and said, "Good Lord, Franny. I'll cut you some more wood."

"You won't cut it right," she said. Her father would know. Better to just leave be. She was indignant. She liked the feeling of indignant. This kind of playing house was more real, anyway, than cooking eggs or bacon on the stove. She couldn't ever remember a time her father and mother worked in the kitchen together. It was her mother, or if her mother was gone it was her father. But they had argued plenty in the kitchen. Part of her secretly hoped Roy would haul off and knock her upside the head. It was a revolting thought that made her plenty angry, and she took not a little pleasure in the heat in her cheeks and chest. The mommy and the daddy.

"I will," he said. "I know how to cut wood."

"Not like my daddy," she said.

He grabbed her by the wrist. "That dog won't hunt," he said. He said it good and nasty, and soft, but deep-voiced, like a grown man. The sound of it was weird. Unsettling, like the dark could sometimes be.

She laughed and tried to push him away. He held onto her wrist and she couldn't get loose. "Let me be," she said. She started slapping at him. "Roy Samuel Prather," she said, "let me be."

But he wouldn't let her be. He dug his dirty fingernails into her wrist and pressed down until she screamed. Then, fast as lightning, he reached down with his free hand and grabbed her by the ankle. He picked her up like that, wrist and ankle. When she tried to kick free he just let her body hit the ground, hard, without letting go of her wrist and ankle, and he dragged her like that out to the front porch and down the four stairs, her shoulder or back or arms knocking against every step.

When he got her out to the yard, he swung her back, then flung her forward as hard as he could. She landed hard, rolling out as best she could, which wasn't much.

He took two steps back, bent down and picked a blade of grass, put it between his teeth and chewed on it. He said, casual as can be, "I give you fifty steps and then I'm gonna come and get you."

By now she was plenty sure he wasn't the same Roy Samuel Prather she had known the day before. She got up and ran with all that was in her, which was considerable. She had long legs and could run fast, and not just for a girl. She was barefoot, but her feet were hard and soft at the same time, feet that did not mind stepping on stray stones the way other feet might. In later years she could not remember whether she said it aloud or not, but she did have the distinct memory of urging her feet on, of speaking to them: "Go, feet, go."

She did not count her steps, but it could well enough have been fifty before she heard Roy give an Indian war whoop and then the sound of his bare feet moving through the grass.

She thought she might lose him in the tobacco field. She did not know what he meant to do, but she had been admiring his new brown belt with its metal buckle the shape of Kentucky, and she thought if they really were going to play house, he might just whip her like a daddy would a mommy, and if he did it with that brown belt he might forget to take off that metal buckle, and wouldn't it hurt to get beat about the buttocks and back by Kentucky.

She tried to keep as low to the ground as she could and still run. She was among the rows of tobacco now. The leaves whipped her face and neck, but she did not raise her arms to protect her head because she needed them to pump. Behind her she heard Roy saying, "Run, Mommy, run!" and she did not know, now, if they were still playing the game or if he was mocking her.

But he was not gaining on her. She was running as fast as she could and she knew she would not tire before he did. It was a good feeling, a safe feeling. She could outrun danger.

She turned a corner at the place where a strip of dirt divided one acre from another, then plunged ahead directly into a row in the new field, five rows removed from where she had emerged. She could hear his feet behind her, hesitating, then choosing a row, choosing the right row, and then the chase was on again, but she had put some more distance between them.

Her plan was to reach the end of the row, then double back toward the house. All that was beyond these fields was mountain, and though she was not afraid of the mountains, she was afraid of getting too far from home, of not making it back in time to cook supper and getting whipped by her daddy.

She made it to the end of the row and made a sharp turn left. She meant to count seven rows, then make her left-hand turn toward home. She was running flat-out, counting—one, two, three, four . . .—and then, BOOM, some large figure, something twice her size maybe, came out from row five and stood still, and she could not slow herself or dodge it in time to avoid collision. Running flat-out, she hit this massive wall, hit the body of a grown man, and just before impact, the man's body jerked its weight forward, into her, and knocked her backward. She landed hard, like a stone thrown straight at the ground, and bounced like the stone would bounce. It took her a moment to clear her head. She heard the sound of footsteps behind her, Roy's, and when she looked up she was facing him, and when she turned the other way, she saw that she was facing something ten times more scary.

Roy's brother Donny. Donny Lynn Prather. The bad seed.

He was chewing on a blade of grass. He chewed it just like Roy. He said, "Well, now, what have we here?"

She did not make a move to get up. She dared a look at Roy, and he was grinning ear to ear.

Donny said, "It's a fine morning, ain't it darling?"

Roy whistled a tune: Shoo-Fly, Don't Bother Me, 'Cause I Belong to Somebody.

Donny took a step toward her. He said, "Now, who do you belong to, honey?"

"Somebody," Roy said. "is me. I'm the Daddy."

"Is that right?" Donny said. He bit off the end of the blade of grass and spit it out. She did not like the way he was smiling at her. His smile wasn't the same as Roy's. For the rest of her life she would remember that smile. It was the smile of a buzzard in the face of a newly coyote-eaten body of a deer, rotting but not quite dead. "What if I said I'm the Daddy."

She looked at Roy. All of a sudden he looked very small. He puffed out his chest and said, "I'm the Daddy, I give the whooping. Like you said."

She cheered a little at his words. Her own daddy could give a whipping like you couldn't believe, and she knew how to take it. A whipping wasn't nothing to her. One, two. No matter. She would close her eyes and take it. But then Roy was taking off his belt, and she looked again at that metal belt buckle shaped like Kentucky, and she knew it wasn't Roy was going to get to whip her with it, but Donny. And what damage could somebody like Donny do with a weapon like that?

Roy was on one side, and Donny was on the other, behind her. She could outrun Roy, she had already proven that today, but there wasn't one way she could think of to get loose of Donny. So she turned around. She intended to tell Donny that, sure enough, Roy was the daddy, and she would take her whipping from him. That was the rules of the game.

But when she turned around she saw that Donny had already taken his belt off. Behind her, Roy was getting steamed. "It's my whipping, goddamn it," he said. "I'm the daddy."

Franny took two steps back, and neither Roy nor Donny did anything to stop her. Donny stepped right past her and yanked the belt from Roy's hand. He had his own belt in the other hand, and then fast as anything he swung first his then Roy's at Roy's back and legs, first one then the other, again and again. The sound of them hitting was terrible, the whipcrack of Roy's belt followed by the dull thud of the belt buckle.

It didn't seem right for him to beat on Roy like that. Franny took a running start. She jumped on Donny's back, and when she did, he threw the belts into a row of tobacco and picked her off his back with one hand and threw her down.

She had lost her wind. Her whole body hurt from being thrown down so hard, especially her left side, where she had hit. She breathed in hard, trying to suck down as much as air as she could as fast as she could.

She could see Roy. He was on the ground, behind Donny, on his butt, shuffling backward. Donny didn't pay him any mind. He looked down at Franny. He said, "Ain't you a lovely thing, Franny Mae."

Then he undid the front of his trousers and took out his worm—she knew what one was but had never seen one before—and it was long and flesh-colored and purple at the end.

"You ever seen one of these before?" Donny said.

It made her ashamed. Roy was still sprawled out there on the ground, looking at them with a big dumb face.

Donny took the worm between his fingers and pointed it at her, and a hot stream of white piss came shooting out at her. She screamed, and he laughed and shook it up and down so it covered her up and down and some of it got on her face. She raised her hands to her face and tried to get up, but he came closer, pissing all the way, and when she was almost up, he pushed her down again.

When he had stopped pissing, he said, "Open up that pretty little mouth, Mommy."

She shook her head no and clenched her teeth and held her lips tight together. She wanted to tell Roy to do something, come help her like she had tried to help him, but she did not want to open her mouth.

Donny reached down and gripped both of her cheeks with one hand and squeezed so hard she thought her teeth would be pushed loose from her gums. He pried her jaws open, and then he put that disgusting part of his body right up to her lips and started pissing again. She tried to shut her mouth, but he was still holding it so she could not. It started to get hard and push against her mouth. The piss was hot in her throat, and it gagged her, and she could taste it most in her nose, where the scent of it rose from the back of her throat like the dust from a field newly ploughed.

Then he lost his aim somehow, and his grip on her face, and the piss splashed all over her face. It was Roy. Finally—*finally!*—he had jumped on Donny's back from behind. When Donny turned around, Roy reared back and punched him square in the nose.

Blood began to squirt from Donny's face. He put his hands to his nose and when pulled them away they were covered in red, and she could see that his nose was bent a little, to the side. He reached up and grabbed his own nose and yanked it back into place, and when he did he made a sound so terrible that it threw Franny into a panic, and she got up again and started to run, but Donny saw it, and reached out his foot to trip her.

She fell hard on her face and knocked free one of her front teeth, a new adult one that couldn't be replaced, and right away she could feel the warmth in her own mouth, the taste of iron overtaking the ammonia musk. As she dug in the dirt, looking for the tooth, she could hear Donny and Roy scuffling, Donny cursing and Roy yelling at him to stop.

She found the tooth and put it in her pocket. She put her tongue to the gum from which it had been knocked to try and stop the bleeding. When she looked up, Roy was on his back, and Donny was sitting with his knees on Roy's chest, his thing still hanging out the front of his pants. He had pinned Roy's arms beneath his legs, and Roy's legs were kicking at the air with no chance of getting the rest of him free. Donny was slapping him in the face—"How's that, you little shit? Does that feel fine?"—pulling his right hand back, then bringing it down full-force on Roy's right cheek, then again with the left, then the right again.

She did not want to leave Roy like that, at the mercy of his older brother. She had to think quick. What occurred to her in later years was that, like it or not, Roy had set her up, and because of what he had done she had lost a tooth and wasn't going to be able to get it back, and that she certainly must have feared losing worse than a tooth. That's how she rationalized it when she was older and needed some way to find peace with herself at having left him to fend for himself against an older brother twice his size, an older brother whose self could not be controlled.

But in that moment, all she knew was the great animal fear that made the deer freeze and the bobcat run. She did not look back. She ran into the rows of tobacco, through one acre and then the next and then on to her own house, and past it, and down the country road, to the house of her mother's cousin, Miss Lucy. The whole time, running, she could not know whether or not Donny was behind her, giving chase, could not have heard the sound of his running if she had tried, not above the din of her own exertions, the labor of her breathing, and the pounding of her heart. She ran as though he was chasing her, did not even look back when, after banging on Miss Lucy's door with her fists, she ran through the open door, right past Miss Lucy, and into the bathroom, and shut the door and locked it and would not come out, not for hours and hours. Not until her mother came by in the early evening and got her out, first coaxing, then threatening, then promising no harm would come to her by way of her father.

By time she left that bathroom, Franny had washed her face clean. She did not, would not speak, and it was not until two days later that her mother discovered that her front tooth was gone. By then they had found Roy's body up in the mountains. By then some dogs had got it, and it was mangled so badly they were hard-pressed to know what the dogs had done and what Donny had done. Everybody knew it was Donny, but nobody could prove it, and when the time came, Donny produced a girlfriend, a truly unreliable witness named Thelma Jane, from up in the hills, from a family well known to let their children run wild, and whose men were all locked up in jails most of the time, most of them on repeated small-time stints in Rowan County Jail, and some doing longer, harder time in state and federal penitentiaries.

For her part, Franny didn't say anything. Not one word. Wouldn't even admit to being there, and even though her parents were sure enough she had been with Roy that day, they did not want any part of the proceedings against Donny. He was family, and it was a family matter, and it was meant to be settled among family. In the end, he was let go for want of evidence. Before his own daddy could get at him to settle it in the family way, he was off and gone, some said to California, others to New Mexico, others to Mexico, out of the country and far away, maybe even as far as Guatemala or El Salvador, or past the equator to Venezuela, Argentina, Brazil.

But Franny couldn't see it that way. She thought about it often as she grew older, Donny and Roy and that awful day, and she wondered what would have happened if Roy had just run off like he could have. Would it have been her they found up that mountain, eaten away by dogs?

It troubled her, and then one day, when she was thirteen years old, she thought of something that troubled her even more, which was that Donny was not the brightest wick in the lamp, and how on God's green earth could anyone be made to believe that he, of all people, could possibly teach himself to know Spanish?

He couldn't be in South America, then. Not there, or Guatemala, or Mexico, or anywhere. And how would he pay his way to New Mexico or California? And what would he do for work once he got there? All he knew was hills, and he knew them the way ants knew their dirt tunnels, could probably find his way through every twist and turn in every creek, knew when and where the waters changed their paths after a rain storm, knew which caves were empty and which bedded brown bears or bobcats or coyotes.

The truth that became apparent to her, then, and which no one else ever seemed to know, was that Donny Lynn Prather, the bad seed, the murderer, was living in the hills that surrounded her. One evening not long before her fourteenth birthday, she was lying in bed in the middle of the night, not sleeping as always, or barely sleeping, sleeping the light sleep that is less like sleep than like worry, when she heard a tapping at her window. Just a slight tapping. Just a little tap. Just a tap-tap-tap. Three taps, a sound like knuckles rapping against a door.

She looked up, and what she saw was nothing. Or nothing she could be sure about. But when she looked down again at her own covers in the dim half moon light coming through her window, she thought she saw—it was not even an impression so much as an impression of an impression, a shadow's shadow's shadow—the figure of a man hovering there. When she looked up again he was gone. When she looked down again she thought she saw the movement. She looked up again, and there was nothing there, and then she was afraid to not look anymore.

So she stared out the window. She lay rigid, alert. Staring. She stayed that way the rest of the night, in that nervous state. It was exhausting to spend the night that way, and when morning came, she was so relieved at the sight of the sun that she directly fell asleep. Her mother came in and tried to stir her when she did not show in the kitchen to help with breakfast, but there was no rousing her. She had only the faint memory of opening her eyes and seeing her mother hovering over like a ghost, her face white against a bedroom that had taken on a strange shade of blue.

After that she thought she saw him everywhere. Saw him without actually seeing. He was the squirrel peeking out from behind the trees, so she stopped going off into the woods. He was the whistle of the wind through the exposed roots of the old cherry tree by the creek, so she refused to cross it to go the well and fetch water. He was hiding behind the wood stove where she and Roy had cooked the bacon and eggs with the wood they had stolen from her father's pile, so she refused to anymore go into the kitchen.

Her world grew smaller and smaller and smaller—her room, the parlor, Sunday church—and then she was old enough to flee. John Wenderoth, a boy at the Free Will Independent Baptist Church, asked her to marry him, and she said she would on the condition they move away—"Anywhere, as long as it's away," she said, when he asked—and as soon as he had saved some money working as a well-digger's apprentice, he spirited her off to West Palm Beach, Florida, where he knew able-bodied men were needed for the construction boom, and then they were gone.

The children came quickly, Eleanor first, and then Millie, and then, after enough years had gone by that they thought they wouldn't have any more, along came John Junior, who they called John Junior until he was old enough to declare himself Jack. The world grew larger again. John came home after work smelling like sweat and dirt, smelling sweet to her taste, like a man should, and she fed him, and together they bathed the children, something other families did not do all together. They prayed at the dinner table, too, and broke bread with great reverence. Life was rich and full.

Eleanor went off to the state university, the first in the family. She did not finish, but then neither John nor Franny had finished high school, and they were proud of their eldest all the same for even going. They bought Florida Gators T-shirts and hung an orange and blue flag from the front porch, parallel to their red, white, and blue American flag.

Then Millie went away, too, to Stetson University, a private Baptist school in the north part of the state, on the east coast. When she told them, Franny thought John would burst a vessel in his brain for worry, but then she said she thought she could get a scholarship, and she did, and the people at the church were so proud that they pitched in for board and books.

Millie finished, too, with a degree in accountancy. John said, "Can you believe it, darling? We don't never have to pay anyone to do our taxes ever again."

Franny beamed. Things were so good. She couldn't believe things could ever get so good.

But then they got better. First, Eleanor married a man from a wealthy family, a dentist named Carl. John said, "Can you believe it, sweet girl? We can get our teeth fixed right." And sure enough they did. Carl pulled all John's bad teeth and fitted him with the most beautiful set of porcelain teeth anybody ever saw. They went to church that Sunday and people were making over him like nothing he'd ever seen. Franny could not believe that porcelain teeth could bring anyone so much happiness.

But then Carl went to work on her mouth. She had been wearing a prosthetic tooth all these years that John had bought for her when they first moved to West Palm Beach, a belated wedding gift so beautiful she demanded he drive her straight home, and when they arrived she led him to the kitchen table. She told him to sit down, situated him just the way she wanted. Then she took off his shoes and his socks and rubbed and kissed his toes and his feet, pulled off his belt and unzipped his trousers and pulled them off, too. Then she rubbed and kissed his legs, just as slow as she liked him to rub and kiss her. Then she did something she had been refusing to do those early months of their union, had been refusing because of Roy and Donny Prather and what Donny had done to her that day in the dirt behind the tobacco field. She put her face right in his lap and took him in her mouth, and the act was to her every bit as cleansing as she imagined the day of her baptism might have been if she had been old enough to know and understand just what sins, past, present, future, were being washed away. When he was finished, she rinsed her mouth in the sink, and then she hiked up her good dress, and—she could hardly believe it—he was ready already, and she climbed up onto the table, onto him, and when they saw that it would not hold their weight for long they made their way into the bedroom.

That's the way Eleanor was made, and now this dentist husband of hers, this Carl, was offering to make a new tooth for Franny, not a prosthetic, but an actual tooth that he would implant in her gum. By now her prosthetic tooth had taken on a blackish-blue cast, a navy blue almost, that stood in ugly contrast against the yellow-brown color of her other teeth. Carl made this new tooth white, and colored the yellow teeth to match it, and when he was done and her mouth had healed from the procedure, she looked in the mirror, John standing behind her. "You look beautiful," he said. He had been saying it for many years, but this time, this once, she believed him, thought herself beautiful. She was almost forty-five years old now, and for the first time beautiful.

Then the hard times came back with a vengeance. The year John Junior turned thirteen, Millie married another accountant, a man she met at work, and for two years she all but disappeared. This man, this accountant, had been rude to Franny and especially to John at the wedding, and made some mean-spirited comments about John's blue suit, which the man considered out of fashion, and on which John had spent two hundred dollars the week before the ceremony. That was the second sign of trouble. The first had been his forgetting to ask John for Millie's hand in marriage, but Franny said that it must have been an oversight, that times had changed and it wasn't Kentucky, and weren't they glad for that. But then Millie all but disappeared, and when Franny did see her, usually in passing at the grocery store, she looked haggard. She had taken to wearing dark sunglasses, even indoors, and to speaking in whispers.

After the third time Franny saw her this way—produce aisle, iceberg lettuce display—she told John she suspected Millie was what they called a battered wife. John could hardly bear it. He did not go to work the next day. She saw him in the back yard, pacing. She let him pace but thought a vegetable drink might make him feel better. His brother Larry back in Kentucky had got his cancer, melanoma of the skin, and beat it after buying a juicer and making three times daily drinks out of lettuce, cabbage, apples, carrots, and lemon juice. John thought it was a good idea, and whether or not the juicer had the power to ward off cancer, he sure did look and feel better, though his skin had lately taken on an orangish cast that the Eleanor's wife Carl said had something to do with the beta carotene in the carrots.

She watched him while she juiced. He looked up and waved a hand to let her know he saw her, and made his way to the door. She met him there, the orange-brown juice in hand. He took a long sip and said, "I'm gonna have to go over there."

She said, "You might make it worse." But she wanted him to go whether it did or not. She wanted to go herself.

He took another, longer sip, and drained the whole thing. She didn't know how he could do it, but it must've given him time to think what he was going to say next. He swallowed, then he met her eyes with a gaze more direct than she was used to seeing from him. It was a little cold, and she remembered what power he was capable of projecting, and what kind of good man he must be to rein it in at home. He said, "If it's gonna get worse, I'm gonna get her out of there myself. And if she's not going to go, I'm gonna get him out. One way or the other."

What happened next it took her some time to piece together. John didn't say much to her, but he did confide in Carl, and Carl confided in Eleanor, and after awhile Eleanor let it slip in fragments, a detail here and one there, until finally Franny was satisfied that she knew. Horrified, too. What happened was it was dark by the time John arrived. There was a light on in the house, and the ugly green curtains were drawn, and he could see Millie and her husband—his name was Erik, the Viking name mismatched with his scrawny body—he could see them in silhouette. He saw Erik's arm reach out and make contact with Millie's head, and Millie pushing back. Erik must have been off-balance, and he fell, and when his shadow rose again, he reached out for the red curtains and ripped them from the wall. When they came down, he could see that Millie was crying. She was standing there, naked from the waist up except for a frilly brassiere, one of her eyes swollen shut. By this time, John was out of the car and racing for the front door. Inside he heard a lot of yelling. The door was unlocked, which was a good thing, because in that state no doubt he would have kicked it down. When he got in the house, he found his daughter backed into a corner by skinny Erik, who was saying vile things. He turned and saw John, and Erik said, rapid-fire, "This is private; this is none of your concern; you don't know what's going on here, what she's done," and by the time he got to who she's fucked, John was across the room. He grabbed Erik by the wrist and yanked so hard he jerked the skinny Viking's arm from its socket. Right away, Millie tried to intervene. She put herself between her husband and her father and said, "Stop it, Dad. Stop it right now. He's my husband!" To John, hearing her saying it like that was like taking a whipping. He took two steps back, looked at his daughter, looked at her husband. All the fight went out of him then, and he looked at Erik and said, "You don't have a daughter. You don't know how it is." Erik didn't say anything. He went into the bedroom and pulled a suit from the closet, walked out the front door, his arm dangling from his shoulder at a grotesque angle, and drove away. Millie was still standing in the corner. John saw her there and it must have killed him to see her like that, wearing that lacy brassiere above her bare midriff, her eye swollen shut. He went into the bedroom and took the orange velour blanket from beneath the comforter and brought it out into the living room. She had sat down on the couch, and he sat beside her and wrapped the velour blanket around her shoulders so it covered her and made her warm. His arm came to rest on her shoulder, and he let it rest there, lightly, and she didn't resist any. They sat there in silence for a long time. Finally, he said, "I'm ashamed, but it's not you I'm ashamed of."

After that, Millie moved in with Eleanor and Carl for awhile. Erik made some overtures toward patching things up, but it was clear his heart wasn't in it. Franny didn't want Millie to even talk to him again except through lawyers, but she knew well enough to keep quiet, and she told John to do the same.

It ended badly, at least as far as Franny was concerned. The dentist who employed Eleanor's husband Carl was nearing retirement age, and his practice was housed on land he owned, land that sat on one of the last mostly undeveloped major intersections in downtown West Palm Beach. The land was maybe twenty or thirty times more valuable than the dental practice, and the old man decided to sell. He offered Carl his client list in exchange for a continuing (and quite large) participation in the business's future income, and Carl gave it some thought, but it would have been difficult to find land to buy or lease in the same part of the city that was affordable enough to ensure the kind of profitability he hoped he might achieve in return for the hassle and risk of taking over the practice.

He would have to move the practice to the suburbs, maybe out west of town to Royal Palm Beach or Wellington, where the young families were moving. But then if he was going to move anyway, and no doubt lose most of the client list, who wouldn't want to make the half-hour commute to the dentist's office twice a year, why give a cut to his old employer?

Carl and Eleanor mapped out their reasons for rejecting the offer over a supper of Franny's famous Hungarian goulash, a recipe she had learned from the Cuban woman next door, and John nodded, and inside Franny was cheering all over again for this man Carl, this dentist who had made Eleanor's life so good, and who even now was making such well-reasoned decisions for himself and her daughter. But then Eleanor said, "Carl's parents say they'll co-sign the bank loan for a new practice in Lake Mary. It's only fifteen minutes from where they live, and it's growing so fast. That's the direction Orlando's growing, to the north . . ."

It was like a blow to the chest. Franny and John both lied and told them it was wonderful news. "Best thing me and Franny ever did was move away from Kentucky," John said—gamely, Franny thought—but after they went home, John said, "Do you think they're gonna take Millie with them?"

The thought had not occurred to Franny. She took to calling Carl and Eleanor's house at odd hours, hoping to catch Millie when they weren't home. But one or the other of them always seemed to be home when she called. When she heard their voices, she hung up the phone, and after the eighth or ninth hang-up, she got a call from Eleanor. "Mom, have you been trying to call here?" she said.

"No," Franny said, too fast.

"Mom, I know you have. We had to get the phone company to put a trace on the call. It cost fifteen dollars. Do you know what a trace is, Mom?"

She could figure it out well enough.

"I don't understand, Mom. You call because you want to talk to me, and then you hang up?"

Franny didn't know what to say, so she hung up.

She leaned on the handset for awhile where it rested in the cradle and looked at it. Then she lifted it from the cradle and called back. Before Eleanor could even say hello, Franny was off and running. You're-ruining-my-life-by-leaving-and-you're-taking-my-Millie-too, and How-could-you-do-this-to-your-father? Then she hung up again.

Then she made a list, a catalog of all the things she and John had done for Eleanor and Millie on a ruled yellow legal pad, starting with eighteen combined months of pregnancy and moving on through all work of infant mothering (item #12: "nursing, no Karo syrup") and getting toddlers ready for school (item #37: "i learned to read better so i could teach it right to both of you") and roller skates and Barbie dolls and braces and even flashy teenage miniskirts ("and I even hid it from your daddy even though it wasnt right to do it") and on and on, filling seven long yellow pages and writing a paragraph on the eighth to the effect that this effort, this "hasty couple pages," was very much an abridgement.

It was Millie who called first. She had been seeing an expensive psychologist, a friend of Carl's, and her mouth was full of three-dollar words. She told Franny what she said Franny didn't know about boundaries. She said what was being forced on her and Eleanor was nothing less than an extension of the guilt-complex Franny had been building in them their whole lives. She said Franny's main goal in life was her own comfort, and that's what all the walking around the house humming and talking about nothing had been about all those years.

"What humming?" Franny said. "What talking to myself? I was singing songs to bring happy to the house. I was talking to you, to cheer you up. It was a habit, a good good good habit."

"It was an unconscious habit," Millie said. "You did it to meet some unmet need in yourself from your marriage or your childhood you haven't found a way to come to terms with." She told her about something called Johari's window, something her psychologist told her, some way of looking into the soul, where there was all different things about you, and some of them were known to you and everybody else, and some you knew about yourself but kept close so nobody else could know, and some were secrets about you, but open secrets that you didn't yourself know but everybody else knew about you.

Or claimed to know, Franny thought, as she listened to Millie go on and on in this high-minded way. Because how could any one person know what was happening inside the mind of another person? What their thoughts were, their intentions, their motivations? Her intentions were pure, she knew that well enough. And her secrets were her own.

Franny said, "Don't throw big words around to try and show me. I'm no dummy. I know what those big words mean. And let me tell you another one I know: Cultivate. I cultivated every one of those habits. For you. So don't try and tell me, just because you're getting too big for your britches. I raised you. I knew you from when you were not but a speck in your daddy's eye. I knew you before you knowed yourself."

Still, it was the first she'd heard of this talk, and she knew after hearing Millie say it that it must have been said many times before. She thought about that Johari's window and the things she must not know other people thought they knew about her, had been thinking about her all along. She knew, then, that her children were ripping her up behind her back after she spent her whole life trying to make theirs good. There wasn't a child on earth loved her parents as much as her parents loved her, Franny knew that well enough, but what about respect? What about where the Bible said honor thy father and thy mother? That was in the Ten Commandments. It was given to Moses from God, and those girls knew it, too. She had showed it to them in the blue Bible storybook probably a hundred times or more when they were little.

It wasn't long after that she started to get bogged down in thinking about secrets and the way they were kept. Long after Carl moved away and took Eleanor and Millie with him to Lake Mary and his new dental paradise, nearer his own wealthy parents, she played and replayed that conversation with Millie again and again in her mind. John did not say much about it, but she noticed that he had been taking care of even more things around the house than he usually did, which forced him to be around more. He was taking John Junior—Jack, he wanted to be called Jack now—to the high school every morning so Franny could sleep in, and picking him up after baseball practice in the afternoons, too, juggling his own work schedule and saying no to good overtime so he could do it. He was making most of the meals, and he was bringing into the house flowers fresh cut from the back yard, and putting them in vases, and changing the water as long as they stayed nice. It was his way; it was what he had always done when he thought she was sad, and kept on doing until her sadness had passed.

But what she was feeling was not sadness. All Millie's talk about secrets and comfort and what is known and to whom . . . all of that had put her in mind again of the Prather boys, her cousins Donny and Roy, and that day Roy had chased her through the tobacco field, toward Donny, who he had to know was waiting there for her, waiting to do bad things to her, even though Roy probably didn't know how bad. The day playing house had gone wrong, and her childhood had ended, and Roy had died.

It was a secret, *the* secret, in fact, of her whole life. She had never told John the story, although he knew well enough about the dog-eaten boy that was found up in the mountain, knew, too, that Roy was her cousin, and that the boy, the brother, who had most likely done it had run off and was never heard from again. But what seemed so remarkable to her, now, forty years after she stopped being nine years old forever, was that her husband John had never once brought it up. Never once asked. Didn't act one bit curious. Wasn't that strange?

Jack came home early that afternoon, saying baseball practice had been cut short by rain and he had caught a ride home with a girl named Julie. That took Franny by surprise. She looked him over as he walked down the hall toward his bedroom and shut the door. Only fifteen, but from behind he looked just like his daddy did when Franny had first met him, except for Jack's long hair. Same broad shoulders, same thick legs, walked the same way. Good Lord, he was almost the same age John had been then.

She walked back to his bedroom and knocked on the door, and when he said, "Come in," she did. He was laying on the bed, propped up on his elbows over a pad of graph paper full of algebra equations. Franny said, "Who is this Julie?"

"Just a girl, Mom," he said, but from the way he said it, she could tell it wasn't just a girl.

"How old is she?" Franny said. "She's older? She drives a car?"

"She just turned sixteen, Mom," Jack said. "She's in the same grade as me."

Franny frowned. She had been so caught up in the lives of her girls, she hadn't been paying enough attention to Jack, not for a long time. He was so quiet, moved through the house like he wasn't even there. You could almost forget he was there at all.

"Don't worry, Mom," he said. "It's nothing."

He turned his attention back to the algebra. She said, "Did you call your daddy and tell him you was coming home early?"

He acknowledged as much with a wave, not disrespectful but not mindful, either, of her. He had been growing less and less mindful of her. It had been going on for a long time, but she only now noticed it as a pattern.

She went through the motions of making dinner, peas and carrots and potatoes and cubed steak, but she did not find any joy in it. Turning on the burner on the electric stove, she noticed that she was humming. A hymn. "Oh, precious is the flow that makes me white as snow . . ." For just a moment it had made her feel better, and she remembered what Millie had said, and then it made her feel worse, her humming to keep herself company and not even knowing it, like everyone apparently knew she did.

When John came home, he went directly to tend to the back yard without saying so much as hello. She thought he was mad at her at first—the whole world was, it seemed like—but after awhile she looked out at him through the window and saw how he was hacking away at the hedgerows that lined the back of their property with his hedgeclippers, but he wasn't doing it right, wasn't doing it slow and careful like was his way. He was going fast, clip-clip-clipping. It looked like he was trying to hurt the bushes. She could see his biceps working where they poked out from his shirtsleeve.

She went outside. He did not hear her approaching. He kept on moving, herky-jerky. She called out his name. She said, "John, honey, John . . ."

He turned and looked at her. He had a strange look on his face like he didn't recognize her.

She said, "John, what's wrong? What did I do wrong?"

He softened at his, let the arm, his right arm, holding the hedgeclippers drop to his side. He was standing there at a half-crooked angle, those hedgeclippers dangling from his right side and his body all slumped to the right like it was following the hedgeclippers. He said, "Oh, shit, Franny."

It was maybe four times she had ever heard him even say a curse word. She could count on one hand with the thumb finger left over.

"Them girls is gonna move away," he said. He said it like they were dead.

She thought on it awhile. He seemed to be looking at her for an answer.

Then she said, "Just like we did."

At that he just nodded his head, slow. Like he was resigning himself to it. He could say a hundred things and more to her without even saying one single word.

Then she said—she could hardly believe she was saying it—"Do you know why we ran away?"

She said it like that—ran away. Not went away.

He picked up on it right off, and said, "We didn't run nowhere at all. We decided. We *chose*. We made a choice, a real good choice, and packed our things, and left in a orderly fashion. We left because you said we ought to, and that was good enough for me, and I stand by it. I'm not ashamed of it."

He must have been trying to make her feel better, she decided. And that's what he would think was called for. That's what he always thought was called for, making her feel better. Good Lord, that was what he lived for. She knew it and had always known it but only realized that she knew she knew it just now. Millie and her Johari window. It was gonna haunt her, and she did not like it one bit.

She said, "That's not what I'm talking about. I'm talking real things here. I'm talking about why we left. Why I told you I wanted to leave. You never did ask. We just packed our things and went."

"And that was good enough for me," he said. "Your word is good enough for me any day of the week."

"No, no, no," she said. Her voice was rising. "I asked you a fair question, and you must have an answer. You, John Wenderoth, are a smart man who thinks of things. And this once I want to know what it is you think. So you tell me. Why did we leave Kentucky?"

He looked down at the ground for a long moment, one that felt like ten or twenty. Then, lifting his head but not connecting his eyes with hers, he said, "Well," and then another long pause, and then he said, "I suppose we left because of your daddy."

He did look in her eyes, then, probably, she thought, to gauge how it was she would respond before he went on. She did not want to give herself away, afraid he wouldn't if she did.

He said, "Your daddy was a mean man, God love him. I know he was. I seen him being rough with people more than once. And you was so quiet. You didn't hardly come out for anything. I saw you there, sitting in the pew at church, and I knew. I knew how it was. He must've been . . ."

Here his voice trailed away, and she knew what he was saying was that all these years her husband John thought her daddy, her sweet daddy, had been beating on her, or worse, the way daddies sometimes did to their daughters in those hills, in those times, the thing that passed among the women in whispers you had to overhear to be privy to, and that was what he meant to rescue her from. She didn't hardly know what to say to it.

He was still looking at her, like it hurt him to almost say it. He said, "It's okay, Francine. He didn't probably mean anything by it. It wasn't your fault. Maybe not even his. It was a hard life back there. People didn't know how to be."

She stood there and looked at him, her secret between them, and all those years, too. One way of looking at it, what she had to tell him was so much worse than the thing he had been thinking all along. But, the other way, it wasn't worse at all. One way it was her cousin did it to her before he murdered his brother, and the other way it was her own daddy did it to her, and murdered her a different way, a way so bad she would have had to keep on living with it. But then she was living with the other thing well on past when it happened, and it hadn't killed her, but then in a way it had, and she had had to resurrect herself, or at least teach herself how to be again.

Around and around she went with herself. Not much time passed, but in the way the mind does when under great pressure, the time inside her grew very slow to her own reckoning even as it must have been very fast when compared to the ticking of the clock on the kitchen wall.

Then she decided. She hung her head. She didn't say a thing.

John walked over to her and wrapped his arms around her, and he said, "It don't matter one way or the other, Francine. You're the whole world and you always was."

She leaned into him in the way he liked because she liked it and told him so. Roy was dead and buried, and if Donny had found a way to live he was an old man now, and not Donny any more. Those girls could move away if they wanted, and soon Jack would be gone, too, but what was past was past. She sealed it off inside herself, and there wasn't anyone could touch her heart in the worst way again. It was a cold feeling.

She didn't have her John for long after that. One afternoon he was working on a construction site in Port St. Lucie, where some developer was building a new baseball park, a spring training facility for the New York Mets where their minor league team would also play during the summer. John was excited about it, working on a baseball park. It meant something to him that office buildings and suburban neighborhoods did not. One afternoon he heard some Mets executives and a few ballplayers would be flying down to survey the progress, and he told Jack to take the day off school and come to work with him, meet the players.

Franny watched them drive away that morning. She watched the way they touched each other when they were walking down the sidewalk to the carport. The good-natured arm-punching and the horseplay. They had something between them she thought she had once with Eleanor, and then Millie.

They got into the car and drove away, and that's the last time she saw John alive. On the interstate, on the way to the construction site, John clutched his hand to his chest. Jack later said he thought, for a moment, his father would lose control of the car; but just as Jack was reaching for the wheel, John rallied, inhaled with great effort—"He was white as a sheet," Jack recalled—and straightened his shoulders and gripped the wheel and steered the car onto the shoulder and then the grass strip beyond. Then, the car safely at a stop, he slumped over the steering wheel. Jack jumped out of the car and waved his arms frantically at the approaching traffic. A middle-aged woman in a beige Datsun compact stopped, and together she and Jack wrestled John from the car. By then he had lost consciousness, and by the time they reached the hospital he had stopped breathing. By eight twenty-two that morning he had been declared dead. Jack called and told Franny what had happened and asked her to come to the hospital, and she said, "He's dead?" and Jack said—he was crying—"Yes, Mom, he is," and Franny said, "Then there's nothing I can do," and she got him off the phone as quick as she could. Then she went into the bathroom and vomited until she was too weak to get up. She lay on the bathmat and let herself drift into something not sleep but like dreaming. She rested there until she had marshaled the strength to get up. Then she got up and went to the kitchen and made some tea. Her hands were shaking. She drank the tea and ate some peanut butter cheese crackers. Then she went into the bathroom, brushed her teeth, and scrubbed the toilet until there was no sign of her illness.

By the time Jack arrived home, Franny had prepared grilled cheese and tomato soup. It was ready for him on the table. He came in through the back door by the kitchen, took one look at the food, then hung his head, went into his bedroom and did not come out until the next day.

Jack never said anything about it, but she always wondered whether he thought her somehow defective as a mother for not going to the hospital to comfort him. He had been sixteen then, and his pain must have been enormous, but what about hers? Who had she had, her entire life, except for John? Eleanor? Millie? For their duration of their childhoods, maybe, but they were gone now, moved away, off to follow that dentist Carl—no better than a kidnapper, that Carl—to Lake Mary, which may as well have been the red planet Mars. What could Jack know about what she had lost, losing John. What could any child know about what a whole life spent with someone means. Especially a whole life that didn't rightly begin until that someone came along and gave it a reason to keep being after years and years of having no reason at all.

The distance between Franny and Jack widened after that. They shared the space of the house, but they did not have things to say to each other. They were not enemies; there was nothing bitter between them. They were more like strangers. And something else, too. As he grew toward manhood, he continued to have some of his father John's features, but as he grew into his face, characteristics from her own family began to assert themselves in ways she could not have expected. His nose and ears grew longer, more like her father's and less like John's. He had been seeing the older girl, Julie—that's how Franny thought of her, even though she and Jack were still in the same grade—and as they grew more serious, there was some glint in his eye that was not of John, some expression of desire she caught a glimpse of now and then when Jack was walking behind Julie and did not know she was watching him. When her son would look at his girlfriend's legs or backside. A directness. Nothing sidelong. An expression of desire that was different in kind from the way she had seen John look at her in the unguarded moments they had shared.

She tried to put it aside, but she could not. She did not remember ever seeing her father in a moment so unguarded, yet she somehow knew it was of her family. She knew in a very general way but would not say to her own self, not even in the privacy of her own mind, that the quality she saw in her son's gaze was in some way reminiscent of something she remembered about her cousin Donny Lynn Prather.

Just once, and only to put it to rest, she put it into words, but not aloud. Only in her head. Just once, just to put it to rest. Because it was not, she knew, any sign of any deficiency in her son. It was just something in the blood, something, in fact, that came from her, that something inside her shared with Donny only because they shared a grandfather. It was not what caused Donny to be what he had been. It was just a speck in her son Jack's eye.

She suspected Jack and Julie were sleeping together but could not put her finger on why. When they went out at night, he always came home at an acceptable hour. He was busy, and stayed busy, with baseball. He had been going to the church more, the Cherry Road Baptist Church the family had been attending ever since they had moved to West Palm Beach, way back when it wasn't even a proper church but instead what they called a mission. John used to stand in the back as an usher one Sunday a month and greet visitors and tell them that he was "a charter member of our church."

Franny wasn't going much anymore. It was too hard to go without Jack. Worse, it made her think thoughts that ended up in bad places. Like, if God is good and loves those who accept Jesus Christ as their personal savior, then why does He allow so many terrible things to happen in the world. And she wasn't thinking about it in the abstract. The beef with God she was trying to avoid was quite personal. As in: If God is good and loves those who accept Jesus Christ as their personal savior, then why is John dead? And why did Millie's husband beat her? And why did she and Eleanor move away? And why was Donny Lynn Prather allowed to kill his little brother Roy on a day he meant to do less?

Sunday mornings Jack would rise early and shower and dress and leave to pick up Julie, and Franny would lie in her bed and pretend to be sleeping.

She went on sleeping in, and not just on Sundays anymore, but also on Mondays and Tuesdays, Wednesdays and Thursdays and Saturdays. Fridays she did force herself to wake, by the alarm clock neither she nor John had needed their whole lives, being children raised in the natural cycles of the sun's rising and setting. Fridays she was in the car by eight-thirty, and off to Claudia's Beauty Salon in the

Cross-County shopping center on Okeechobee Road, where she got her hair done and listened (without participating) to the neighborhood gossip, this ungrateful child and that one, mostly, and wondered at her own restraint, for she by now had as much to say on the subject as anyone.

Jack graduated from high school and went on to college at Stetson University, same as Millie, and he, too, planned to be an accountant. Julie followed him there, and by sophomore year they were married. At the rehearsal dinner the night before the ceremony, Jack sprung on Franny the news that he had changed his major from accounting to something called Bible and Religion, and it was all she could do to keep from screaming in protest: "And how will you feed your family?" Already he was up to his eyeballs in college loans; six months later he told her he was thinking of attending the Dallas Theological Seminary in Texas upon graduation, which he said would now take five years on account of his changing his major so late in the game.

Three years passed. Jack and Julie moved to Texas. Eleanor sent a card every year for Christmas. Millie remarried, a partner in Carl's dental practice named (and this was funny) Dennis, but didn't send Franny an invitation. The backyard ceremony grew nearer and nearer—Franny heard all about it from Sally Cunningham down the street, whose daughter was Millie's lifelong best friend—and finally, when Franny couldn't take it anymore, she called Millie on the phone and said, "Your old mother can't come to your wedding?"

"I sent you an invitation, Mother," Millie said. She said it cold like that. Mother. What kind of way was that to talk?

"I never saw no invitation," Franny said.

"Well, I sent it," Millie said. "And, anyway, you're invited. I'm inviting you now."

But the invitation never came by mail, and to Franny that was message enough. She did not want to go any place she wasn't wanted. If John were around he would've smoothed it over, called Millie, calmed Franny, arranged for an invitation to be sent. But John was not around. John was dead and gone and everything good with him. Franny did not go to the wedding, and after that she and Millie did not speak at all.

Franny went out less and less. She stopped getting her hair done once a week. It was a vanity she did not need to indulge, and anyway she was tired of hearing about everyone else's children, what they had accomplished. Now she got her hair done once every three weeks at Mary's Beauty Salon on Military Trail, but the talk there was almost more unbearable, everyone prattling on about their grandchildren and passing along pictures.

What did it say about her that her children, all married, had not produced any grandchildren? Sure, Eleanor and Carl had the good excuse that they weren't able, a problem of Carl's, not Eleanor's. But was this not the age of science, like they said all the time now, and technology? Surely, with the kind of money a Lake Mary dentist must be pulling in, they could afford some of that in-vitro fertilization. Shelby Crockett's son-in-law had been shooting blanks all along, but all he did was get his brother to go in a cup, and then they implanted his seed in her daughter, and it was as though the baby was all theirs, instead of three-quarters.

But Millie, well, Millie said she wanted no part of any childrearing. And Jack and Julie had been married going on four years now, and still no news. That saying, no news is good news? Well, it's not so. No news is not good news. Good news is good news. Franny waited and waited, but the good news never came.

Then one morning Jack called, and he said, "Mom, I have some good news." This was it. She was sure of it. She was so excited she began to squeal and jump up and down.

She said, "Oh, oh, I'm so happy, I'm so happy for you. For us."

Jack said, "Well, wait a minute, Mom. I haven't told you yet."

And she said, "I'm sorry, it's just I get so excitable these days." She dabbed at her moist eyes with a handkerchief. She sat down in the chair by the kitchen phone and waited to hear it. She wanted to savor every second. In that brief moment she felt forty-five years old and beautiful. She wished John were here to share it with her. She bounced up and down in her seat like a schoolgirl.

"It's me and Julie," Jack said. "We have a big change that's going to happen in our life. We're moving. Back to West Palm Beach. I've been called to be the pastor at the Cherry Road Baptist Church."

She put her hand over the receiver and began to sob, silently as she could. She was shaking at the shoulders.

"There's a few formalities," Jack was saying. "I have to come down and preach. There has to be a vote. But, I mean, they know me and I know them, and I don't think there will be any sort of problems."

She regained her composure. He was waiting for her to say something. He would want her to tell him how wonderful it was, and how happy and proud she was, and, really, it was true, the part about it being wonderful. It was wonderful that one of her children would be moving home. She could be happy about it. It was something to be happy about.

She said, "Jack, I'm happy and I'm proud. The news you are saying is wonderful."

He said, "I want you to come see me preach, Mom. I want you to be there."

She said, "I'll be there, all right. You just watch. I'll be there on the front row, saying Amen. Me and Julie, and, who knows, little John Wenderoth the Third maybe . . ."

She went on at some length about what it would be like to be a grandmother. John, for his part, did not say much about it. When he said he had to get off the phone, had to go attend to something for Julie, she still had more things to say, so she called Eleanor on the phone. Carl answered and tried to exchange some pleasantries, but she said if he didn't mind would he get Eleanor on the phone, because she had some important and exciting news to share.

As soon as she heard Eleanor's voice, Franny told her tale, first the news from Jack that he and Julie would be hearing God's call on their lives to come on down to the Cherry Road Baptist Church—that part she told real fast—and then a whole lot of speculation about what it would be like to sit on that front row, in a seat of honor, right there alongside Julie and little John the Third, and, who knows, maybe some little girl, maybe named Francine Mae, after her.

Eleanor interrupted. "What's this about John the Third and Francine Mae, Mother?" she said. Mother. That again.

Franny began to lecture. "That's what people do when they meet and marry and settle down," she said. "That's the normal, healthful, God-ordained way of things."

"Well, what does that say about me and Carl?" Eleanor said. "We don't have any children."

"Well," Franny said. It was her way of saying that she understood the rebuke and did not accept it. Eleanor had crossed a line she should not have crossed. She was the daughter, after all.

Eleanor's voice softened. "Look, Mom," she said. "I don't think you should be saying things like that to Jack and Julie."

"And why is that your business?" Franny said.

"I don't suppose it is," Eleanor said, keeping an even tone. That was even more infuriating than if she had been yelling. It was a point of pride, Franny supposed. Refinement. Class. All those things people think they acquire so they can be better than other people. "But I'll tell you anyway, because I don't think it's fair for you to assume that Jack and Julie are going to move down there and make their choices just to please you."

"They are not going to have any children?" Franny said. "You know this? They told you it?"

"They're busy with their careers," Eleanor said. "The same as a lot of people. Jack just did his internship at First Baptist of Dallas and he was working eighty, ninety hours a week. And Julie's doing the crisis pregnancy counseling. That takes time. You get these poor black girls who don't have anyplace else to go and the man who got them that way sees he can pay a couple hundred dollars for an abortion or spend the next eighteen years paying child support or more likely running from it. You know how they are. That's a lot of pressure she has to try and combat. And they're all confused about love, like any girl that age knows the first thing about it. It takes a lot of time to avert a crisis like that. It's life and death, Mom. She's out there on the front lines of it, and sometimes it keeps her away all hours."

"You're lecturing me," Franny said.

"I'm not lecturing you, Mom," Eleanor said. "I'm telling it to you straight."

And right away, thoughts began to consume her that she could hardly bear. What kind of mother raises three children who themselves think so little of children that they do not want to have any of their own? What kind of trauma do they think they survived? What do they know the first thing about survival anyway? They had it so easy, these children. John working a good job, and Franny staying home and tending to everything. So easy, and the warmth of family all around them, and now every single one of them acting like family itself was some kind of poison they needed to void from their systems.

Franny went to see Jack preach his try-out, but she sat in the back row, not up front with Julie. It was her way of protesting, but no one seemed to notice. Jack acknowledged her from the pulpit, asked her to stand, said, "That's the woman who raised me, who I owe my very self to. I want to say it publicly. I love you, Mom." Then everyone applauded, but it wasn't for anything she had done. It was because that's what they were supposed to do. It was a dog and pony show.

When it was over they voted him in two hundred and four to sixteen, with four abstentions. That was as close to unanimity as the Cherry Road Baptist Church had ever seen. Franny herself abstained, which would have brought the total abstentions to five, except her vote was invalidated on account of the last time she set foot in the church was seven and a half years ago for the Easter cantata. She was still a member, a charter member at that, but not in good standing. But the act of attending made her eligible to vote again for at least the next five years, and for the rest of the years she lived in her own house, the one she had shared with John, she never missed another vote. She registered strongly her support for air conditioning improvements and her opposition to hiring a music minister who did not also want to work with the youth, often enough heading up a stubborn bloc of old-timers against Jack. She did it for the same reason she had abstained the day he was voted in. It wouldn't be right to cast a favorable vote just because the pastor was her son. That would be nepotism, and it just wouldn't be right.

Still, there were advantages to being the pastor's mother. Jack was well-liked. Women she had known her whole adult life would come up to her and compliment her on her raising him so well. "He's grown into quite the gentleman," they might say, or, those so inclined: "He's grown into quite the mighty man of God."

She began to attend the Wednesday morning women's prayer meetings, which she found were quite useful for catching up on everyone's business. Everyone talked bad about gossip, even while they were doing it. Marjorie Phillips would say things like, "I want to offer a request for intercessory prayer for Mary Jo Abdo. I was at the beauty shop last week and I heard her spreading all sorts of gossip about the women of the church. I want to pray for Mary Jo, in the spirit of love, that she might turn away from idle chatter and toward more edifying kinds of words."

It was delicious. Franny joined in, too. She resumed her weekly hair appointments so she would have more prayer requests to share. Often she was the first to know about illness, divorce, and all kinds of other miseries, which she offered up for prayer. Mary Jo Abdo began coming to prayer meetings and before long told Franny that she considered her to be an A-1 All-American prayer warrior, and something of a mother to her in the faith.

Tuesday evenings she went over to Jack and Julie's house for dinner and they made over her. Sometimes Julie grilled steaks on the back porch, really nice tenderloin cuts Franny and John never would have bought, and sometimes Jack made some kind of Mexican food, or Japanese food, always something new he was learning from someone he went to visit. He said it made people feel more comfortable if they had something to do with their hands, and it made him more comfortable, too, so when he went to visit people, if they weren't too ill, he would ask them to teach him how to make their favorite meal in the kitchen. He would even offer to buy the ingredients, though almost everyone refused to let him.

One Tuesday evening Julie was out back grilling. Franny and Jack were sitting in the comfortable chairs in the living room, and she was telling him about how Mary Jo Abdo had met a gentleman in his fifties—"A younger man," she said, eyes bright: "The scandal!"—when Jack interrupted her and said he wanted to check on Julie, that he'd be right back.

He was gone a little too long, and she began to worry. If life had taught her one thing it was that the good times don't ever last, that the bad times come and take them away right when you least expect it. She waited another minute and then she got up and walked toward the back door. Just then, the door opened, and Jack and Julie walked in pushing a brand-new bicycle, a beautiful old-fashioned kind, with high sloping handlebars and a basket and a red horn. "For you, Mom," Julie said, and that was almost better than the bicycle, her calling Franny Mom. It was the first time she had ever said it.

She began to ride the bicycle in the early afternoon. It felt good to move around some every day. She was sore at first, but then her body adjusted, and then she began to ride in the mornings. Once a week she undertook a long ride to the airport and back, growing fond of passing landmarks like the old army barracks, the bomb shelter, even the strip clubs and their pink facades.

July 4, 1996, the church gathered at Okeeheelee State Park for an Independence Day celebration. They started early. The men played softball and later basketball, even though it was hotter than blue blazes by nine-thirty. There was a potluck lunch followed by a potluck dinner. Bill Miller brought his famous banana pudding. There were lawn darts and horseshoes, tetherball and badminton. The older women served the food and rested between meals in plastic lawn chairs beneath the shade of the palm trees. At nightfall the children traced their names in the air with sparklers. At nine o'clock the fire department brought a skiff out onto the lake where the water skiers practiced and shot off fireworks. Oh, what a sight. Red, white, and blue. And then the grand finale, explosion after explosion. Franny covered her ears and dropped her jaw the way the men who got back from the war said people did in London during the air raids. Then, just when the music had stopped and the last lights burned out in the sky, the music started up again, a massive chord played on maybe ten pianos at once, and dozens of fireworks, one last round, went up into the sky, and burst into color simultaneously. The pattern they made was the American flag.

When it was over, everyone sat in stunned silence for a long, long time. Then someone put their hands together and began to cheer. That's all it took was one person, and everyone was cheering, up on their feet applauding and whooping like there was no tomorrow, or, better yet, like tomorrow was going to be even better than today, which was saying a lot, because today was as good as it gets.

That was the night she slept in her own bed for the last time. In the morning she woke up feeling fine. She made a cup of coffee, put sugar on her grapefruit and dug the flesh from the rind with her spoon. Then she got on her bicycle and set off for the airport.

She saw them up ahead, at the corner of Seminole and Cherry. Two Guatemalans—pickers, no doubt; day laborers, like her father had been; but not like her father at all; dirty and unruly—trading blows. The bigger man had the smaller one in a headlock and was punching away at the top of his head with his free fist. The body of the one in the headlock was flailing all around, kicking his legs in the air, trying to spin out of the hold or get the bigger man on the ground, and he was delivering short blows to the kidneys with both hands.

She slowed down, wanting to see what would happen. Her money was on the one in the headlock, the little guy. He had fight; it was plain to see. It was all she could do to not shout her encouragement.

And just then, the smaller man got his legs hooked around the larger man's legs and swept them out from under him, and they went down together on the sidewalk. The smaller man's head hit the concrete first, and right away split open, ran red on the sidewalk. Then the larger man came down on top of the smaller man.

It was horrible, sure, but it was beautiful, all that blood, and the sickening crack of the smaller man's skull as the larger man came down upon it. She was reminded of something she had all but forgotten from when she was very small, a story her father told. There had been a terrible passenger train accident, a section of track just west of Rowan County that had not been mended. Her father happened to be nearby. He was very young, maybe fifteen; she couldn't remember. He was hunting deer with his father. They both saw it happen. The train derailed, and forty people died, "But I could see the faces, all them people looking out at me and my daddy through them windows like they never had seen two men holding hunting guns before. Like we was the most beautiful people that ever lived on the planet earth. I don't reckon I'll ever know that feeling again."

And that's how it was for Franny. That Guatemalan picker hit the sidewalk and busted open his head, and then, just briefly, his eyes met hers, and he must have thought he dreamed it, an old lady on an old-fashioned bicycle.

She thought that the man might die, so she held onto his gaze as long as she could. She held onto it, and the act of holding onto it made her forget to keep her eyes on the road ahead. The bicycle rolled slowly into the intersection at Seminole and Cherry. There was the sound of squealing brakes. She looked up and saw a green pickup truck as it clipped her front tire. She lost control of the bike and fell, and the last thing she remembered was a dull cracking sound not unlike the one the picker's head had just made, but coming from the direction of her right hip. Then a searing pain in that hip as it went stationary while her shoulders and head continued their fall. Then for some reason the smell of bay leaves and cinnamon. Then blackness.

She woke to a strange parade of strangers, vagrants in white coats, faces from her past—neighbors, relatives, schoolteachers, themselves but not. She found herself in great pain, the worst of it in her hip and running up and down her leg. She was haunted by the long dead. They spoke to her, and she was confused because their faces did not match their voices and they had not aged in the years since she had known them in her youth. Time had ceased its orderly way forward. She could not walk, and men came to kidnap her, and when she tried to scream they strapped her to a gurney and injected her with something that caused her to lose consciousness, but not entirely.

It happened again and again. She could hear them speaking though she could not move. Once she heard them say that she was suffering from some sort of stroke-related dementia and near-paralysis. But she knew that it was the world that was changing and not her. She had *clarity*. Once, opening her eyes, she saw that the youngest of the doctors— how could this be possible?—was Bruce Macholtz from Mt. Sterling, Kentucky, one of the doctors who had tended to her when she had the chicken pox at age six. Dr. Macholtz, but younger now than he was then.

And where was her John? It was time for him to come rescue her. She called out for him, or tried to, but her lips would not properly move. She was saying (but not saying),

Let's do it again, John. Take me away from here. Take me any-
where. We can start over again.

She remembered a magazine picture of a beachfront
town near Georgetown, South Carolina. Debourdieu. Oh,
it was so beautiful. Beach houses on wooden pilings two
hundred feet from the Atlantic Ocean. John appeared to
her once, calling her Momma, and she knew it must be a
dream. Debourdieu; she had seen it in *Better Homes and*
Gardens. Why would John call her Momma? *Sweet girl*, she
wanted to say, to John. *Tell me I am your sweet girl.*

In Debourdieu the alligators occasionally approached
from the brackish swamp water just north. Mary Jo had
told Franny about Debourdieu, had shown her the pictures
in a *Better Homes and Gardens* magazine, but the alligator
talk she heard from her friend Arlene, who had vacationed
in Georgetown. Alligators, walking the streets and beaches
of Debourdieu. They had to get the Negroes and Chinamen
who worked the rice paddies to come wrangle them away.
Oh, for some Indian alligator wranglers. Old fashioned cowboys
and Comanches, John Wayne in a white hat, Tonto. Shirley
Temple, remember her? She was a sexpot, a five-year-old
tramp in saddle shoes, and no one was allowed to say it.
The old men drove to Lexington to see her shake on the
silver screen. It was her eyes, Shirley Temple. They spoke
lewd things to the old men, those eyes. Oh, in Debourdieu,
there, no Shirley Temple would tap her jig. They would
feed her to the alligators, and then the Negroes and the
Chinamen would hustle it all away.

She and John, there in Debourdieu, growing old,
away from their horrid daughters with their dentist
husbands, their rejections. But first she would have to find
a way to escape. She woke as from a dream and saw the
white flecked with black in the ceiling tile squares. White
florescent lights ran the length of the ceiling. The terrible

new Negro music blared from the television. The talking over the boom-boom-boom. Two of them in the room, talking, so not watching. First about men and their bodies. Delicious men, hard men who could be soft as cotton candy. Men worth their runnings around, but just barely. Then praying together. One said, "Take my hand, Sister Charlene," and then: "Oh sweet Jesus, we come to you now with heavy hearts. We lift up our Sister Charlene in her time of trouble . . ."

The television still running. That dialect she could not bear, and the music, or what passed for it. She tried to cry out, to scream. Oh, sweet Lord, what if I have been taken from your bosom because of my secret. Because I have lied to John. Where is the fire and the brimstone? The heat and the sulfurous smell that lays waiting for the unrighteous?

The days and the nights intermingled. The woman came and said, "It's me, Mom. It's me, Julie." Called her Mom. Took her away, but not to Debourdieu. To a house that seemed familiar, which was a comfort, but which she did not recognize. Often in her life she had recognized places she had never been. There was a word for it, in the French. She couldn't remember.

On New Year's Eves she had often longed for confetti, at Christmas for snow to fall in Florida, every other day of the year for Christ to come back on his white horse, the sky to turn red, her to be bodily raptured to be with her Father in heaven and all the saints. In this new place, she slowly realized that she could not any more control her body than a small infant could. She'd once heard a preacher say that from dust to dust there is a fall to match every rise. I know I am not dead by my pain. I know where the branch creek meets the larger creek that flows into the river at the bottom of the mountain and I am walking with my father. I am a good girl and have not known a whipping for more than a week. He has not said go choose a switch from the tree.

She knew the tree. She knew it was better to pick a stiff switch, one without any give. But not too stiff, because then it would break against her backside, and, "Franny Mae, you're in for a world of hurt now."

She was wearing her red housedress, and this Julie was taking it off and bathing her. The water was not cold and not too hot. She remembered Goldilocks and the Three Bears, and isn't it nice to have something that is just right. And isn't it nice to feel the warm washcloth against your skin, and the water, and to be lifted bodily from the water and feel the towel around your shoulders, and the hands of the young woman drying you.

The pain was worst in the middle of the night when she was alone and tried to call out and no sound came, so no one came. Then one night the worst of all, the thing she thought she had laid to rest.

Donny Lynn Prather, looking in her window.

He mocked her by standing still, watching and not watching. She could not lift her head to see the window, but she could feel him there, staring, not moving.

One evening he found a way to speak to her so she knew he was not moving his lips but was just speaking from his mind to hers. A violation he had achieved how? He was not using words but instead a liquid fear. She could feel him seeping it into her through her skin and skull. She worried it would melt her.

He was sending her a message and sending. A message he was sending but she could not know the words and what they stood for.

Sending and sending.

And then, all at once, she knew and it was worse than the melting of her skin from her face, though that was part of what he was promising. The words she could not know because they were spoken in Spanish, so he had gone to Mexico after all. He was saying, You thought I was a dummy, little girl, but I got something for you. He was saying it in Spanish, but she was hearing it in English. He had been taken by devils for sure. She remembered the preacher when Eleanor was a baby who came one Sunday night to the Cherry Road Baptist Church and said that these devils were all around us, standing on our shoulders, wanting to poke at us but for the blood of Jesus, and it was not that they had got to Donny Lynn Prather just now or even when he was on the run in Mexico. It was that they had got to his momma before he was even born and taken residence in his soul.

Every night he came to her window but did not show her his face by coming in the room. Just let her know he was there so she could not sleep.

She could feel a growing tightness in her chest. She spent most of her days wrung out and half-alive, slumped sideways in a La-Z-Boy chair until the woman Julie brought some couch pillows to prop her up. Like she was a rag doll with sagging flesh, discarded victim of love like the Velveteen Rabbit. Perhaps a dog would come and take her in his jaws and drag her away.

Then one night Donny Lynn came to the window with a new message. Do you wonder where your John is? he said but did not say. Yes, I do, she said. They were talking this way often. They were bound up together now in such a way that neither had need of voice. You have him, don't you, she said. You have taken him.

There was a long silence.

Then Donny Lynn Prather went away. He did not say anything. The absence of him was worse than his presence, because he was gone and he had John.

Ten days passed, or ten years. She could not be sure when Donny had found a way to reorder time. A day with the Lord, the preachers would say, is like a thousand years. But what about a day with Donny?

She could see him whipping that little boy, Roy, his little brother, in that field, curse that field, with both belts, knocking that belt buckle the shape of Kentucky into his head, and Franny was standing to one side, no, sitting, in that woman Julie's La-Z-Boy chair, slumped to one side, watching Roy's head cave in slowly, while all around her she could hear string music that sounded like heaven, and Julie saying, "Mom, it's Vivaldi, it's so beautiful, isn't it, have you heard it before?" and Roy crying out to Donny, pleading for his life, singing for it—Shoo-Fly, Don't Bother Me, 'Cause I Belong to Somebody—and then Roy looking at her, saying I'm not being no Mommy.

Then, a time of amazing quiet. She fell asleep one evening and woke the next morning. That evening she fell asleep again, and did not wake until the morning. Mornings she sometimes woke soiled by her own urine, sometimes even her own excrement. No matter, the woman Julie would come and tend to her. Bathe her, dry her, brush her hair.

She came to think of herself as a child, and Julie her mother. It was not true—she was not a child, and her mother was long gone—but then, in its own way, it was true. In her heart she was growing to love Julie.

One afternoon Julie left her in the care of another woman. She said she had to go to the store to pick up a few things. When she returned, she was holding a metal cage, and inside the cage was a green parakeet. She held it up so Franny could see it. The parakeet jumped from its perch to ring a bell near the top of the cage. "His wings have been clipped," Julie said, "but he's not any less lovely, is he Mom?"

That evening she went to sleep and woke the next morning reeking of drying urine. She waited for Julie to come and get her, but Julie did not come. She waited for a long time. She could hear the parakeet stirring in his covered cage. The daylight from her bedroom had reached him through the white pillowcase meant to comfort him and keep him quiet through the night.

She began to worry about Julie. The Florida sun burned through the window, the heat rising enough she could notice it every few minutes. She worried the parakeet would overheat and die. Tiny birds are fragile. Little green birds.

The door opened. She heard it open, and the relief settled into her. Julie's being there.

Then a voice. But not Julie's. A man's voice, saying Julie's words. "Let's get you cleaned up, Mom."

She had been conscious, sometimes, of the presence of a man in the house. It was not her business. Julie, kind as she was, could do what she wanted. Any comfort there is in the world . . . how could any of it be bad when all we are doing is waiting to get old and die? She wanted to help that parakeet grow its wings and give it the run of the house. You couldn't set a thing like that free, because some cat would get to it, or some bigger bird.

The man leaned over her, and she did not right away recognize who he was. He was so familiar she should have known, but what in the world is easy to know when it is so hot in the room?

He reached his arms under her and picked her up. He was not gentle enough. His way of lifting her hurt her. Hurt her legs and hurt more under her armpits where he was carrying too much of her weight. Who was he? And why was he moving her instead of Julie?

He carried her into the bathroom and sat her roughly on the toilet, then knelt at her feet. She could not hold up her weight, and she slumped to the side. She had the terrible pain in her hip. He reached up and grabbed her by the shoulders. As he leaned back she caught her first glimpse of his eyes.

It was the eyes. Something about the directness of his gaze. Even for just a moment, so direct. So familiar. It was then that she knew who it was who had come for her, after all these years.

It was Donny Lynn Prather. He had come and took John, and then he had come all those nights to scare her at her window. If he was here, what had come of John? What was he planning for her?

Donny said, "Mother, I'm going to take off your shoes and socks now, all right?" And it was not his way of talking. It was the way the younger people talked in this part of the country.

It was a matter of pride had led her to this. She had all those years thought Spanish was beyond him, but he had learned it. Now he had learned to talk like the people all around. He was like one of those lizards that could change color.

And he was calling her mother. She remembered the words so burned in her memory: *Open up that pretty little mouth, Mommy.* What job had he come to finish?

With the greatest force of her will she tried to scream in protest, but no words would come. His hands were on her shoulders. His hands were so close to her throat. Then he knelt again and was strangely silent. She could hear only the small sounds of his moving.

"Your shoes, mother," he said, and she felt him take the slippers from her feet. She wondered if he was going to kill her why did he not kill her, and then she knew he had made up a ritual to make her afraid.

She was afraid.

Then he did something to her foot. He hurt her so bad she lost her air. Her throat closed up like it sometimes did without her wanting it to.

He said, "Does it hurt, mother?"

She tried to still herself. Her chest was burning.

He said, "Does it hurt?" What did he want from her. How could she keep from him the pleasure of letting him know her pain?

He stood, and again those fearsome eyes locked onto hers. "Mom," he said—in his mouth, the word was a curse—"Does it hurt?"

Some signal, any, to make him stop. She tried to blink her eyes. She could only feel the right one, could only see out of it. She blinked twice.

"I saw that, Mom," he said. "Can you do it again? I want to be sure."

In hostage situations, give the captor what he wants. That's what they said on the evening news. She did it again, but her muscles got angry and her eye fluttered and she thought it might pop out at him. Any other man would feel horror, but he might find satisfaction. She did not want him to be satisfied.

He began to taunt her again. He was cruel. He said, "Well, that's something." He must have thought it was funny to see her like that, not able to move her body like she wanted. "Okay," then louder, to intimidate her, the monster: "Okay."

So she tried to blink again and was relieved that it at least stopped the fluttering. "I see it," he said. Oh, he was cruel.

Then he began his lies. "I don't want to hurt you," he said. Had he said it to John, too? "I'm going to wash you now. I'm going to do it, but not if you don't want me to. I'm going to take that sock off by unrolling it from the top, all right?"

Rape. She had been avoiding the word all her life, and now it popped up from the place he had planted it. Her body offered nothing for him. What pleasure was left in her old body? This was only violence. Only cruelty. Only the pleasures children find on their way to evil, as when they string a cat from a tree, and flay it open, strip its skin, and let it die of exposure. Like they say Donny did when he was a small boy. They say, "Why, we knew then he was a bad seed." They say it, they said it, but here stands Donny, and all them dead, and still he only a little older than he was then, to judge by his talk and his eyes. He found a way in Mexico. Must have. Here he is. Here, standing over her.

He was waiting for something. She blinked one more time, to pacify him. That seemed to be what he wanted. He lowered himself again. She felt him touch her on the calf. His skin on hers. He was taking off her sock, like he said. If this was the end of her, he was going to drag it out. She was like that cat, but not kicking. Her body betrayed her.

"Mom," Donny said, "you've got a nasty sore down here. On the arch of your foot. It's bruised. It's a bad one." Then he struck her three times, just enough to hurt, on the calf. "The other one now," he said, "Mom."

Mom. Mother. He kept using the words. He was taking off her shoes and her socks now. Sometimes in the years after he had run off into the mountains and far away she had suffered from terrible dreams—she in a canoe with Roy, paddling downstream, and suddenly the water filling with snakes, and both of them trying to beat them away with the paddles, but there were too many, snakes filling the canoe, snakes wrapping themselves around paddles, snakes wrapping themselves around limbs and chests and necks, snakes hissing, snakes opening their mouths, snakes showing their fangs, their forked tongues—and there would come a time when she realized she was asleep and dreaming, but that did nothing to make the snakes any less real. She would try to wake from those dreams. She would fight as though trying to escape from her own skin. She would fight and fight, a feeling not unlike trying to get above water to avoid drowning, and the fighting would exhaust her. She would wake alone and wet, her muscles tense, her blood rushing like whitewater rapids.

Her body, now, was not unlike her young girl's body had been in those long moments of not-waking. But now she could not wake. Her body had become divorced from her. It functioned to the extent that it functioned and no more. She could not will it to do much more.

She tried to resist the urge, then, to swim upward through herself and try to escape through whatever surface it was that separated her self from her body. Like a swimmer underwater, she could see through the surface well enough to know it was there, to see the light play upon it.

He kept up his patter. "The other one now, Mom," he said.

She began to pray: *Lord, if it is Your will take me now. I've seen enough of this life. I don't want to suffer any more. Not at his hands.* She did not believe her prayer would be answered. She had been told that faith the size of a mustard seed was enough to make heaven move. Her experience of life said that was not so.

He said, "Mom, have you noticed the shower curtains?" What did he want with the shower curtains? "They're starting to yellow, and that's the problem, I think, with translucent shower curtains, the way they yellow with time. Julie was thinking of buying some shower curtains to match the hand towels . . ." And at this she thought she might vomit. What was he threatening? Take me, take me, what life do I have left for living? Julie, she is so kind, so kind . . .

Now she could not hear the words he was saying, so loud was the sound of the screaming in her own head. The screams got trapped inside when she could not give them voice, and inside they reverberated as in an echo chamber, and multiplied, grew louder and louder until all that was in her seemed to be screaming, crying out as the rocks might but in anguish, not in praise.

She waited to hear the sound of water running, knew he was capable of drowning her, knew how little it would take if he lay her face down in the water. In Rowan County she had known of at least three children drowned in less than three inches of water in nearby creeks. She had known of cats wrapped in burlap sacks and weighted down, dropped in only a bucket of water and killed that way. Donny himself had at age twelve buried a wounded dog up to his neck in sand and brought over chickens to peck at his eyes and deeper, killed him that way. There was no one way to kill a feeble creature.

Donny began to hum. The song he was humming was carnal. She could feel it in her bones. Could tell from the way he was humming it, the sharpnesses and roundnesses of notes, the way they refused to flatten-out, the kind of music that was the opposite of hymns, that carried with it the mark of the silvery tongue.

She heard it, knew she was getting bound up, worried that she was giving him what he wanted. He could take her life if he so pleased, but with the least pleasure possible. Right then she tried her best to think of things outside herself and long ago. The moment John Junior took his first steps at Connie and Millicent Pomeroy's house. They had brand new white carpeting, made to look marbled on purpose, and Eleanor was so excited at the baby's steps, she ran into the living room carrying her cup of grape juice and spilled it on that carpet, and John said, "I'll buy you new carpet. I'll install it myself!" And he would have, gladly, but Connie said he had extra, would he just patch it, and John did, with Connie's help. She could see them, those two men, cutting a careful square that white carpet and matching the extra just right, matching one end of the marbling pattern to the other so you couldn't tell unless you put your nose right up to that carpet, and then standing back, taking such satisfaction in what they had done, with their hands, with their heads.

The memory calmed her. She could feel it, and hoped Donny could see it, hoped it sped him on his way to whatever it was he intended to do to her, then sped him ever quicker to hell. Surely someone would find her body and go looking for him. Justice was harder to escape than it used to be. They had more than dogs. They had helicopters and computers and television programs. She had watched them every Sunday night, hoping to catch a killer.

She heard the sound of the faucet turning and the water beginning to run. He was still talking but she was refusing to listen to the words he was saying. She had survived him once before, and she would not be afraid of him now.

The phone rang. She heard him turn off the water, wondered if he would leave her to get up and answer it. Fleetingly, she heard Julie's voice, which alarmed her because what if she was in the house?, but it was the answering machine, because she heard the beep, and then some sort of wrong number, a woman talking the way one woman talks to another, but saying in the course of her yammering, "Bring me the man of God!"

Then Donny said, "Art Miller. Now there's one guy who can wait."

He had turned on the water again. He was looking at her. And then she knew. He meant to kill not just her, but others, too. She tried to pull herself together, but the fear was beginning to rise in her again. She thought of the little green parakeet, and that affected her somehow more than Art Miller. Like people used to say, "Somebody else's baby dies, you wear black to the funeral. Your dog dies, you wear black for a whole year."

That wasn't right, she'd always thought. Now she knew it didn't matter if it was right or not. Like a lot of things. It was so. It was what it was, and there was no changing the ways of people. The way of a man is righteous in his own eyes, like the preachers say. Oh, to save that little green bird.

He turned off the water. She was aware that he was staring at her, with those cold eyes. She could not see those eyes, but she knew. It was just like those long nights when he waited at the windows, or those long-ago afternoons when he stalked her tree to tree. She could not hear his voice anymore and knew he was keeping it from her to prolong the silence and create an empty space in it for her fears.

Finally he spoke. "Now, Mom," he said. "After I stop the tub, okay?" As though he were asking for her consent. The sincerity of the venomous snake, its bright colored markings covered in mud. And he put his body near hers, his face near hers, so close they were almost touching, so close they were breathing in one another's air. Close like lovers, his eyes probing hers, his eyes winding their way inside her.

He said, "I'm going to give you a bath now, momma," and surely this was her end. There was a strange light in his eyes, something stranger than the familiarity. A sadness, almost. Judas kissing Jesus, compelled by some force stronger than his own love. She could see in that moment something of love in Donny's eyes, and the sight of it, the sight of love, was more frightening than anything she had seen in her life. To know that the very face of evil was love. To know that every boundary separating every one thing from another could be wiped away in the last moments of life, which she knew these would be. The true nature of the world letting itself be known in this last hour.

Then he began to undress her. He worked his way down the front of her, button by button. He was pulling against the housedress as he went. She could feel the pull of the fabric against her back. He crouched down, and the dress went open, and his eyes, now, would be gazing upon the breasts of which she had become first ashamed then indifferent. He continued to unbutton, the waist, the lap, the knees, and then the housedress came undone and fell to her sides. He was seeing for the first time the hidden parts of her. She wondered what it meant to him and knew it must thrill him now even more than it would have when she was very young and he meant to ruin her and did.

Then he picked her up again, and she felt a burning in her chest, a great pain. He lifted her, and as he lowered her to the water, he said, "Shh, shh," and then, "Mommy, Mommy. It's all right, Mommy."

Then she began to shake. Then she felt a great pain in her chest. She had always feared she might die alone, but she was not alone.

A Love Story

obody abused me. Nobody touched me or fondled me or any of the things they tell you about in counseling. I never stole or wore or laundered my mother's underthings. I had a good father who never hit me, who hugged me maybe too often. He did not die young. He is still alive, and even now when I drive out to Inverness to see him and my mother, he greets me warmly.

Even though they couldn't afford it, they sent me to the Good Shepherd's Academy in West Palm Beach, Florida, kindergarten to grade twelve. In March of my sixth grade year, our principal Mr. Ratliff pulled all the boys out of class and marched us into the old gymnasium and gave us what he called his Fireside Chat. We sat on those hard wood bleachers and heard his confession about how his wife had left him to be a Navy captain's mistress, and how he was raising two children on his own. "I still love her," he said, "and even today the door to my heart and home is open, waiting for the prodigal to come home."

This, he said, was a picture of what Christ had for us. We had gone astray and he waited for us with open arms. But all that was prelude to what Mr. Ratliff really wanted to talk about, which was sex. "I'm not ashamed," he said, "to say that I was a virgin before I was married, and that I have not been with another woman besides my wife, who is still my wife in the eyes of God."

Then the lights dimmed and Mr. Lewis, the art and P.E. teacher, put up pictures of the male and female reproductive systems on the overhead projector. Mr. Ratliff walked us through the mechanics of each one, and talked about how sex was a beautiful gift from God, but only for a man and woman within the bounds of the marriage covenant. "I have to warn you," he said. "There are plenty of perversions out there. The world is full of them. Men lying with men and women with women. Children being born out of wedlock. One night stands in dirty motels.

"Do not be deceived," he said. "God is not mocked. For whatsoever a man soweth, that shall he reap. Keep yourselves pure unto God."

He went on to say that talk about sex, even perhaps the talk we were this very day talking, could stir up powerful feelings inside us. "That's only natural," he said. "If those feelings weren't powerful, nobody would have any reason to bring babies into the world." The thing to do, he said, was to avoid talking about sex or thinking about it, as much as we could. When we went to the bathroom at home, we ought to leave the door open a crack to avoid the temptation to touch ourselves. When we went to bed, we ought to pray ourselves to sleep, and lie flat on our backs and keep our hands crossed over our chests.

That evening I lay flat on my back in bed and kept my hands crossed over my chest and thrummed with all that had been stirred up not by the talk of sex or the drawings of reproductive systems, but rather—and this had been happening more and more often—by the memory of the charge that lit that room for me, the bodies of all those other boys in the un-air conditioned heat, and the sound of the metal fans turning near the ceiling, and the smell of sweat and bodies they stirred. I lay there for a long time, holding my breath for longer and longer intervals, feeling something build up inside me that I knew to be dirty but which did not seem so dirty as I imagined it ought. It did not seem right to pray amid all that, and when I tried it seemed I let go whatever bodily control made possible the holding of hands to chest, and then I found myself praying for deliverance from my own hand, and with the pleasure I brought myself came the worst kind of defeat, and I wept myself to sleep.

We had a tradition at Northern Illinois Bible College by which roommates set each other up with dates of their choosing. Sophomore year, twenty years old, I shared two hundred square feet with Steven Whitley, a graphic design major from Marion, Indiana. "Marianne Wright," he said, and made her shape in the air with his hands.

None of us were allowed cars, so I picked her up on foot. It was December, and snow was falling, and she was stunning, her red velvet coat, blue jeans, and brown boots against the white clapboard dormitory and the white ground and the rapidly whiting-out sky. It was a ten minute walk down one hill and up another to Sir Walter Raleigh's, known for its three hundred twenty-five varieties of ice cream sundae and one-third pound hamburgers they would cut in half so two people could share.

"Don't expect romance," she said, slipping her arm in the crook of mine, and it put me right at ease.

"Just warmth," I said, and she smiled and leaned closer as we walked against the wind. It felt good, walking with her like that, and it was not to be expected. It raised a hope within me.

At Raleigh's, she ordered the cherry-lime with almonds, and I stuck to my old favorite, chocolate. "Three hundred twenty-five varieties of ice cream," she said, "and you choose chocolate?"

The service was fast at Raleigh's, and just then the girl at the counter slid us our bowls. Hers was a deep dark red swirled around a too bright green, pitted with chunks of almond. Mine was a deep chocolate, scooped in a shapely way. Mine looked as lovely as I knew it would taste, and hers was unsightly. I looked down at her bowl and made a face I meant to mean *that's why chocolate.*

"Fair enough," she said.

We sat down at one of the long wooden booths in the far corner, where just the yellow stained glass light fixture hung over the table, a dim green bulb casting a dim and eerie light, pleasant for its dimness. "Tell me about yourself," she said, in her direct way.

I began to talk about West Palm Beach and my school and family. The acoustic guitar. College football— the Florida Gators, not the thuggish Miami Hurricanes— and tennis and swimming. The darkroom at Good Shepherd, where I developed pictures I took in Palm Beach, out near the pink seawall. A black and white of a soldier on Worth Avenue made of clay pots, unkempt plants growing from the joints of his armor at every odd angle. "It won me a prize," I said, "a blue ribbon," and for once I did not feel childish for speaking proudly of it and meaning it.

She reached over and touched my arm, her way of saying *go on, I'm interested.* And then, before I knew it, I was telling her things I had never told anyone about before, the reasons, I was coming to realize, that had led me to Northern Illinois Bible College in the first place. "My family moved," I told her, "in the seventh grade. Not far. Just twenty-five miles west of West Palm Beach, to what they called The Acreage. Before that we went to a Southern Baptist church of the nastiest kind. Every Sunday night some different preacher came from out of town with pictures or a film or a sound recording of some horrible Satanic thing, always talking about the Antichrist or *Psycho* or, once, how this kid watched the movie *Night of the Living*

Dead, then went to sleep, and when he woke up something was biting him up and down his arm and ripping away his flesh."

As I was saying these things, it occurred to me that this was not first date talk. The way she listened, with her eyes locked on mine, was not far removed from talking, and something briefly clouded them when I mentioned the gremlins.

"I'm sorry," I said.

"No, no," she said. "It's just I heard these stories, too, at my church."

"We should be eating ice cream," I said.

"Do you believe in demons and the Antichrist and all that?" she said.

I told her sure, of course I did, everyone did. "It's just the dwelling on it all the time. Especially around children. I don't think children ought to have to hear so much of it."

"I had nightmares," she said. "Four straight years. Age six to almost ten. I slept with a bed full of stuffed animals and held my head under the covers, not that it helped."

"I used to wait by the window," I said.

"The red sky," she said. "The horsemen, the bowls."

"Wow," I said. Her, too.

"I know," she said. "So. Your family moved."

"I think my parents were getting tired of the whole thing."

"The Southern Baptist thing?"

"No," I said. "Just this one church. The people there. Moving was the excuse they needed to make the break."

"We had something like that," she said, "except I was in ninth grade."

"Where was this?"

"You first."

"Okay," I said. "The new church was Southern Baptist, too. But it was brand new. Not even a church yet when we got there."

"A mission," she said.

"Right. And the preacher, Brother Marshall, was about twenty-five years old, and he already had three kids and a fourth on the way. He had this thing he said: You can live the turkey life or the eagle life. The eagle is soaring, not letting the things of life get him down, not living by guilt and fear. The turkey is always going around with his head down, plucking at the ground."

I waited to see if she was on board with this kind of speech-making. She leaned forward, listening.

"You could see my parents loosening up," I said. "Not so much the way they treated my sister and me, which was already mostly good. But just the way they carried themselves. My mom came from a family where there was a lot of yelling and throwing things, and it's like she was on edge all the time, and my dad pretty much lived to make her feel comfortable. But there was this window of time, these two years under Brother Owen, things just kind of leveled out. We were going to the beach on Saturdays. My mother was packing coolers with turkey and provolone cheese. Things we hadn't done before that.

"All this time," I said, "we were meeting in an elementary school cafeteria, and then one Sunday, Brother Marshall said we had to step out in faith and purchase this model home complex down the street that was up for sale, and turn it into our church home. God was providing this opportunity and we had to recognize it."

"You bought it and it tanked," she said.

"It took about nine months," I said. "It was summer. People were on vacation. We missed payments. But here's the thing I remember."

I was conscious, even as I was saying it, that I was speaking something into being that I had been mulling over in my head but to which I had not given voice. "A few months after everything went south, I was cutting my old Sunday School teacher's yard for maybe ten bucks. Brother Marshall stops by. He's in town to pick up his stuff from storage and put it in a U-Haul and take it back to Texas, where he's from, and he's stopped by to see old Russ. He sees me there, and I turn off the lawn mower, and we start talking, and he's asking about school, and then he's asking about what I want to do with my life, and out of nowhere I say, 'Actually, I was thinking about maybe being a preacher.' And when it comes out of my mouth he gets this sad smile on his face, but it covers his face—it's a genuine smile for sure—and he says, 'It's not for everyone, but if you're called to it, it's an honorable thing. God will honor it.'"

Across the table, Marianne Wright for the first time smiled for me the smile of comfort I would come to associate with her all our years together, and she reached across the table and grabbed my hand with hers and said, "Then you knew," and I said, "No, I'm not sure I knew except for now, saying it. It's a scary thing to say."

By then we had long since ceased eating our ice cream, and we hardly knew each other, and I could not account for why I had told her all I had told her except that maybe she was the first person I had met who had seemed ready to listen.

We stayed at Raleigh's long enough that the manager came over and said if we wanted to keep tying up the booth, we'd need to buy something else, so we ordered the one-third pound hamburger and split it as she told me about her own family, her father a Southern Baptist preacher from Americus, Georgia, who moved the family every two years or so as he bounced from church to church, trying not to get fired or made to resign. "There was a window of time," she said, "when he was ready to hang it up. I was in the ninth grade. We moved back to Americus, where I hadn't lived since I was a baby, and where I didn't want to go on account of it was so small and we had been living in suburbs of major cities, mostly. He took a job at a lumber store, spent all day measuring and cutting and stacking and selling lumber, and, thing is, there was a man there, the man he worked for, Allen Jones. He was bivocational. He ran the lumber store and he pastored the church where my dad had grown up."

This Allen Jones was a quiet healer. "I hadn't noticed it," she said, "but Daddy had developed a hunched-over way of walking. It happened over years so none of us really noticed it. But all of a sudden he seemed taller. We'd go visit him at the store, and he wouldn't know we were there, and he would be humming to himself while he ran the saw."

That evening when I walked her home, I felt more warmly toward her than I had ever felt toward a girl, and when we reached the door of her dormitory, she said, "Because I'm terribly forward, I'm going to tell you that I wouldn't mind if you leaned down here and kissed me on the mouth."

I thought my heart should be pounding. Maybe because I have always been a person who likes romanticizing things, I was waiting for some tremor in my hands or some indication that soon the earth would move beneath me, or at least that something would stir in the nearer parts of soul or body, but nothing happened inside me. She was standing and waiting, and I liked her and wanted her to like me, so I bent down and kissed her lips, and felt nothing except the warmth of her mouth. When I put my arms around her, I could tell that she was trembling, and when we parted she said, "I would never have thought a roommate date would be this wonderful, and I hope this isn't too good to be true, because I just broke eight or eleven of my own rules about getting to know people," and when she said it I wanted not to disappoint her.

It was the Wednesday night after that, though in my guilty memory sometimes I remember it as later the same night. We had the mid-week prayer meeting, and it wasn't the pipe organ and some old preacher friend of someone on the faculty yammering on. Wednesday nights were student-led, and the music was good. Jesus music, still. This was 1979.

I played the acoustic guitar and then when the music was over I gave the sermon. It was my first time to do it, and I brought with me my baseball mitt and a ball and threw it back and forth with a theology student in the front row while I talked about the story of the Good Samaritan, and how the priest and the Levite passed by without helping the robbed and beaten near to death man in the road, and how it was this passing man from Samaria—I characterized it then in terms I wouldn't now, as the Harlem of Palestine— so the dirty man, then, the unclean half-breed, who was willing to rescue the poor man who would have under other circumstances spat in his face, and carry him to an inn to recover, and pay his way in advance.

My reasoning was that if I played catch while I preached, I could distract myself from my own nerves, and distract my audience, too, by way of something visual. It had nothing to do with the story, or the message of the story, and I justified it in the sermon by ending with a lame metaphor about how when we give selflessly of our love it comes back to us. But what I discovered, that night, had little to do with the Good Samaritan, and more to do with my own gift. Turned out the ball and mitt were completely unnecessary, because something happened in me as soon as I climbed the stairs and got behind the pulpit. I had always been middling as concerns social skills, but as soon as I took that stage, it was as though I was smarter and smoother and more handsome than I had ever been, in the way I had always wanted to be. Right away I abandoned my prepared sermon and spoke nearly the same one, but from the gut, with a conviction I took for the anointing of the Holy Spirit. I was electric. I glowed with it. I was possessed for the first time of an energy I had never before known but which I could even to this day summon at will if you gave me a microphone and a stage and an audience. I had found the one thing in the world that came naturally, unbidden, and I took it as affirmation of a calling.

When I was done, another student came on stage to lead the prayer. I sat down on the wooden pew on the first row, where the visiting preachers always sat, and as I leaned over to pray, I felt the warmth of a hand on the back of my shirt. In those days and in that place, it was not uncommon for a person to lay a hand or two hands on a person's back or shoulders during prayer, as a blessing, and also as an affirmation of the family we meant to be in prayer. The laying on of hands was something I had always enjoyed, had always felt reassured by, and almost always the hands were the hands of other men. This, though, was a smaller hand, a woman's hand, and I had to resist the urge to turn around and see who it was, and I hoped it was Marianne Wright, and then, when the time of prayer was over, I turned around, and it was. She leaned close and whispered in my ear: "You killed."

Other students, now, were making their way over to offer their congratulations or to voice an agreement with some point I had raised, or, for all I knew, to argue. That kind of thing happened then and still happens now, and I had seen it enough to know to expect it. "Your public awaits," Marianne said. She kissed me on the cheek, then made her way against the forward movement of the students who were already beginning to surround me.

Stephen Whitley, my roommate, made it to me first, and punched me soft on the bicep. "Marianne Wright!" he said, just out of earshot of the others, then, "Next time, buddy, leave the ball and glove at home."

Then he was gone, too, and it was twenty minutes after that of Praise Jesuses and Amens and all the things people say to let you know they are on board with the spiritual program you've been selling, and most of it, I still say, sincere. It was exhausting, that first time, but thrilling, too, and while it was all happening I raised a silent prayer for humility, in fear as I was of how good it felt to shake all those hands and hug all those necks.

When I returned to the dormitory room, Stephen was holding a wooden back massager. It had been a gift from his mother, sent in a care package from his hometown of Sikeston, Missouri.

"Check it out," he said, and threw it to me. Four lathed and polished wooden spheres the size of oversize knuckles attached to a larger, palm-ready sphere by thin wooden dowels. "Go ahead," he said, and turned and took off his shirt and offered me his back.

I ran the knobs up and down him, twisting from the palm sphere, and putting some good pressure to it. "You killed," he said.

"That's what Marianne Wright said."

He leaned back into the massager. "She's hot for you," he said.

"She does seem to like me," I said.

"She's hot," he said. "I did you right, buddy." He was moving his shoulders now, guiding the massager to where he wanted me to put it. Red tracks raised from where I had pressed.

"Mmm," he said. "Right there." I pushed harder into the muscled groove beside his left shoulder blade and worked the massager up and down. Then he made the sound again: "Mmm."

After that his breathing changed and we stopped talking, and when he lifted his shoulder a little and I couldn't seem to get at the knot with the massager, I put my hand beside it and rubbed with my hand.

He was going all loose, and my breathing, then, began to change, too. Then he lay down on the floor, and I followed him down and dispensed with the massager and began to rub the muscles of his back and up and down his spine with my hands, and in the grooves beside his shoulder blades, and then I sat down on his buttocks and moved down closer, and our breathing began to sync up, and not on purpose that I can remember. By now the blood had rushed to the center of my body, and he must have felt me hard through my pants against the back of him, but neither of us said anything about it, and I felt as though all of me would explode from the confinements of my skin and there was a lightness in my head, but not a dizzy one. Rather like all I was was body, and all my body was was whatever it was as it pressed against his.

All at once he stood up and backed fast against the wall, and he was breathing fast, almost panting. "I have to . . . I'll be right back," he said, and went out the door of our dorm room to the floor bathroom and did not come back to the room for a long while, and I felt a dull ache in my lower extremities and somehow full and empty all at once, neither feeling good. He was still in the bathroom, and I didn't want to see him when he came back to the room, so I grabbed my coat and went downstairs and out into the snow and walked in the dark until my legs were numb with the cold and the moisture from the snow as it melted under my feet had seeped into my boots and through my socks. By time I returned to the room, my toes were blue, and he was asleep with his head under the covers and had not bothered to turn the lights out. A few days later he moved out of my room, and into one of the single units up on the fourth floor.

The college had a counseling department of one—Don Trilling, the campus pastor—and it was widely known that the job was his because no one else had wanted it, and also because the counseling and campus pastoring kept him out of the classroom, where his ideas and influence—he was considered something of a liberal by Northern Illinois Bible College standards—could be kept from a wide audience. Firing was never at issue, though it might have been if he had been anyone but Don Trilling, because he was widely liked and because in many ways he lived his life in service of the other faculty members. Seventy years old, he rose before dawn on snowy days and carried his snow shovel to the houses of colleagues twenty and thirty years his junior and cleared their sidewalks and sprinkled salt. Infuriatingly considerate things like that, and then he would claim that he was only doing himself a favor, because at seventy he could only continue to do these things because he had forced himself to always continue to do them.

We talked about Don Trilling, and not kindly. He had become isolated, and we derided him for his theological softness, and now, the day after the encounter with my roommate Stephen Whitley, I went to see him for precisely all the reasons I did not respect him, and with one pragmatic notion at the fore: He would not see to it that I was kicked out of school for what I was about to confess. No one would have to know.

I told Don Trilling my story, and then he leaned back in his chair and ran his fingers through his thick gray hair.

"Who have you told this to?" he said.

"No one," I said.

"You think what you and your friend did is a sin?"

I thought about that for a moment. "To think it," I said, "is to do it. Right?"

"I'm asking you, son," he said.

"It's committing adultery in your heart," I said. "You know: to look at a woman with lust in your heart is to commit adultery in your heart."

"Well," he said, and smiled broadly. "No one's married as far as I can see. And no one's a woman."

He was splitting hairs with Scripture, and it didn't seem right. "To lay with a man . . ." I began.

He held up his hand and leaned forward. "But you didn't lay with anyone," he said. "You didn't know anyone, as the Biblical terminology has it. It's not black and white."

"I'm afraid," I blurted out, "that I might be gay." There, I had said it. There was no relief in saying it. I felt nauseous.

Don Trilling looked down for a moment. A silence of no comfort followed. Then: "Let's put that aside for a moment. Let's talk for a moment about love. What's love to you?"

"Greater love," I quoted, "hath no man than this, that a man lay down his life for his friends."

"All right," he said. "That's one kind of love. I don't know what it has to do with romantic love."

"Romantic love is a fallacy," I said, now parroting preachers I had known rather than the King James Bible. "Love isn't feelings. Love is a choice."

Don Trilling nodded slowly. "What I'm hearing," he said, "is a lot of talk where everything is this or it's that. How old are you, son?"

"Twenty years old," I said.

"Well, I'm seventy years old," he said, "and that doesn't make me any smarter or better able to understand anything than you, and maybe in some ways worse, because I've long since made up my mind about far too many things. But one advantage it does give me, those extra fifty years, is a lot of extra time to see a lot of things and people, and the one thing I've learned is that things aren't as this or as that as everyone says they are."

"That's what they say you say," I said.

"Don't I know it," he said. "I'm three feet from being booted from the door, they say. Right?"

I couldn't meet his eyes at that.

"It's all right, son," he said. "I've been here longer than most of them, and I'll outlive most of them, and I love them all the same. Listen. About love? It's romantic, and it's a choice, and it believes all, and it sometimes will lay down its life for a friend, and everything else they tell you. It will send some people to their heights, and other people it will ruin. I've seen it again and again, and you can't predict any of it. Love is all the things love can be, and ten other things too, and all of them at the same time. You follow?"

I didn't.

"What you need to do," he said, "is just put this massager incident behind you. Just forget about it. It's nothing. Don't beat yourself up about it, don't dwell on it, don't think twice about it. Just put it aside.

"Then," he said, "what you need to do is go get yourself a girlfriend and make this choice you're talking about, and love her, and get married, and have babies, and grow old together, and try to be good to each other.

"Okay?" he said.

Marianne Wright and I were married eighteen months later, and the next year we moved back home to West Palm, to my home church, where Brother Marshall's successor, Pastor Mike, soon to light out for mission work in the Philippines, had handpicked me to take his place. He introduced me to the congregation with his farewell sermon. "This young man," he said, "is more or less the same age I was when I came to you, and three times as wise." He spoke about how none of that mattered anyway, that all the members of the church were meant to be ministers, and that it was now their duty to labor alongside me, and to help me succeed.

That evening he stood alongside the church elders and led me through the ordination service, all of them laying their hands on my head and shoulders and speaking prayers of consecration to God.

"There was a warmth I can't explain," I told Marianne, after we were home from the ordination and the late celebration dinner at Denny's that went on until eleven that evening.

We were sitting on the couch, and she leaned her weight into me, and I put my arm around her. "God was in that place, is all I can chalk it up to."

She leaned her head lower, against my stomach, and she put her hand to my zipper, and pressed against me with her fingers.

I put my hand against her hand, not pushing her away, but not pressing her to me, either.

She looked up at me. "No?" she said.

"It's not no," I said. "It's just I'm tired." I had been putting on weight, too. We had eaten greasy food that evening. There was the matter of moving my way of thinking from the spiritual to the physical. I couldn't say why it would be a problem, but it was. This happened all the time.

"Well, maybe, then," she said. She unzipped me and lowered her head and put her mouth against me and then put me in her mouth. It felt good the way it would feel good to have anything warm and wet around me, but I did not feel, and I did not like the way it felt not to feel.

Still, there was a stirring. The sensations were pleasant. She worked at me for a long while, and I did not want to do what I often had to do, which was think of Steven Whitley and the wooden back massager, or think of R-rated movies I had seen, where a man and a woman were making love, his body moving above hers, or think of pornographic movies I had seen in the Bible college dormitories, in other people's rooms, where you could see more of the man's body as the woman did whatever she did to please him, or two women. Once I saw a scene where two men and two women traded partners three times, and this I could recall so easily, and I could remember nearly every detail of everything they did, none of it loving exactly, I remember thinking, but all of it exciting. One of the men had a Donald Duck tattoo that covered the muscles of his right shoulder.

But this is what I gave myself over to, these thoughts and these memories, and it seemed to please Marianne, but when I was done, she went into the kitchen and rinsed in the sink, and when she came back into the living room, she was carrying two glasses of wine. This was something we allowed ourselves without guilt, although some people in the church we knew would never approve. We kept it to ourselves, under the principle that one ought not cause his brother to stumble.

She handed me the glass and I began to drink it, but I drank it uneasily, because this was a prelude, I knew, to reciprocation. I kept a toothbrush and toothpaste under the bed for occasions like these, but I did not want to follow her into the bedroom.

We were silent for awhile. She tried to look into my eyes, and I tried to look back into hers, but even with some of the wine in me, I would not will myself to look at her the way I knew she wanted me to look at her, and I focused on the place where her nose met her left cheek.

"You don't want to come with me into the bedroom," she said.

"That's not true," I said.

"It's all right," she said, but she drained the wine glass the way she did not, which is to say she tilted it back and drank what was left, which was most of the glass, in one swallow. Then she kissed me on the head, said good night, and went into the bedroom.

I did not want to follow her and hear her crying again, so I lay on the couch and turned on the television and spent the last few minutes of my ordination night watching *The Tonight Show with Johnny Carson*.

Three years into my pastorate, it was Deputy Frank Laimbeer, a marginal member of our congregation, who told me about Tamarind Avenue. "I see them all the time, these goddamn rednecks—excuse my French, pastor—come down Tamarind Avenue and drive up and down with their passenger side sun visors down in the middle of the night. It's down if you want a woman, diagonal if you want a man. You pull them over and say, 'Why's your sun visor down in the middle of the night?' and they say, 'No law against it,' and then they drive away, and you and them both know you were doing them a favor, stopping them before they got the whore in the car and not after, when you could haul them away."

"Frank," I said. "It seems frustrating." I leaned forward, so I could look him level in the eye. He had two inches on me, but his height was all in his long legs.

"It's more stressful than you think, pastor," he said.

"Frank," I said. "Do you think anything good can come of taking it out on your wife?" She had been showing up for choir practice with too much makeup over and under her eyes, but you could still see the swelling.

He bowed up. I could tell he wasn't going to do anything. Why was he even sitting in my office? "Things aren't the way you're saying they are," he said, and gathered up his things and left my office in a quiet rage, and I hoped he was not going home to her.

A few weeks later—it was Friday, first night of the weekend women's retreat to St. Augustine, so Marianne was gone—I drove down to Tamarind Avenue, but I left my sun visor up. I just drove around, and then a black woman in high heels motioned me over, so I pulled over and rolled down the window. "Ten," she said. "Fifty for the whole shooting match."

"I'm not here for that," I said. It sounded ridiculous as it came out of my mouth.

"What the fuck you here for then?" she said, and slammed her hand on top of the car. "Shit," she said, walking away.

I looked around. Tamarind was where people got shot, and it's true there were people—mostly black people, if not all—walking around. Too many to be walking around at night in any neighborhood where I had ever lived. But nobody was hurting anybody, and the people who were yelling, it seemed to me, were yelling because that was how they communicated.

I left the car running and got out and left the door open. Now people were staring at me. "Wait," I said, to the woman.

I started to jog after her. She turned around fast and pointed at me and said, "Sit your ass down," and I don't know why, but I did. She walked toward me but didn't get too close. "What kind of crazy motherfucker are you?"

"I don't mean you any harm," I said.

"You don't mean me no harm?" she said, the sound of her voice angry, but I didn't think she really was. She took one step closer. "It's twenty now," she said. "Twenty and a hundred." She crossed her arms over her chest and threw her shoulders back. She had been here before. I reached into my back pocket, and she moved closer and put her hand on my elbow and said, softly, "Not here, baby, not on the street."

I opened the car door for her, and she looked around then got in.

I slid into my side and closed the door and said, "How do you know I'm not a cop."

"You're too crazy to be a cop," she said. "You got everybody on this street scared of you. Drive."

We drove a ways. I didn't know where to drive her to.

"Take a left here," she said, and I turned into a blind alley, then: "There." We pulled behind a dingy two-story house. Two Dobermans barked from behind a chain link fence. "Now I'll take your money," she said.

I reached into my wallet and took out a twenty, and she took it and stuffed it in the strap of her right heel. She heaved her chest, which was considerable. "Might as well give me the whole hundred now," she said. "Once this shit gets started, you're gonna want it, and I'm not giving you no twenty dollar discount then."

"I just want to ask you a question," I said.

"I'm out of here," she said, and opened the door and slammed it behind her and started walking away, fast, toward the gate and the Dobermans.

I reached over and rolled the passenger window down. "Wait," I said. She turned, gave me a scowl I interpreted to mean she thought she should know better, and wanted me to know she knew better.

When she reached the window, I began to whisper.

"Speak up," she said, loudly.

"I wanted a man," I said. It surprised me, hearing it from my own mouth.

"Shit, honey," she said. Now she was laughing. "That ain't nothing. I'll get you a man. You just sit tight. Shit."

She went back to the gate and opened it, and the Dobermans greeted her, and she rubbed their noses and between their eyes as they followed her to the back door, and then she closed it behind her and left me alone in the alley.

You're far from home, buddy, is what my father used to say when I did something wrong as a child. I pictured that back door opening, a man coming out with a smile on his face and a knife in his back pocket. *You're far from home.*

I backed the car out, and drove out of the alley and onto Tamarind. I drove a little ways, and then a sheriff's cruiser was on my tail. He followed me when I turned onto Okeechobee, and then, after about a half mile, turned on his blue lights.

I pulled over. I hadn't been speeding. I rolled down the window. By time I found my license and registration, the deputy was at the window. I looked up, and it was Frank Laimbeer. He looked at me, and then he took off his glasses and looked at me some more. "What you're going to say," he said, "is that things aren't the way I'm gonna be saying they are."

I didn't say anything.

He put his glasses back on, walked back to his car, and drove away.

I'm leaving out the good parts. The parts, I mean, about the good things that happened and the good that was done. We added over a hundred families to our congregation in those first five years.

At Bill and Tracey Meadows's wedding, her stentorian father danced for the first time. He said it was not a dance, but a children's game called A Pig in A Poke. While his hands moved, and his feet, and his knees, which he raised, despite his age, to waist level, he said to his daughter, "You have always brought me great joy."

At the Christmas pageant, Herman Davies rode his horse through the center aisle of the church, upon a path of palm fronds, to simulate the Triumphal Entry into Jerusalem, and no one complained, at least publicly, about the horse.

We built a school, pre-kindergarten through third grade, and made half the enrollment available to poor kids, mostly Haitian, from the neighborhoods from which our own church members had long since fled.

They let us into the prisons once a month, and we stayed for three days each time, locked into the chapel with fifty prisoners whose behavior warranted the trust, and held a retreat to rival any anywhere for its warmth and power. In the late evenings, before we lay down on our sleeping bags, the lights overhead bright all night as they must be, under such circumstances, we sang "To God Be The Glory, Great Things He Has Done," and in the mornings I preached a message of hope and love and possibility. Sometimes, after parole, we would welcome one of these men or another into our congregation, and hope for the best. Sometimes, after we helped a man find a job and a place to live, start a bank account, the man would live uprightly for a long while, and then, after three months, five months, a year, would inexplicably hold up a convenience store clerk for less money than he could make in an afternoon of painting or roofing, and then he would disappear again into the system. It made me angry, when a man would give up like that, would do what he had to do to ruin his life again after he had taken such long strides to leave behind whatever made him ruin it in the first place.

The Sunday after Frank Laimbeer pulled me over near Tamarind Avenue, his wife wasn't sitting in her usual spot on the third row, and we never saw her there again.

That gave me something to think about, and it ate at me. I wanted to talk it through with Marianne, but there was no way I knew to talk it through with her that wouldn't raise all sorts of questions I wasn't prepared to deal with myself, let alone with her.

Marianne noticed right away that Frank's wife was gone. "You think it's the counseling?" she said.

"I think maybe I pushed too hard."

"How hard is too hard, when it comes to something like that?"

"I don't know," I said.

"You think we ought to call the police?"

"I think they'd just as soon come get us as one of their own."

"Jesus," she said, then bit her lip. She rarely swore, and didn't appreciate it when other people did.

"You think I ought to go over there?" she said.

"I don't think I'd want you to go over there alone," I said. "And I don't think I'd be welcome, anyway."

"I wanted you to say why don't I go over there while he's at work," she said. "At least talk to her."

"I can't tell you what to do," I said.

So she went, but when Frank's wife came to the door, she said, "I'm not letting you into this house," and Marianne said, "Why?" and Frank's wife said, "Because I don't want you to get hurt," and I let Marianne go on thinking that Frank's wife meant a literal hurt and not the worse kind.

It wasn't long afterward I stopped by our house in the middle of the day, to pick up the clergy parking tag I needed so I could get in and get out of Good Samaritan in time to catch a Spring Training game, Expos and Braves, with the retired men's fellowship, a group I liked because they preferred baseball games and golf to brunches and luncheons.

When I opened the door, there was a rustling from the direction of the kitchen, and I thought I must have startled Marianne. Usually when I left the house in the morning, I was gone for the day. "It's me," I said, and the rustling continued and even seemed to get more frantic. "Marianne?"

When I appeared at the threshold, the rustling stopped. The kitchen table was covered with bags of potato chips and potato chips in bowls and French onion dip and Italian dressing in a bowl with potato chips in the dressing, in the bowl. Also: sugar cookies, chocolate chip cookies, chocolate donuts, a glass of milk, nearly empty, with pieces of cookie soaking in the bottom.

"It's not," she said, but didn't finish the thought.

I didn't know what to say. She gathered herself, then, and began what she had started when I heard the rustling, which was to roll down the tops of the bags of potato chips, and secure them with clothespins. Then she took down Tupperware containers from the cabinets and put the cookies in them and sealed them. The dips she covered or rinsed down the sink. I wet a paper towel and said, "Is it all right?" and she nodded, so I wiped down the kitchen table, which was fairly covered in cookie crumbs and stray shards of potato chip.

While I was wiping down the table, Marianne went into the bathroom and put on her makeup. When she came back out, I was sitting down, waiting for her. She took a seat across from me and said, "Well, you had to know, anyhow."

It's true that she had been steadily putting on weight, in her hips and buttocks, around her waist. But her mother was the same way. It didn't seem to me to be an unusual thing, or anything to worry about, given the genetics.

This I did not say. What I said, instead, was, "I'm not sure what there is to know."

"What's horrible," she said, "is that all I can think about, while I'm doing it, is how you already find me unattractive."

"I don't," I said.

"You don't have to lie about it," she said. "It's all right. I find myself unattractive, too." She said it matter-of-factly, without a trace of self-pity in her voice.

"I've reconciled myself to that," she said. "It's all right. It's better than what a lot of people have to deal with. You don't beat me."

"Score one for me," I said.

"You don't beat me, you don't shout at me, you don't belittle me, you don't even use me for a sermon illustration," she said. "But what it makes me think, sometimes, is maybe you don't think about me at all."

"It's not so," I said.

"It doesn't matter anyway," she said. "This is our life, and this is what it's come to, and it's not so bad."

But later that evening, after I got home from the Spring Training game and she made pasta Fagiole and we ate it, she said, "I still want children, you know," and then, "It wouldn't be much for me to lose twenty or thirty pounds, get down to the optimal weight before I started putting more on," and then, "Do you ever think about these things? Because I think about them all the time," and the television was tuned to *Wheel of Fortune*, and I pretended to be engrossed in the puzzle, and pretended not to hear what she said, but she knew well enough what I was doing, and my silence was answer enough, and she went to her bed early, and it took me a long time to fall asleep on the couch, which by now had worn divots the shape of my hip and shoulder.

Ten years passed. We did not have any children. I did not return to Tamarind Avenue. We never heard from the Laimbeers again. Marianne gained weight and lost it and gained it again, and so did I. The church continued to grow in numbers. Gray crept into our hair, premature, and both of us took to coloring, touch-ups every six weeks. Sometimes I think about what it would be like to have a son of my own to take with me to baseball and football games, or to play catch in the back yard, or to tuck into bed at night. I wonder if he would be like me, would want to spend his days around people, helping people, sure, but mostly just being around people because it would be in his nature. Or whether he would, because of me and what life with me would require of him, choose spend his days doing some kind of solitary work, perhaps a trade, perhaps plumbing or carpentry, which are jobs many of the men in our church worked, or had worked, if they were retired. But, more likely, some kind of white collar work—accounting, architecture—or maybe some kind of artist's craft—painting or the piano. More likely one of these, because he would not have been raised to work hard with his hands, and we would value school, let him know from day one how important it is to learn how to read and to think, pass along to him the prejudices about labor we hide from the people in our church who work with their hands, on account of respect, and on account of love.

But that, again, is more than likely me, bringing my own romanticism to bear upon something I don't know enough about. Because what I have found, from counseling, and from the talk grieving people talk the day after funerals, is that children are no more angelic than little old ladies are sweet. They spring from the womb with their grievances, with their needs and desires, and mostly with their wants, and as often as parents speak of their pride in their children, they bear the wounds of their children and their unreasonable demands, and their constant reappraisal of their childhoods through the lens of whatever opportunities are denied them as adults because of the failures of their upbringings. With children, there is always blame.

I say this to comfort myself, but I say it, too, to forestall the leap this story must make if it is to be the true story I mean to tell. This was a little over a year ago, toward the end of 2006. We had just come through a difficult season. The big church out by the highway put what it called a "satellite campus" three blocks from us—a predatory and wholly unnecessary practice, if you ask me—and we started losing families the same way churches all around the county were losing families to this newer, bigger kind of church. If you asked the pastor of the big church, he would tell you what he told all of us, which was: "Less than ten percent of the people in your zip code regularly attend church services. We're not going after your people. We're going after the unchurched." The first part of what he said was true, but the second part was a baldfaced lie, and I believe he knew it and knows it.

I worried the losses more than I should have. Most of my life I have worked long weeks, but now it was eighty hours, ninety hours a week. I was trying to get into the home of every family on our mailing list, over 800 people by then, and spend some time with them, and—to be honest—to give them the personal attention I thought might keep them from leaving.

By the third month of this—February—I developed a terrible sinus infection, a pressure behind both my eyes, and I ignored it the first few days, and pushed through the pain, and kept pushing until the pain became so intense that it would force me to vomit several times a day. By time I made it to the doctor, he was worried enough to hospitalize me. While I was in the hospital, he pulled Marianne aside and told her that if I didn't get some time away, to rest, it was likely she would be a widow inside of five years.

Of her own volition, and without my knowledge, she met with the board of elders and persuaded them to grant me—to mandate, really—a five-month sabbatical, the first week of which was to be spent at a pastor's retreat on St. Simons Island in Georgia, alone. All of this was decided before I was brought into the conversation, so I could not do what I wanted to do, which was to declare all this against my will, and speak of bad timing, and speak in the ways I knew would move them where I wanted them to be moved: talk of faith and perseverance and sacrifice and the will of God.

I had been a half hour at the retreat center at St. Simons—long enough to find my room and unpack my clothes into drawers and wash my face and brush my teeth to refresh myself from my twelve hours on the road. It was six o'clock, which I had been advised was the time dinner was served downstairs. Out in the hall, I saw a man sitting in a chair by the elevator, studying a map. He looked familiar, and he looked for all the world like Steven Whitley, my old roommate from Northern Illinois Bible College. He was older, heavier, thicker in the face, his head shaved bald.

"Excuse me," I said. "Are you Steven Whitley?"

He looked up at me, and I could see that he recognized my face. Then he stood and reached out to embrace me, which took me by surprise, but I embraced him back.

"The food here is terrible," he said, "but I know a place. You like seafood?"

He took me to a place on the beach. We sat on the open patio, which had been wrapped entirely in Visqueen and heated against the late February chill and the wind off the Atlantic. He was wearing blue jeans and an Oxford shirt under an overcoat, which he draped over the back of his chair. He had a small diamond stud in each ear.

"How," I said, "does a graphic designer make his way to a ministerial retreat center?"

"It has been awhile," he said, and laughed, and took a sip of his water. It was college, he said, senior year. "There was a nursing home near Woodlawn Cemetery."

"Meadowbrook," I said.

"That's the one," he said.

"I went there Thursday afternoons with Don Trilling, junior year," I said.

"His practicum," Steven said. "I did it senior year. I needed one hour to graduate, and that was the only one hour class."

"It smelled terrible in there."

"Awful," Steven said. "These days they'd shut it down. Or maybe they wouldn't." He took another sip of water. "I hurt my back," he said, "playing intramural basketball. I went to the sports trainer, down there in the trailer where they had the Health Center."

"They tore it down," I said. "You should see it now. There's a three million dollar wellness center where it was." Our church alone had gifted sixty thousand to the debt reduction campaign.

"Well, this trainer said he couldn't help me because I wasn't a varsity athlete. That's all he was paid to see, varsity athletes. But he suggested I go down to the YMCA on 7th and Vine, and they had some massage therapists there who worked for a reasonable fee."

"What's a reasonable fee?"

"There wasn't one, as far as I was concerned. I was flat broke and told him so. He must've felt bad, then. He reached into his back pocket and pulled out a hundred dollars and said if I negotiated it up front, I could probably get five sessions, and if that didn't do the trick, I needed to see a chiropractor.

"So I went down there and the guy at the desk called up, and this man named Clarence came down, a little guy, maybe five feet tall. Napoleon syndrome. Barked instead of talking like a normal human being. I told him what the trainer had said. I was naïve. I didn't know to take a strong negotiating position and then come down from it. He said it was insulting, what I was saying, and he left in a huff.

"By then I was running late for Meadowbrook. The boy at the desk leaned over and said, 'He's just doing what he does. Just leave me your number. He'll call you back, and he'll do it for a hundred, trust me.' So I did. I left my name and number and went off for Meadowbrook.

"And here's the thing. The drawing wasn't going well. I didn't like to look at the CAD screens, because they hurt my eyes. I got tired, to be honest, of the way everyone was around the art department there, how superior they all were, and I didn't like the hours. People were in those labs, upstairs—"

"Shockley."

"—the Shockley building, right, just working themselves to death, and I got to where I didn't want anything to do with any of it anymore.

"But Meadowbrook, shithole that it was—and make no mistake about it, it was a terrible, terrible place—became something of a haven for me. We would go in there with Don Trilling and one guy with an acoustic guitar, and we'd take requests room to room, or we'd go bother the ones who were so far gone they couldn't talk, and sing to them, hold their hands, let the nurses know when they were covered in their own excrement, and stay there until someone came to change the sheets. Sometimes we would help change the sheets, if they let us.

"It was a good feeling," he said, "to know that one time, once a week, I could go and do something for somebody else and it didn't have anything to do with painting or drawing or CAD or that constant pushing, that constant pressure of competition I was always feeling."

Our orders arrived—fresh snapper on a bed of rice for Steven, shrimp and steak for me—and he paused to chew, and I watched his still-familiar mouth, and between bites he sucked on the lemon from his ice water to refresh his palate.

"So Clarence, from the YMCA?" he said. "He calls me back a week later." Steven eyed me carefully. "He said he was going to take pity on me, a poor college student, and he was going to give me five sessions for the hundred.

"So I went in there, and I took off my clothes and lay there on my stomach with the towel around me, like he told me to do. It hurt, what he did. Some of it did. The deep tissue work did. My back was in knots. And Clarence, he said, 'I don't think all of this is from intramurals.'

"I hadn't given it much thought until then, but it sounded true, what he was saying. It was true. Another thing: Clarence seemed to care about his work. No more Little Napoleon act. He was working hard. He was sweating, I was sweating. He said, 'You might feel sick tonight when you get home, but don't worry about it. That's the toxins in that deep tissue, working their way out of your body. In a couple days you'll feel better than you even know you can feel.'

"Then he told me to turn over." Here, Steven paused. His pause was a form of communication I knew well from all my years counseling. Men did it, especially. What the pause was, really, was a way of asking permission. A confession followed, usually. I had learned how to grant this permission, to indicate that I was willing to carry whatever burden was about to be transferred to me. A widening of the eyes, a slight downward tilting of the head, a nearly imperceptible nod.

"Well, I did," Steven said. "I turned over and I took my towel with me and draped it over the front of me. I had come to feel so comfortable with Clarence that I had stopped being self-conscious of my body, even though I have always been self-conscious of my body. When I was a child, I had surgery because I was growing breasts where I should have been growing a chest. Did I tell you this, when we were roommates?"

"No, you didn't," I said, softly.

"Of course," he said. "I wouldn't have." He shook his head. "Anyway, when I rolled over, I became conscious of my body again, and, more, I became conscious of his, of Clarence's. This had happened before, this deep, intense sort of consciousness of another man's body, when it was close to me." I remembered that evening, our last evening as companionable roommates, the wooden massager.

"He was leaning over me," Steven said, "working his hands up and down my legs, and I began to get an erection."

"That could happen to anyone," I said. "You didn't have any clothes on, and there was that skin to skin contact, and at that age."

"That's true," he said. "I know that's true, now, but then it was terrifying. Everything about my body was terrifying. Everything about my sexuality was terrifying." He paused again, and I knew that he was going to report on a homosexual experience of one sort or another, and I knew, too, that my worry was not that I would not judge him, but rather that I would continue to be as interested as I was already, which was too interested.

"He saw it—he had to've—but he didn't say anything, just kept working on my legs. His touches had got softer. Then he crawled up onto the table on his hands and knees so he was straddling me, his body over mine, our bodies not touching except where his hands were working, and he began to work over my chest and my stomach and my arms, and then he took each of my hands, one at a time, in both his hands, and rubbed my palms with his fingers, and rubbed through the webbings of my fingers, and by now, forgive me, I was aching.

"He said, 'If I don't release that tension for you, you will have blue balls for the next week.' The way he said it, he let me feel like what he was doing was just another clinical procedure he could do with his hands, like the rest of the massage. Like those ladies you hear about in the late 19th century who used to go to the doctor to get their weekly preventative treatment against hysteria, which was, if you said it or thought about it the way they wouldn't have, just the doctors giving them a weekly orgasm their husbands paid for.

"So I let him do it, and, to this day, it was the most extraordinary experience of my life. I felt like I was being lifted out of my body."

He took a deep breath. "I would imagine," I said, tentative, "that this experience you're talking about would have caused you some problems later. Some worries."

"We're talking Bible college," he said. "We're talking me, who I was then."

"What did you do about it?" I said.

"Well, I went to Don Trilling. I trusted him, by then, because of Meadowbrook."

"What did he say?"

"He said, first, it was not that unusual for a young man in college to have an experience like the one I was describing. He said not to worry, that I was not gay, that these things would work themselves out. He said I should just forget about it, that I should find a girl and court her and get married and get on with my life, the way we all must do."

"So you found a girl and got married," I said, sure this was the answer.

"What I did," he said, "was keep on going to Meadowbrook on Thursday afternoons, and keep on going to Clarence. After awhile, I was seeing him twice a week and sometimes three times, if he had room in his schedule. I got a job waiting tables at the Olive Garden, to pay for it."

"Wow," I said. I didn't know what to say, and wow, I had learned, could stand in for anything without committing me to anything.

"That's what I did for a long time," he said. "Four years went past after graduation, then five. I stuck around town. I had an apartment not far from the chapel on Vine, where Don Trilling preached on Sundays, and I waited tables, and sometime in there he started passing off the Meadowbrook ministry to me, and I ran it, ran the practicums for him. He was getting older. Slowing down, if you can believe it.

"Then I was running the counseling office at the college. Then, last year, he died. By then, everyone knew I was running things, and I was well thought of, so they told me if I'd just enroll in seminary, they'd go ahead and ordain me and make me the campus pastor."

"Do they know?" I said.

He leaned over the table. "I got nothing to hide," he said. "Not anymore. If they know, they don't ask me, and I don't tell them, like the military. Exactly like the military, if you think about it. And it works, okay? Because all those Bible department guys want to do is sit up there in their ivory tower and think lofty thoughts, teach their classes and fill everyone's head with whatever their particular theological bullshit is and try to avoid attracting attention, because, let's face it, a lot of those guys have moral problems of their own."

"Plus," I said, "if they canned you, they'd have to listen to people's problems all the day."

"And run the practicums at the nursing home and the hospital," he said. "Your Greek and Hebrew won't take you so far there."

"Still," I said. "The churches. The donors." The college was less than thirty years removed from its great scandal, wherein a marginal pastor in South Carolina photocopied pages out of human sexuality textbooks and sent them around to every retired minister in the country, with a letter saying the school was promoting pornography, and got the school to run off its longtime president and ban life drawing classes for the art majors.

"They aren't paying me enough money to worry about it," he said. "I don't need much money, anyway, and if I need it, I know how to make it. The part of my job I like is going to Meadowbrook, going to visit sick people, bringing the hot meals and all. You don't have to have a title or a license to do any of that."

I had both title and license, and I had to force myself to do all of that.

"You still see Clarence?" I said. This part of the story disturbed me more than the rest. I was sure the answer was yes.

"I stopped seeing him around the time Don started slowing down," he said. "It wasn't healthy, and it was sort of sad, and it made me sad knowing I was doing it, and it makes me sad telling you right now. I'm celibate, if you want to know the truth. Not out of piety, I mean. Not out of choice."

He let that hang in the air.

I did, too, longer than I should have.

Finally, I leaned over the table and took his hand in mine, brotherly, maybe fatherly, the way I would any man who had trusted me with a deep and abiding secret. "Steven," I said, "what you told me I will keep in confidence.

"Steven," I said, a formality creeping into my voice even as I felt his pulse through his hands, "I want to visit with you some more this week, but it's been a long day of driving. I need to get back to my room and get some rest for the evening. Would you mind if I led us in a word of prayer?"

He said sure. There was something of resignation in his voice. I left the ending of the prayer open-ended, in case he wanted to pray, too, but he just closed it with Amen.

I had come to St. Simons Island to rest, and I intended to rest, and I lay down in the hotel bed that evening to rest, but I could not achieve anything like rest. There was still light through the window from the direction of the hotel pool. I got up and walked to it and saw fathers splashing in the pool with their children, and young men roughhousing in the hot tub, and, on the beach beyond, a man and woman walking very close together, hands clasped, and beyond that the darkness of the ocean, and the pinpricks of light from whatever fishing boats or pleasure craft were drifting out there.

My thoughts ran in the direction of Steven Whitley and all the things he had told me at dinner, and also toward Marianne, whose love had seen me away from her and toward this hotel room. I thought, too, of the church, and the work we had done in our years there, and of what it said about their regard for me, that they would send me here at their expense, and offer me—require of me—a five month paid vacation, for the sole purpose of my own health.

I knew and know how strange it might seem to hold all of these things in tension, to think of them with gratitude while at the same time entertaining the darker things this quiet was bringing up alongside them. I wanted, yes, to knock on Steven Whitley's door and confess to him that the feelings he had were a whole lot like the feelings I have always had, and to confess to him that I wondered why God would create a man with an empty place in the center of his being, and make it clear inside that man's self that the only thing standing between him and happiness was the love of another man—erotic love, yes, but also a spiritual communion akin to what the union of man and wife had not brought into my life.

But there was the matter of my own capacity for self-deception. The one doctrine of the church that seems to me to be forever verifiable is the doctrine of original sin, the idea that we are born with selfishnesses beyond measure, and that we can do any number of increasingly complicated contortions in our own minds to justify whatever cruelty, whatever pettiness, whatever selfishness appeals to what Christian tradition calls the flesh, that part of us that is carnal and separate from spiritual transcendence.

The selfishness at hand was twofold. If I did what I wanted I would hurt Marianne, and if I did what I wanted I would hurt the church.

The church, it seemed to me, would bounce back. I had not created a cult of personality around myself. I had, all these years, trained the people to create for themselves a community of faith, mutually supporting and loving and uplifting, and I had always told them that every person they would ever meet was capable of failing them and would, in fact, fail them, me included. It was the incontrovertible truth life had taught me. People will fail you.

So the deeper problem was Marianne. Menopause had come to her mother early, and her grandmother before her, and her grandmother's mother before her. Marianne had always wanted children, and I had not, and now, as she reached the end of her childbearing age, for me to leave her would be to inflict the deepest sort of wound. Out of love for me, a love I had pledged to permanence, she would have given up her childbearing years, and her most physically attractive years, and the years in which it would have been easiest to find another love that could carry her into old age. Marianne, who had worked at understanding despite all the disappointments I had brought into her life, and who loved me despite all the ways I had failed in love for her, would take this, I knew, as the ultimate betrayal, and it did not seem in any way melodramatic to consider the possibility that she would not survive it.

With all of this knowledge—so much of it terrible knowledge, really—rattling around inside me, I began to pace. I walked from one side of the room to the other and back again, and wished that this retreat center had a television. Certainly the reason they did not was because a television would be a distraction from the business of spiritual renewal, but like all prescriptions, this one failed to account for its shortcomings. If there had been a television in the room, I would have watched it until it drugged me groggy, and fallen asleep at one or two in the morning to a forty-year-old rerun of *The Andy Griffith Show*.

Instead, I got dressed, and walked down the hall in sock feet, and knocked on Steven Whitley's door.

He came to the door barefoot, in boxer shorts and a white T-shirt. "What brings you by this fine evening?" he said.

"Can't sleep, Steven," I said. "I been looking out the window at that beach and I think I might like to walk on it, out by the water. You want to walk with me?"

He studied me. "Come on in," he said. "Let me get some pants on."

I went inside and let the door shut behind me and sat on his unmade bed while he took down a shirt and pants from the hanger and then he sat down in the chair across from me and put on his socks and shoes.

"I'm kind of surprised you came by," he said.

"Couldn't sleep," I said. "No TV."

"I gave up the TV years ago," he said. "Developed a taste for reading."

"That's what I should have done," I said. "Use that time to improve and preserve the mind."

"I like to read spy novels and military thrillers," he said. "John LeCarre. Tom Clancy. *The Hunt for Red October.*"

Now we were walking down the hall, down the stairs, through the hotel parking lot, out to the sand. We took off our socks and shoes—"Funny," he said, "that we just put these on to walk on the newish carpet, and now we take them off to walk on a beach that could wash up jellyfish, broken glass, used needles"—and walked up the beach, in the direction of the pier.

We walked in silence for awhile. The ocean breeze was cool but not cutting, and the sand, too, was pleasant between the toes, although I could tell, already, that I would be sore in the morning from the extra lift each footstep required.

"Something is on your mind," he said.

"How do you know?"

"This is what I do," he said. "Forgive me. I don't mean to presume on you, but I guess that's what I do, too. Something is weighing heavy on you."

"I've been thinking about the principal at my old school," I said. "Mr. Ratliff."

"High school?"

"It was kindergarten through twelfth grade, inclusive," I said. "Same guy the whole way through until the last semester of the twelfth grade. Brain cancer."

"I'm sorry," he said.

"No, it's not the brain cancer I was thinking about," I said. "It's the story of his life. Have you noticed everyone has a story of their life?"

He nodded. "Everybody's story, to them, is the most important story in the world."

"Have you noticed," I said, "that they're always the same stories?"

"That's not precisely true," he said.

"Love, sex, death, family, betrayal," I said.

"Well, when you put it that way."

"Mr. Ratliff's story was that his wife left him young. Ran off with a Navy captain."

"She married a Navy captain?"

"Not to marry him. She ran off to be his mistress."

"A kept woman," he said. "Juicy."

"Kept nicely," I said. "They say he put her up in a million dollar apartment on Palm Beach. So all these years, she's living the life of luxury a twenty minute drive from Mr. Ratliff."

"It drove him crazy?"

"It drove him to the strangest sort of sanity I've ever seen," I said. "He kept his job, stayed home, raised his two kids—they both turned out to be more or less good, kind people—and waited."

"For her to come home."

"Yes. For her to come home."

"I bet she never did," Steven said. By now we had stopped walking. We were standing side by side, the ocean in front of us.

"Mr. Ratliff never dated, he never remarried, he never said a foul word about her except to explain why he was still a bachelor—or, to say it the way he said it, why he was not a bachelor at all. How they were still married in the eyes of God."

"That story," Steven said, "is sad in about forty-three ways."

"What I've been wondering lately," I said, "is if he didn't get it wrong. About love, I mean."

"I don't know," Steven said. "That's one of the most classic love stories I've ever heard told."

"Think about if you were his wife," I said. "You live your life the way you want, but knowing he's not living his life at all. He's waiting. And everything you do to live your life will be interpreted by him as another injury love must sustain. So the romance of you gets greater with every transgression, and the reality of you diminishes, until all you have become is some kind of principle. He doesn't even know you at all anymore, doesn't know anything about you. All he knows is what you used to be, and he goes through life telling himself that what you used to be is what you really are, and if he waits long enough, you'll come into what you are. And he also goes through life telling himself that what he used to be is what he is, only stronger, when, really, there's less and less of him all the time. That's the saddest part to me."

Steven picked up a seashell and skipped it across the surface of the water. It skipped twice, then went into a small wave. Then he picked up another. Then another. Then I picked one up. We were skipping these seashells, and the whole conversation seemed unreal against the seashell skipping, until he stopped abruptly and turned to face me and said, "The saddest part to me is that he couldn't get past his principles and go find love and be happy."

I stood facing him, with the seashell in my hand, and what I was thinking was *will I tell Marianne?* and what I found myself doing was letting him lean into me and kiss me.

✿

It occurred to me, later, lying in his bed at six o'clock the next morning, that nothing irrevocable had been breached. Like they say in the movies: What happens in Vegas stays in Vegas. That if I told Marianne a lie, it would not be the first time I had ever told a lie, nor would it be the worst lie I ever told, and it would be told on account of noblest purposes. Truly, I did not want to hurt her.

Steven went home two days later, which left me with some time to think about my life, and what I had been, and what I might become, and what might become of me and Marianne. I went home a day early, and I confessed everything.

We were sitting in our kitchen. She was very quiet. She listened and she shed no tears. When I was done, she said, "Will you leave me?"

"I don't know," I said. I couldn't meet her eyes, which were fierce.

"What will you tell the church?"

"I don't know."

"This was sprung on me," she said. I noticed that she did not say, *You sprung this on me.* "I need to think about this," she said.

She left the house. I heard the car roar away in the driveway. I wondered where she was going, and who she would tell, but when she came back, twenty minutes later, I knew she hadn't gone to see anyone. There wasn't time. Probably, she just went for a drive.

I was waiting for her at the kitchen table. I figured it was better not to bring this into any of the other rooms and sully them by association. I didn't know what to say.

"I have come to a decision about you," she said. "Here is what I think. I think you are starting to think you know what you are or who you are. I don't think you're confused or having a midlife crisis or anything like that. I just think that life is a disappointment in general, and you're just coming to knowledge of it later than the rest of us."

I let her speak and tried not to show agreement or disagreement.

"I think that eventually you will decide to do whatever you decide," she said. "I don't have any control over it, but that's nothing new.

"So here is the question I want to ask you," she said. "Have I loved you?"

I did not hesitate to answer her. "You have been nothing but love to me," I said.

"Have I been good to you?"

"Of course," I said. "Of course. Jesus." My shoulders now were slumped. She was standing tall over me, and I was sitting in the kitchen chair.

"Then, by God, take your time," she said. "Take your time and make your decision, and then I will decide to forgive you, one way or the other. I will decide, and it will be hard, but whether you stay or whether you go, I will be the same person I am and I have always been, and I will give this to you. I will forgive you, and let me tell you, it will be the hardest thing I have ever done in my life, because right now I hate you."

She took my face in her hands and she kissed me fiercely on the lips, and then she left the room. Perhaps she left to weep in a place I could not see her. I don't know. She left again in the car and left me, but only for a few hours.

All of these things happened a year ago today. It is Saturday night. I am standing in the hallway corridor, watching her watch television, and it occurs to me that I have never given her an answer, nor have I provided one for my own self. Soon I will go back to my study and finish my Sunday message, and see if I can find a way to offer up again the peace that passes all understanding.

goodbye Hills, hello night

Here's the plain truth of it. I never killed no one. You want to talk murder, you talk to Jim Bailey. He didn't mean to, neither. He's the one done it.

In the newspapers they said we was bum bashing. They called it that—bum bashing—and other times they called it crashing. That don't sound right to me. We was rousting. My daddy uses a word: Roustabout. You know it? It means a rough person, a person who's only going to be around for a little while, a person prone to raising some hell. Pile four or five boys into an old green Impala, white leather seats, old 8-track player, wake some up some vagrants. That's rousting.

That night there was a party at the Hills—you wouldn't know the place, it's gone now—but out behind the old Royce Hotel there was a big sandpit, hills and hills of sand they'd dumped to raise a foundation for some tower they never built—and all around it the pines grew thick enough you couldn't see inside from the street, but low enough so the cobalt streetlights could sneak over the trees, light the place up.

Our plan was to drive around for awhile first. You don't never show up to a party early. I liked to show up last, give a war whoop, a Banshee cry, make my arriving known. So quarter past eight Freddy Bailey shows up at my house, him driving, his brother Jim in the front seat telling him where to go, Billy Jones in the back, his hand wrapped around one of the baseball bats like he'd ever have it in him to swing one at anything but a baseball.

"Badass Billy Jones!" I said. "Move it on over." And I slapped him upside the head because that's how we did him, and he wouldn't expect nothing else. Freddy thought this was funny and got to laughing, and Jim slapped his ear with his hand cupped shape of a C. If you slap somebody's ear like that it rings for hours, and Jim knew how to do things like that—he done it to me and said it was to show me how. Jim Bailey knew how to hurt people a hundred ways and more.

The week before I gone to the Farmer's Market, big old warehouse on Congress Avenue, and I bought some protection. The streets at night can get scary, cocaine niggers and worse, and we'd had a bad scare already. You heard of a transvestite? That's a man done up like a woman. We'd saw one a few weeks before, walking up and down Florida Mango, drinking from a brown paper bag, and on that night it was just Jim and me and John Streeter, big dumb offensive tackle, and Jim was driving and pulls the car over and throws a beer bottle out the window. It bounces off the guy's head and shatters into pieces on the sidewalk. Before I know it Jim's grabbing our shirts, John's and mine, and pulling us out of the car, and we're running toward this big ugly woman who's cussing and screaming bloody murder, and Jim's yelling, "Bring it on, freakshow," and big John Streeter's outrunning both of us—he's in football shape, been running laps, and we're already losing our wind, running so hard—and John, who's only a little bigger than the transvestite, he gets there first, and then the transvestite does some kind of judo move, sort of steps out of the way and yanks on John's arm at the same time, and John goes flying and lands ten feet away in a heap. And then me and Jim jump at the old bag. More judo, and we're on our asses, when John jumps her from behind, and they roll around for a minute, tangled up in that big old skirt, both of them so big it's scary, and next thing you know John is laying on his stomach, blood soaking through the back of his shirt, and the hag running away, screaming, "I was in Vietnam. Viet-fucking-Nam, motherfuckers." Then she was gone into some alley, took her knife with her, and we took John and dumped him at the emergency room doors and drove off before anyone could ask what happened.

So after that, like I said, we all got some protection. Jim Bailey sawed the handle off a shovel and duct-taped one end, made himself a billy club. Freddy Bailey bought some brass knuckles from a colored kid, and Billy Jones, he didn't know what to do, so Jim told him to swipe some baseball bats from the equipment shed at school, said might as well get something for all the time he wasted at practice and riding the bus home all night from games, but I think Jim just said that part on account of being jealous of Billy always being in the newspaper—no-hitter this, and home run that—and because Billy didn't know better than to rub it in our faces when the scout from the Cincinnati Reds come to watch a couple games. John Streeter, he didn't buy or swipe nothing. He said he was finished with all that business, and getting near stabbed to death saved him, tell you the truth, from being in Jim and Freddy's Impala that night, from ending up like us. I can't say that none of us blamed him, or even said one word about his getting nearly stabbed to death by a man in a dress. We was ashamed of that ourselves. We didn't tell nobody.

And me, I marched on over to the Farmer's Market on Congress and bought a blackjack, a real nice one, eight inches of leather, lead ball embedded in the mouth. That's what I swung at the one who didn't die. I never touched the one who died. That's why I got eighteen months and three years probation instead of twenty-five to life, like Jim, who, like I said, didn't mean to kill nobody, same as me. I got wise to something in the penitentiary, and I'll tell it now: the difference between one kind of life and another comes down to a moment no person can control. What if instead of buying a blackjack I made me a billy club instead, like Jim? What if we each of us run off toward a different vagrant—that's the word the lawyer said to use, and I been using it ever since, vagrant—what if Jim got the nigger instead of me, and I was the one went after the Indian? What then?

That night we drove around, Jim and Freddy and Billy and me, waiting for some time to pass so we could show up late to the Hills and see some girls drink from the kegs and make ourselves known. Jim and Freddy only had about two 8-track tapes, both Kenny Rogers, but one of them Islands in the Stream with Dolly Parton, and nobody wants to hear that, so we was listening to Coward of the County over and over, and singing along, too, singing into the blackjack and the billy club and the baseball bats like they was microphones, loud as we wanted, because it was funny to sing loud and bad, especially out the window at other cars when we stopped at red lights, and especially to hold out a long note when the music faded down and the track changed and then the music faded back up again at the place where it left off.

We drove back into a side neighborhood over there near the airport, you know, the one behind the Verdes Tropicana bowling alley where all the spics live, and one of the streets run along by a canal where this Guatemalan was fishing. He was squatted down, and sort of leaning forward, like he was gonna think some fish into jumping onto his line, and it was too good to pass up, him leaning forward like that and squatted down, so I told Freddy to slow down, and I reached up to the front seat and grabbed hold of Jim's billy club, then leaned my whole body out the back window and gave him a tap on the backside, just a little love pat, just enough to help his body move in the direction it wanted to move already. That fisherman didn't know what happened. He just fell forward, dove really, right into that nasty brown canal water, and we nearly doubled over laughing, it was so funny. Jim said it served him right for fishing in that canal where they probably pumped sewage and who knows what else, and for all our laughing we stopped paying attention to Freddy for a moment. Freddy always needs babysat when he's driving—he hardly ever pays enough attention regular times, forget about laughing times—and then Jim sees how the road is about to dead end at the bend in the canal. He starts yelling at Freddy, grabs the wheel and turns it while Freddy slams on the brakes. Goddamn, I thought we was going into the canal. But the car spun out so we was sideways and stopped just in time to see that Guatemalan climbing up the canal bank, madder than hell. He come running at us, and Jim must've been thinking about that man in a skirt, because he wasn't itching for no fight like you'd've thought. He told Freddy to get the hell out of there, and Freddy turned the wheels around and hit his foot on the gas and damn near ran that Guatemalan into the water a second time.

Jim said we better be on to the Hills, and I think he was a little shook up even though he wasn't acting like it. Under his seat he always kept a bottle of Jim Beam, and he pulled it out and made a big show of flashing it in front of the window like he wasn't scared of no cops. My daddy's a highway patrolman, and I know how it ain't smart to call attention to yourself, especially by waving around a bottle of bourbon in a car. I told Jim to put that thing away, but Jim just put it to his mouth and tilted it back. Took two big swigs. Then he turned around and leaned over the back of his seat, got right in my face and said, "Russell, pal, I like you, you know it? But don't you ever say nothing to me about nothing." He had a big, ugly look on his face, smiling like a Rottweiler who's spotted a trespasser. Some smiles don't mean nothing joyful. Half of me wanted to knock that dog smile off his face, take a couple teeth, but I knew well as Jim did how he could break me into small, tiny pieces, real fast. I seen him beat bloody grown men twice his size.

I backed down, and he patted me twice on the cheek hard enough so I knew he was being nice. He handed over the Jim Beam and I took a long swig myself and then passed it over to Billy.

It'd been dark for a couple hours when some blue lights come flashing behind us and right off I thought that Guatemalan must've lived close by to where he was fishing and called in on us, and I could know right then what was on Jim's mind, that he was gonna tell Freddy to go faster or turn into some alley and try to get away. And I knowed from my daddy how there ain't no getting away, and it's best to just let them get you, to go quiet and be agreeable and say yes sir and no sir. Sometimes we'd have five or ten state troopers over to the house, all of us eating around the big oak table, and they'd be sipping on red wine—all except Daddy, he's a deacon at the Baptist church and won't drink a drop—and making jokes about how sophisticated they'd all become, all of them now turned into wine sippers, and they'd make a big show of holding their pinkies up in the air while they held their glasses—their goblets, they'd call them—and it being funny because with the other hand they'd be stuffing their mouths with barbeque, and after a few hours of wine drinking, they'd get to bragging about hauling in this assailant or that criminal, and the most happiness they'd show would be when they'd talk about some colored kid resisting, and then of course they'd have to show him who was boss or beat some respect into his head, and whenever they were talking about it I'd think how they really liked being disrespected, on account of it gave them a chance to kick and punch on somebody for awhile.

So behind us those blue lights come flashing, and Jim starts yelling at Freddy to step on the gas, and I'm yelling *no, no, keep it steady*, and all the while the siren getting louder in our ears and the blue lights getting bigger in the rearview mirror, and Freddy screaming *I'm gonna turn, I'm gonna turn*, but not turning or anything. By then the whole inside of the Impala was all lit up blue, them blue streaks flying across the white leather seats every time the lights rolled around. I could see Freddy was about to run, the way his body went stiff—he was telegraphing it. Like my daddy says, there ain't no mystery with that boy. And just then, them blue lights right up on us, that cop car swerved out into the lane beside us and kept on going, fast as a rocket ship, not after us at all, as it turns out.

Everybody starts laughing, and all is forgiven, even though my first thought was Jim might turn around and sock me in the jaw for arguing. But he wasn't always like that. Sometimes Jim could be a real nice guy, and right then he slid over to the middle part of the seat and put his arm around Freddy and tussled his hair. "I'm hungry as hell," he said. "Hamburgers on me, for everybody."

Freddy pulled into the drive thru, and after we all got our burgers he got all brave and started talking about how he was gonna score with Allyson Dedo, which was bullshit and we all knew it, because her daddy was a famous boob doctor from the island, from Palm Beach, and we was just white trash far as she was concerned, and she probably didn't even know who we was. But Jim was still being nice then, chewing his hamburger, and he said, "I don't know if it's gonna happen tonight, Freddy boy, but I'll tell you this. I seen Allyson Dedo looking your way at school. She's been watching you for half the year now, and I half can't believe it took you this long to see how she's all up in your shit. It ain't gonna happen tonight, probably. You gotta grow some testes first, be nice and take her to a movie, feed her some fancy shrimp or something. But soon, baby brother. Soon."

You should've seen how Freddy perked up. You could tell how much Freddy really wanted Jim to believe in him and Allyson Dedo, and it got me to thinking—then, not now—how nice it would be if Jim was my big brother, instead of Freddy's, or if I just had a big brother like Jim who was closer to my age, and home instead of in prison like my brother Emmett. But that's a whole nother story I don't want to get into right now on account of as it turned out it was a good thing for me that Emmett was in jail when I got there because it gave me some protection right off that neither Jim or Freddy ever had. To this day I know they give Jim an awful time inside, and he still has a long time to go before it's over if he don't kill himself first, which wouldn't be no surprise..

We got to the Hills around quarter past nine. Freddy drove the Impala on around the back of the Royce Hotel. There was a little dirt turnoff at the back end of the parking lot, a path that was wore away by them dump trucks that hauled up all the sand. I was finishing my last bites of hamburger and Jim was giving all of us a hard time for checking our teeth in the rearview mirror, even though he was doing it, too. Nobody wants to greet the ladies with beef between your teeth.

Them trees did their work. Outside you couldn't tell nothing was going on, but inside the Hills was lit up like the Fourth of July, the cars and trucks all lined up in a big square, their headlights facing in toward the mounds of sand, and lit from up top by them cobalt streetlights. It was kind of eerie, too, how the white light from the headlights reflected off the white sand so bright you could hardly stand to look at it straight on, and then up near the top of the mounds how the streetlights gave everything sort of a blue glow, like in horror movies, you know, how the spirits of little children come to visit and have them auras humming all around them? That's how it was, only everybody looked like a spirit, because after you'd had a few taps off the keg that bright white tended to give you a headache, so before long everybody was moving up to the top of the mounds. That was the big joke, you know? *I am the Ghost of the Hills.* Jim liked to say it just like that, and then he'd let out this long, dark laugh, and for half a second you'd be afraid even though you knew he was pulling your leg.

You got to imagine how big the Hills was. You might think there'd be four or five little sand mounds and everybody partying all close together. But it wasn't like that. There was probably twenty sand mounds spread out over maybe two acres, and they was tall enough that you could go between them and find a nice dark spot, spread out a blanket, make time with your girl. Plenty of people did it, and even though there was probably a couple hundred kids around, you knew you could get a quiet space for yourself if you needed. That's why it was no use to have a Hills party without a whole bunch of people, because it took a lot of headlights to keep it all up.

So Freddy pulled in, and a rich kid, pretty boy name of Tom Schoepf, come up to Freddy's window and asked how many of us in the car, and Jim leaned over and said, "Oh come on, Tom, we ain't got it," and Tom said, "You guys aren't gonna drink anything?" And Jim just flashed him a big grin and said, "No, sir, we ain't," and Tom just kinda tapped his foot like he didn't believe it, and finally

Jim said, "Oh, all right. Here's your money," and handed him the twenty bucks he collected from us earlier—five dollars a head if you brung headlights, seven bucks without. Tom stuck a piece of white paper on the window, and that meant we was free to have all the beer we wanted until it all run out, which was never, on account of Tom's daddy owned twenty or thirty Schoepf's Grocers and sold him kegs at cost, so cheap Tom could clear six or seven hundred dollars on a good night.

We got out and right off head up the nearest hill, because that's where they put all the kegs, up top. There was a mess of trash all the way up—old paper and plastic cups and bottles and drive thru bags—and we was racing like always, and Billy Jones was starting to get ahead partway up the hill, because, like I said, he was in baseball shape, and Jim wasn't having none of second place. He grabbed Billy's leg and tripped him up, and Billy went down hard in a wet patch strewn with cans. Jim passed him by and ran on up top first, yelling, "King of the mountain," and we wasn't far behind him, but when Billy didn't get up real fast I went back down to see why. He was bent over his knees holding his face, and when he looked up at me I saw he was bleeding from his eye. Or that's what I thought at first, that his eye was bleeding, but he wiped at it with his shirtsleeve, and I could see he'd got cut by a piece of broken glass above his eye, below his eyebrow, real close to his eyelid. It sliced him up real good, and some girls caught wind of some trouble and first ran away, then ran back over. Jim saw the girls, and then he got all concerned, too, and ran down the hill to check on Billy, Freddy tagging along behind him.

"Billy. Jesus, God," Jim said, and he was looking real intent at Billy's eye, but also I could tell he was scanning around to see what girls had come over. It wasn't any girls he cared about, mostly some fat girls that always hang around the baseball games and pine away for Billy Jones anyway, but still, they was girls, so Jim took off his own shirt and pushed it up against Billy's eye to stop the bloodflow. He yelled at Freddy to go run to the car and get the duct tape from the trunk, on account of he had some left over from wrapping the shovel handle. Jim put his hand on the back of Billy's head and said, "Listen here, pal. You're gonna pull through. We'll patch it up right." Jim had pretty good pectorals, and I could see he was glad to have his shirt off, so he could flex for them girls.

More people come over because they heard there was a fight, so when Freddy come back up the hill he had to push and shove some to get through with the duct tape. Jim made a big show of holding up that bloodsoaked shirt and handing it to me so he could play paramedic. He grabbed the skin on both sides of Billy's wound and pressed them real tight together, which made more blood run into Billy's eye. Then he had Freddy tear off a little piece of duct tape, just a half of a half of a little piece, and he taped Billy's head shut and wandered off to the dark places with one of the fat girls who was making a fuss over him.

There wasn't no fight, obviously, and everyone who'd come hoping for a ruckus went away all disappointed. I stood there holding Jim's shirt, Freddy was twirling the roll of duct tape around and around on his finger like he didn't know no better, and Billy shot us the shit-eatingest grin and said, "How bout we get some beers before they're all gone." He didn't look like nobody the Cincinnati Reds would want, that line of not even dried blood all smeared across his face, and I think he might've liked it that way, since he got to look like he'd been slugging it out without having to actually slug it out.

We got us some plastic cups and kicked back for awhile waiting for Jim. Before long we started whooping and hollering and carrying on, and I got to noticing how even with all them headlights below and the blue light creeping in from over the trees, there was a place in the sky where the ground lights didn't reach no more, and it got darker up there with nothing but a skinny old moon, and you could see all the stars like you couldn't usually when you was lower to the ground. It reminded me of when I was a little boy, right before Emmett went to jail—hell, he was probably the age I was right then—and my daddy come home one weekend and said he was gonna take us out into the woods. We packed up two pup tents with no ground floor or nothing, and we didn't even use them on account of it was a nice night and we was wearing warm shirts. I didn't hardly sleep at all that night. Me and Emmett just stretched out opposite ways there on our tarps. Our heads was close together, and every once in awhile he'd lean over and take a dip or spit some in his coffee can. You could hear Daddy snoring, and we didn't say nothing to each other, mostly, but I remember it was the same as that night on the hill, just a nice peaceful feeling, tiny little moon, and all them stars where you could really see them. I'd have to say both them times was the high points of my life so far. It's funny, because right after both those times life got real bad.

Jim come running up the hill mad as hell, huffing and puffing like I don't know what. At first I thought somebody jumped him, but he didn't have a mark on him, and his fists wasn't bloody or nothing. "We're getting the hell out of here," he said, and right then I knew something went wrong with that fat girl. It ain't often you got one over on Jim like that, and I couldn't resist saying so. What I said was, "Old fatty kicked you to the curb, hey Jim?" and I thought he was gonna light me afire right then and there, especially after Freddy started laughing even though he was trying not to, and then Billy Jones got tickled, too, and started making humping moves with his hips and talking in a girly voice, saying, "Jim, Jim, Jim," and then Jim got real sore and told Billy to give up his shirt since Jim had got his all bloodstained from fixing Billy's eye.

"No sir, I ain't giving up my shirt," Billy told him. "Goddammit, Jim, you the one pushed me down that hill."

By now a bunch of the fat girl's friends come around to see if they couldn't taunt Jim until he lit into somebody, Billy probably, and I figured I was the only one on earth knew how to handle the situation. I walked up to Jim, right in front of all these girls, put my arm around him, and said, "Ladies, I'm sorry to interrupt, but Jim Bailey's services is needed elsewhere."

Jim could hardly get enough of that kind of talk. He tipped an imaginary cowboy hat to them, and I steered him in the direction of the Impala. When we got out of earshot, he said, "What the hell was that all about," and I said, "Jim, buddy, the night is young, and we are fearsome young men."

"We gonna clean up the streets tonight?"

"Yeah, Jim, buddy," I said. "You gonna lead us into action."

Then we all started howling at that little sliver of moon. Freddy Bailey put on this little tiny voice: "We're going rous-tiiiing!"

And we all answered, "Rous-tiiiing!" and put our hands to our mouths and war-whooped the end part like we was playing cowboys and Indians, and had us a footrace to the car, and Billy Jones didn't run his hardest but didn't let us win neither, and Jim knew better this time than to trip him up from behind.

We piled in the Impala, and Freddy revved up the engine a couple times, threw us into reverse and gunned it. For a minute I thought we might get stuck in the sand, but them tires caught hold and we was out of there, goodbye Hills, hello night.

My great granddaddy, my daddy's daddy's daddy, told me a story before he died. He used to live up in the middle of the state, what they call the Chain of Lakes that runs on down to the Kissimmee River. He lived up on Lake Pierce, which is still a special place, a wild place, but not so wild as it used to be when my granddaddy was young. By the time of his story, there wasn't no more problems with the Seminoles. There was some around to say prayers and do dances around the mounds there, where their dead kings was buried. But mostly they was from old Indian families everybody knew, and they'd as soon hunt and fish with the people who lived around the lake as one of their own, and that worked both ways. They was only good Indians around Lake Pierce. The problem, my great granddaddy told me, was Yankees. They'd come down to the lake and throw money around and fool around with the women and go back north before anybody even knew how much damage they'd caused. So after awhile people got sick of it. There was this hermit named Scroggins who worked for the state—his job was to measure how high and low the lake water got to be at different parts of the year—but mostly he just lived close to the land, pitched tents out on the islands and sometimes found a woman to bring back and set up house with for awhile until they got tired of one another and went their separate ways. Everyone was a little bit scared of Scroggins, because he wasn't just partly crazy. He was also partly smarter than everybody else, and a smart crazy man, great granddaddy said, is a lot more dangerous than a dumb one. So my great great granddaddy, my daddy's daddy's daddy's daddy, he knew about Yankees from fighting them in the war, and he also knew how to live like an Indian, same as Scroggins. So he rounded up some other men and formed a posse and they went on down to Snodgrass Island where Scroggins was staying, and they made themselves a plan to rid the lake of them Yankees once and for all. What they did—and you should've seen the look on my great granddaddy's face when he told this, like he was fifteen years old instead of eighty—was they got hold of some roots and berries and made some face paints and then they'd go to whatever place some Yankee was staying, and they'd break in sometime in the middle of the night and get themselves arranged all around the bed, and then they'd start hollering all at once, all around the bed, and dancing and kicking up their heels. They'd rouse that Yankee right up from bed and slap him around some, and shake him, and my great granddaddy said that Yankee wouldn't hardly know what hit him since he just got up out of sleep and so was still half-asleep in the deep black as it was, and then before too much more time they'd run off into the night, and maybe leave some old arrowheads splayed out there by the door as a reminder. "Them Yankees never would come back," great granddaddy would say, and he'd slap me hard on the back the way old men do when they're showing how they like you.

Ever since what happened that night under the overpass, lots of people've asked me what the hell I was thinking, going around with those boys, roughing up bums and vagrants. And mostly I don't know what to tell them, but I've been thinking on it a lot—I've had a lot of time to think—and I guess the best I can do to is say that all the newspapers and the people on TV, my momma, my daddy and all his trooper friends, the preacher at church—everybody was always talking about what they was calling the homeless problem, and everybody was trying to pass laws or getting on the backs of the police and whatnot to do something about all these stray men passing through town and breaking into

buildings like my momma's beauty shop and even sometimes beating somebody up at night, but nobody was doing
nothing about it. And at the time, I guess I was thinking
about my great granddaddy and Scroggins and how they
was men of action and intent, willing to do something about
the Yankee roustabouts that come in and disrupt their way
of life. So, that's one part of what I was thinking. And the
other part is, I wasn't thinking at all. We was just having a
heyday, and wasn't nobody gonna stop us until things gone
too far to fix themselves.

   We left out from the Hills and the Royce, and our
first thought was to hunt down that Guat fisherman. Jim
was bragging about how we run him off the road one and
a half times already, and the story'd almost grown to where
he'd fell in the water twice, not because we believed it, but
because it was more fun to tell that way. If you could've
taken a look around the inside of that car, you might've
understood how real and make-believe didn't seem so far
apart. You'd've saw Freddy Bailey driving, blowing into a
empty bottle of Jim Beam like he's playing in a jug band,
and Jim Bailey, his shirt long gone, his nipples getting hard
from the blowing of the air conditioner, singing Coward of
the County for the eleventh time into a Billy club made out
of a sawed-off shovel handle wrapped in duct tape. You'd've
saw pretty old Billy Jones, his face and shirt all smeared
with dried blood, the skin around his eye all lifted up funny
from where Jim had taped his skin together, baseball bat
between his knees, and me, Russell Gibbs, foolish and feeling
fine, whacking that blackjack against my hand, feeling the
sting of that lead ball against my palm, pretending like I
was my great great granddaddy, ready to raise a ruckus,
ready to get on with the rousting at hand.

   Freddy turned into the neighborhood behind Verdes
Tropicana bowling alley, and we drove all along the canal

and the side streets, down the rows of houses painted up like whores, pinks and bright greens and what they call fuchsias, every kind of flag but American hanging from above the front door, and little runty dogs running every which way. All we saw was some old men smoking on their porches, and a few women peeking at us through the slats of their window blinds.

We didn't even see a single Guatemalan the whole time, and them window blind women was making Jim worried we might get more blue lights called on us, so we hightailed it out of there, and stopped by Verdes Tropicana for a slice of pizza, said hello to some old boys we knew there. Judy at the counter—she owns the place and lives upstairs from the soda fountain—got on Jim for coming in without a shirt, but nothing too severe. She wouldn't serve us no beer, and we knew it and didn't even ask, but we did get some Cokes and some of them pretzels with the extra big pieces of salt poured all over one side to take for our ride. We got back in the car, and Freddy was saying we better not spill nothing on the white leather seats, and Jim slapped him—not hard—upside the head and said how this Impala was older than Jesus, maybe, and them seats had worse than Coke spilled on them and held up just fine.

We got back onto Belvedere Road, and it wasn't but about three miles in the direction of the ocean, just right within spitting distance of my momma's beauty shop, where we saw them, two vagrants, snoring away under the I-95 overpass. "Pull over in the grass," Jim said, and when Freddy didn't do it fast enough, Jim grabbed the wheel and pulled it over himself. Billy Jones didn't have a good enough hold on his Coke, and he spilled it all over his pants and got some on my good slide shoes.

There wasn't time to think about it, though, because Jim had already opened his car door and was running up the concrete incline toward where the two men were sleeping, and there was two of them and one of him, so I kicked off my slides in the floorboard and grabbed hold of my blackjack and run up the hill after him.

I got up there, and it was real dark. Jim was already going through the motions of what he called interrogating the prisoner. He was standing over the Indian, slapping his face, saying, "Wake up, Chief. Wake up, Tonto." The Indian wasn't stirring much. He'd fell asleep with his hand around a bottle in a paper bag, and I figure he was passed out from drink.

Jim didn't approve. He ripped that paper bag bottle out of the Indian's hand and started beating him with it, hitting him on one side and then the other, and that got the Indian roused a little, but Jim still didn't have his attention, but he had already made a hell of a lot of noise. Even with all the sound of the interstate traffic going over the bridge right above us, I could still hear the thud of that bottle connecting with the Indian's body, so I figure Jim must have been wailing on him something awful.

The colored man must've heard it too, because he started waking up, and he didn't seem quite so out of it as the Indian. Jim yelled at me and said I better go take care of business, so I went and stood over the colored man and started slapping him around and telling him to wake his ass up, and while I was slapping his face I give him a speech I used to give about how some roustabouts come and broke into my momma's beauty shop and how my daddy was a state trooper so wasn't nobody gonna come rescue him. He took notice of that and didn't fight me too much. He just put his arms up to cover his head, and when he opened his mouth he was speaking Creole and I saw that he didn't have no teeth. I thought, here is a man who has taken some beatings in his time and knows how to take one proper.

When I thought of that, I didn't really want to beat on him no more—I only even whacked him one time with the blackjack—and I looked over and Jim was really going to town on the Indian, and I wondered how come Freddy and Billy wasn't coming up to help, so I looked away toward the car for a minute, and BAM! That nigger sprang up out of nowhere and sucker punched me in the mouth, and right off I could feel my lip rising up into a big bubble, and before I could do nothing else, he run off—he was fast, faster than you could've expected—into the night, and they never did find him again. He never came forward or nothing.

Things wasn't going good for me, but Jim seemed like he had his situation with the Indian under control, although I did think he was beating on him maybe too hard, so I ran back down the concrete to see why the hell Freddy and Billy was still in the car, and there they was, cleaning all that spilled Coke off the white leather seats with their shirts. I said, "What the hell are you doing with your shirts off? Jim's gonna kick your asses for not helping out," and Freddy said, "This is my daddy's car, and there ain't no beating Jim could imagine could compare to the shitstorm my old man would kick up if I brung this leather back some other color than white," and while we was arguing I looked up the incline and saw Jim reach behind him. He had stuck that shovel handle billy club in the back of his pants, and now he pulled it out and hit the Indian on the head with it once, and it made a dull sound, and then he hit him again, and I heard a crack and knew Jim had broke his skull.

Jim raised that shovel handle a third time, and for a second I could see the side of his face and I could see he had lost himself. He was gonna break that Indian's head in two.

I ran up the incline again, and I was yelling, I was screaming, "No, Jim, no!" but he wasn't even hearing me by then. He brought that shovel handle down a third time, and there was another sickly crack, and that Indian's head broke open like a fountain, blood just everywhere. Jim didn't even seem to notice. He raised his weapon again, and by then I'd reached where they was. I grabbed his arm, and he like to flipped out, just started flailing himself in all directions until I thought he was gonna wail on my head, too.

Freddy and Billy had run up the hill by then, and they was yelling, "Jim, stop! Stop Jim!" and something seemed to break in Jim, some wild fire left from his eyes. He turned around and looked at the Indian and said, "Oh shit. Is he dead?"

Billy went up to feel his pulse—his mom is a paramedic so he knew how—and he said, "He ain't dead yet," and Jim got his senses back and said, "Let's get the hell out of here before he is."

You know what happened after that—anybody ever read a newspaper or watched TV knows nearly much as I do. It was morning before they found him. Billy's mom and her partner was first on the scene—I always thought that was strange and awful—and that Indian wasn't dead yet, but he might as well have been. He was gone before they made it to the hospital.

They locked me up for eighteen months, and Jim, he'll be in prison until he's old and gray. Freddy and Billy they gave probation in exchange for telling everything on us, which I would have done if I was them, too. Billy never was allowed back to play baseball after that, and he already tried and failed at hanging himself in his momma's closet. He won't never amount to nothing probably. Baseball was all he had. Everyone tends to dwell on that. They think it's so terrible that he lost out on baseball, and they don't see what's more terrible, which is none of the rest of us ever thought we had anything to lose out on at all.

After the cameras and the news people all left—and before they all came back again in time for Jim's and my trial—there was a few months of, well, quiet but no peace. I didn't have nothing else to do but run errands for my momma, take things back and forth from the house to the beauty shop mostly, and so three or four times a week I found myself driving right under that overpass, where everything happened.

Every time I'd drive by, I'd see in the light what I never could've saw in the dark. That Indian must've bled a lot, because there was a big crimson stain running from the top of that concrete incline on down into the strip of grass at the bottom. Every time I'd see that crimson stain, that sickly trail of blood, I'd get sick to my stomach and feel the need to pull over and vomit, but the only place to pull over was that grassy strip where Freddy had pulled over that night, so I'd just throw up a little in my mouth and swallow it, and that's the thing I remember most about those quiet days, that awful taste in my mouth and the smell that got all up into my nose, and the way my whole face would burn for hours afterward.

One day, toward the end of the quiet, when things were about to wind up toward the trial, I drove by and saw that right under the bloodstain, someone had taken a spray can and painted *LEST WE NOT FORGET* in big block letters.

I couldn't help myself. There wasn't nothing else to do. I pulled over in that grassy strip and puked and cried until there wasn't no fluid left in my body. Then I walked down the road a ways, down to the electrical workers union building across the street from the beauty shop. I knew they had cans of paint stored away out back, and I swiped four gallon buckets of concrete gray and two paintbrushes, and walked back under that overpass and started painting.

A state trooper car come by, and I thought I was gonna get taken away again, but the door opened, and it was my daddy. He got out and walked up the incline where I was painting with two hands at once and didn't say nothing, just looked at me for a long time. And finally I couldn't look at him no more. I took the paintbrush I'd been using with my left hand and dipped the bristles in the bucket and handed it to him. He got down on his knees and started painting.

We painted all the rest of the afternoon, together there on hands and knees, painted over the blood and painted over the letters. By time we finished it was dark, and he said, "Why don't you follow me home." We got in our separate cars and turned onto Belvedere Road. Above us was a tiny little sliver of moon, and the stars all shining.

The Navy Man

After Chekhov

Talk around the island said a new man, a Navy commander on leave, was poking around the docks, looking for a fishing boat. Genie Ratliff, who had already been two weeks on Islamorada and was beginning to fancy herself a local, kept an eye out for him. Sitting at Wahoo's, eating blackened Mahi Mahi, she saw him—it must be him—walking his Chinese pug out on the boardwalk and looking down toward the water, probably at the long white fish that lounged beneath the pilings.

She kept seeing him after that, once at the movie theater two islands over, twice again at Wahoo's, a few times standing on the beach with the dog. He was always alone, and although everyone was talking about him, she never saw anyone talking to him. Even standing on the beach, unobserved so far as he probably knew, he stood straighter than any man she had ever seen, his shoulders wide and his chest pushed out, out of habit she thought, which didn't make him any less handsome for it.

There was no woman with him so far as she could tell, though he did not seem lonely. He must be a man who did not mind being alone, who sought after solitude. She imagined him on the bridge of some ship at night, the captain asleep in his quarters. His would be a quiet bridge, certainly, and no one would talk of feelings.

She was fleeing talk of feelings. Her husband Leslie, a principal at a private Christian school near West Palm Beach, was always taking her emotional temperature, and then he would want to pray together about whatever he could wring out of her. She was not yet thirty but already he had made her to feel like a very old woman, and the pleasure he took from anything motherly she did for their two small children—Anna, five, and Les Jr., two—seemed as far removed from the life of the body as anything she could imagine.

She was coming into her body. She was as beautiful as she had ever been, and she was beginning to know that she was. Here, on the island, she knew she could have the men who looked her over, and it felt good to her, this knowledge. She felt like she was on the edge of something, some new kind of life that had been deprived her.

Twice, already, she had fooled around on Leslie. Once in Honolulu, on a trip like this one, working on a Budget Travel guidebook, with an older man she met at the hotel bar. She was not an experienced drinker—her family and Leslie's were independent Baptists from South Carolina, and so teetotalers—so even though she was only into her third Scotch and water, and more water than Scotch, she was feeling it, the pleasant thumping of the drink throughout her. He said his name was Alvin, "But you can call me Al," he said, and his was Texas talk, big, all swagger, drawl, and gesture. She let him touch first her shoulder, then her leg, at the bar, and then, in the hotel Jacuzzi, she let him put his hands between her legs and kiss and touch her until she came, although she did not go up to his room like he wanted her to do, and she was surprised and a little frightened at how he pressed the issue. Still, upstairs in her own room and away from him, all he was was what he had been for her in the Jacuzzi, and she knew this was something she could do again.

The second time was last March in Cozumel, the hotel a cheap tourist trap that catered to college students on Spring Break, and she was pleased to know that she was wanted as soon as she set foot in the bar built to look like a Tiki hut, where the girls lay on the table, and the bartenders poured shots into their navels, and the boys leaned down into their long tan stomachs and drank. She had never known this kind of living, but now she wanted to try it, so she hoisted herself up onto the table, and watched the college boys fight over her, and found it pleasing that she could choose—"You there," she said, "the pretty one"—and then there were more of them, their faces stubbly or clean-shaven against the middle of her, a night of this, and dancing, and then the choosing—choice itself an intoxicating sort of novelty—and the trip upstairs with lean, shapely David, and all they did there, which she had lately been replaying in her mind as often as she wanted, which was often.

And then, a Thursday evening, she went out onto the beach at dusk to walk and watch the sky turn orange, then pink, then purple, then black, and the Navy commander came out onto the beach with his dog, and surely he was Annapolis, surely well-off, money in Blue Chips, and alone here, and surely married, and surely worldly enough . . . And these were the Keys, after all, although the whole time she had been here she had heard plenty of talk about wild nights on this beach or in the hotel rooms behind her, of secret trysting places and so on, but the talk was idle so far as she could tell, it was the talk of old women whose best days were behind them, or of young women whose best material came from books and movies, because mostly not much happened in the world, or not as much as people liked to think happened to other people.

She found herself whistling, then, not at the man, but at the Chinese pug, and when the dog came over, she reached down to pet it, but it growled at her. She snapped her fingers at it.

"He doesn't bite," the Navy man said. He was holding a Ziploc bag full of dog treats.

"May I give him one?" she said, and he gave her a green one shaped like a bone, and she gave it to the dog, and heard herself say: "Have you been on the island long?"

"Three days," he said.

"Which is how long I have left to stay," she said. For awhile, they looked out at the water. "Tell you the truth, it's boring here," she said. She didn't know why she said it when it wasn't true.

"It's not," he said, but not aggressively. Softly. The sky, now, was truly amazing, the last light stopping not at the water but at the bottom of the shallows below, because of the angle of the light and the clarity of the water, and it was not hard to think that in some ways it was the edge of the world. "Forgive me," he said.

"I'm sure it's just you spend too much time around sailors," she said, as though she had known plenty of them.

"Sailors," he said, as though the word was unfamiliar on his lips—did they call themselves sailors?, or was that the word officers called the enlisted men?, or what were the words they used?, when it came to these matters, she was lost—and she admired the square of his jaw when he smiled. Leslie's face was round.

They stood quietly until the sun went down. Then they were walking. It was because of the dog, or rather it was because the dog gave them a reason. He asked her how many sailors she had known, and she asked him how many Budget Travel correspondents he had known, and they went on like that for awhile, asking questions and giving no answers, brightly, until he was telling her that, sure, he liked being an XO, and she said, "Anyone would," and he said not anyone, many people didn't like it, chafed at it, wanted their own ship, and that he was lucky because he had been under the command of good men, friends, really, and that he didn't itch for action like many men he knew, even though it was said to be the ticket up. "It seems you've moved up anyway," she said. He couldn't have been more than forty years old—"Thirty-six," he said—and she did not say it must be because he was tall and handsome and well-spoken, with that square jaw and that smile. Men responded to the same things women responded to, gave power to other men who were attractive in the ways he was.

And then she was telling him about her mother, who handmade the dresses she was made to wear growing up—"Hideous, really," she said, "floral prints, usually, and no shape to them at all, and never slacks, only these sack dresses, which got worse and worse the older we got"— her sisters and her, she meant, and he asked about them, and her oldest sister Flora was his favorite already, he said. He liked the way Flora sneaked around with the boys who lived on the dirt road, how she came in through the upstairs window by way of the roof, and: "How did she get up on the roof?" Genie told him about how her father had measured wrong when he was building it, didn't account for the upslope of the hill behind their house, "A happy accident," she said, "because you could sit up there in the cool of night, or if you just needed to get out of the house," and there, a vista, the farmland spreading out around them, and the red clay trenches between the rows, "so much like the ocean, I'm noticing," she said. She told him her name was Genie, and he told her his first name was Everett, "but it's not a name I like," he said. "It's not a name that suits a man, so I go by my middle name, James." If he had a wife, he did not mention her, and she did not say anything about Leslie, but only because he hadn't come up in the conversation.

That evening, in her hotel room, she thought about him—James, Everett James. No doubt she would see him again tomorrow. He would find her; she wouldn't have to look for him. She meant to call Leslie, to check in and check on the children, but it was ten o'clock, and he liked to be asleep by eight, since he was up by four to prepare for the school day and to pray and read his Oswald Chambers and all the things she had tried to do along with him their first year of marriage, but which she couldn't, not at four o'clock, although she did remember with fondness the times she had, the dark and the quiet and the two of them holding hands the way they seldom did now, and the warmth of his body as she leaned into him . . . And of course it could be that he was awake now, waiting for her to call—that would be like him, would be the kind of thing he would do— and she wished, if he were waiting up, that he would be watching television, something late night, some comedian doing a monologue, wished that Leslie would be laughing at something that he thought he should not be laughing about, that he would feel that freedom, there and alone, without worrying about what she would think of him for laughing the way any other person would laugh.

She did not call. Instead, she turned on the television and found a comedian on a cable channel, and she listened to his monologue and knew that his jokes were funny but did not find in herself any reason to laugh at them. She thought of James and how she had felt walking alongside him, and of course he was married, and of course he had traveled the world, the XO, Annapolis, sharp in the uniform. These were not things she knew about, but what came to her mind was Lisbon, Rio de Janeiro, Dubai, Macao, Okinawa. Dots on the map, but now all of them full with James and with women of all kinds, and which kind did he prefer? She got up from the bed and stood in her underwear and looked at herself in the mirror, and admired her own shape, and remembered what it was like when she was seventeen and Leslie called to ask her to be his date to the junior-senior banquet—a banquet, because there was no dancing at their Baptist school, so no prom—and after Leslie's phone call she stood like she was standing now, in front of the mirror in her underwear, but not with the pleasure she felt now, looking at herself. That girl was fat in the wrong places, there were skin problems, moles. What did that girl look like? She couldn't remember anymore. Maybe not so different from the way she looked now as she might have thought. How much of her life had she thrown away on account of her own thoughts?

Two days passed. It was Saturday. Lunchtime he was waiting for her at Wahoo's. She got the table beside his, but then moved to his table, and he asked about her father, and she told him the received story about her father, the one that came from her mother, which was that he had loved her more than anything in the world, that when he died, when she was eight—combine accident in his own fields, foggy rural roads, her mother dragging his body across the field and somehow getting him into the back seat, the family car stuck behind a tractor on the rural road, and no way to safely use the passing lane; maybe he would've made it if they had lived near a hospital—anyway, that when he died, the last words on his lips were of her: "Tell my Genie . . ."

"But, really, my mother was a liar," she said. She never talked to Leslie this way. James lowered his head a little. The way he listened, without probing, opened things up. Genie lowered her voice a little. Why did it matter? She would never see any of the people in the restaurant again. But still she lowered her voice. "My mother had a saying: If you can't be nice, at least have the decency to be vague. And other times she lied flat out when it suited her idea of nice. I was there at the hospital when her mother died, and by then my mother hadn't been to church for ten years and never went again. But her mother said, 'Give me some peace before I go,' and my mother said, 'Jesus is the dearest thing to me, mother,' and, 'I've made my peace with God; I've prayed, and he's heard my prayer,' and she promised her straying days were over. So I don't know anything about my father, James. For all I know, he wanted a son and died of grief for having me."

"I have two daughters," James said. "No father dies of grief for having a daughter."

"Perhaps," Genie said. She was saying too much. Outside it began to drizzle.

"Did you ever think of chalking it up to compassion?" James said.

"The lies?"

"Her kindness," James said. "Her decency."

"So you have daughters," Genie said. "You're divorced?"

"I'm married," he said. "Eleven years, to Valeria."

For some reason, this thrilled her.

"You have children, too?" he said. Texas Al had not asked questions like these. David the boy, neither. And her mother was not in any way noble.

"Anna and Les," she said, leaving off the Jr., somehow knowing he wouldn't press, anyway.

The drizzle turned to rain. Briefly, she considered how easy it must be for him to say kind things. She pictured him in Rio, in Dubai, listening the way he was listening, but to some Brazilian woman, some wealthy Arab business-woman. Surely it was cultivated. She needed to know that that she knew he was practiced.

"I'm afraid of lightning," he said, and reached his right hand across the table and put it on her left. "This isn't that kind of rain, though, and would you like to take a walk under the umbrella?" She found herself rising with him, her right hand cupping his for a moment, so she was holding his hand between hers, and then she let herself look at him for a moment, stand and cup his hand and forget that there were people in the restaurant who believed they knew something about her, and now perhaps that they knew something new, and she didn't mind giving them something to talk about to whomever they talked to, the same way they had talked to her when she had first come to the island two and a half weeks ago, which seemed, now, holding his hand and looking at him, like two months ago, or two years.

He took his umbrella from the rack at the front of the restaurant and they waited for the cars to pass, then crossed the street on foot and made their way to the beach, and he suggested they take off their shoes and walk on the wet sand in their bare feet. She thought he must be kind to his wife and not talk about the things that, anyway, surely she knew went on. They would be separated for months at a time when he was at sea, and she was learning how people made arrangements, sometimes without saying anything about them. Perhaps his wife had lovers, too.

They began to walk in their bare feet. A week earlier she had walked the same beach, in the rain, without an umbrella, she didn't mind, and the sand was the same consistency, the same wet. But now, walking with him, under the umbrella, she was aware of the skin on the bottom of her feet, her awareness heightened in a way she had not known before in her life, and she felt the cold wet rain where it hit her arms when she swung them outside the shadow of the umbrella, and she felt his skin brushing hers, his arm and her arm, and she felt her whole body, the weight of her breasts, and the muscles in her face, and between her legs. And she felt the walking, the way the blood pumped through her, and the breath in her lungs. They were walking briskly, not like lovers, but like people enjoying a brisk walk. She did not struggle to keep up with him, but if he had walked any faster she might have lost her breath. But her breaths were deep. She thought of the word oxygen, and then there were thoughts of red blood cells and arteries. A phrase from junior high life science: Capillary action.

She stopped him, then. Put a hand on his shoulder and turned him around. Leaned up and kissed him on the mouth, under the umbrella. Pressed her lips to his and kissed him hard, and he put his hand to the small of her back. "My room . . ." she said, meaning to say that it was nearby, but then he had taken her hand in his, and they were walking in the direction of her hotel. "Our shoes," she said, and hoped he would say leave the shoes, he would buy them new shoes, but then she worried he would want to retrieve them, so she said, "Let's leave the shoes. I'd like to buy you new shoes."

She wondered briefly about the dog, and asked, and learned that the dog was waiting in his room, that the room was air conditioned, that there was food, and that he left the television on children's shows, which the dog liked, and this pleased her. She unlocked her room, and they walked in barefoot, and he was careful to step over the carpet at the threshold and onto the tile of the bathroom, so he didn't track sand on the carpet.

She followed him, and turned on the water in the bathtub, and she wondered if he would take her foot in his hand and rinse her feet. She thought of Leslie, the way he would sometimes look at her when she was undressing, and how something in him sometimes seemed unable to act on whatever she stirred within him. She always had to give Leslie some signal. He would wait for her signal. And he would not come into the bathroom when she was using the toilet, even though she had no qualms about walking in on him, and even though they only had one bathroom.

She put her feet under the water and looked at James, and he sat on the edge of the bathtub next to her and put his hands on her feet without her asking him, and he rinsed away the sand from them, and then he was facing her, her feet in his hands under the water, and one of his feet in the water next to hers, so their legs were touching.

She thought of her husband, and knew she was betraying him. This feeling had not come to her with the boy or the Texan, but the Navy man filled the room in the way they had not. Where before she had felt only excitement, now she felt like she was breaching something—she tried to push the word promises from her mind—and then she was in South Carolina, in the summer heat, beneath a tent, a gathering of all girls, and a woman—not a preacher; women were not preachers—but a woman who had been a missionary's wife in South America, whose husband had piloted a yellow plane, had been killed on the narrow strip of sand along the river where he had landed the plane while trying to bring the Gospel to a lost Amazon tribe said to be cannibals, "And purity," the missionary's wife was saying, "purity unto the Lord," amidst surprisingly frank talk about the passions men could arouse in women, talk like Genie had never known before, My goodness, I must have been seven or eight years old!, and then the call to purity, to "passion and purity, my beauties," all of the girls under the tent standing, then, and walking forward, crowding around the missionary's wife at the front of the tent, and she stepping down from the wooden platform, coming down to their level, and everyone holding hands together and singing, "You're my brother, you're my sister, so take me by the hand . . ."

James put a hand on her shoulder and said, "Did I lose you?," and, yes, she was defective. She considered the women of his she had been imagining. Lisbon, Rio, Dubai. His wife, Valeria, dark, certainly, with jet black hair and piercing dark brown eyes. A slightly older woman with a stomach like a washboard, who spoke three languages, who had not spent her childhood summers beneath tents in South Carolina.

How would a woman like that hold her head, her shoulders, her body? Who taught a woman to be a woman like that? What kind of life was possible for a woman like that?

James took one of the towels from the rack above the toilet and laid it on the floor, and then he took another, and swung her legs out over the floor, and dried her calves and her feet with the towel. He was crouching down now, not kneeling, but crouching, the weight of his body balanced on the balls of his feet. He was looking up at her, not smiling exactly. Expectant might be a better word for what it was, and not expectant in the way she might expect from Leslie, who carried his worries with him wherever he went, including their bed. This James was fully present. She considered that he did not hold any thought in his head at the moment except for her. Perhaps it was not true, but whether it was or was not, the way he crouched at her feet, drying her legs with the hotel towel, looking up at her, he made her feel as though he did not hold anything but her.

Perhaps this was how to be true to whatever person you were with, in whatever moment you were with them—to put aside anything but the present, and to know enough to enjoy it, and this, she decided, was how she would live her next few moments, with this man who made her feel as though, in the here and now, she was all there was.

The next day they sat on stools in a cabana bar open to the water, the Chinese pug at their feet, and she said, "It's good that I'm leaving," and he did not say anything, which she took as his way of disagreeing, or at least she wanted to believe that he disagreed.

It occurred to her that she had not met up the next day with the boy or the Texan. She had nothing to say to them, and though she did not have anything in particular to say to James, she felt as though there was much that had passed between them, and that there was no need to give words to any of it, that sitting next to him was enough.

They sat until it grew dark, their legs touching, and then he put his arms around her, and she pushed her bar stool next to his, and he turned his body so that she could lean the weight of her body back against him. He held her for awhile and kissed her neck and put his face in her hair, and she was sure to hold the moment close and hold other moments from the past and future away from her.

At home in West Palm Beach, Leslie rose early and went to work early and came home early to cook dinner and spend time with the children, and then he went to bed early. When he asked her, now, how she was doing—how she was really doing—she said she was really fine, she thanked him, she kissed him on the cheek, she helped him chop the vegetables and put them into the Crockpot with the roast and the sickly smell of it filled the kitchen.

Sometimes, standing with him in the kitchen when the children were already asleep, in the hour before he went to bed, his hands in the dishwater and hers on the dishtowel, drying the plates and the silverware, she found that she really was fine, that she could allow him to be the man with his hands in the dishwater rather than the man who rose at four in the morning to pray and read Oswald Chambers, and that she could herself be the woman who helped him chop the vegetables rather than the woman whose father built the house with the roof you could climb upon, or the sister who worried the eyes of God watched her keep secret Flora's nightly escapes, or the daughter at the tent meeting giving herself to the words of the missionary's wife who lost her husband near the yellow plane.

She began to do things for Leslie that Leslie had mostly done for her without her noticing. Often before she woke, he would run their clothes through the washer and put them in the dryer and then take them out later in the evening when he arrived home from the school, and press the dress shirts and put it all away. Other women she knew complained about their husbands, that they did not help with the laundry or dusting or vacuuming. Perhaps they grilled steaks. Leslie did not grill steaks. One Thursday morning she took the children to the day care, then bought two choice cuts of filet mignon, and marinated them in the afternoon, and grilled them so they were ready to eat when he walked in the door.

The minister who married them required six premarital counseling sessions of them, and she remembered that he told her that the feeling of love would fade, that it was chemical, that this was the natural way of things. When the feeling of love fades, he said, service is the pathway to rekindling it. Certainly Leslie was responding to the things she was doing for him. In the evenings, after the children were asleep, he wanted to make love more often rather than going to bed early. He left notes for her around the house, handwritten notes thanking her for all sorts of favors real and perceived, and pledging undying love and all the sorts of things she knew should move her heart with love toward him.

In time, she thought, the Navy man would recede in her memory, and perhaps he would only come to her half-formed in dreams, the way her grandparents sometimes did, or old boyfriends, or people she must have known when she was very young, in kindergarten or the first grade. She joined the women's group at the church and participated in things she had avoided her entire adult life, such as making pies for auctions to send high schoolers to third world countries, or canned food drives, or something called the Angel Tree, meant to make Christmas merry for the children of prison inmates by filling their stocking with possessions.

But another month passed, and Cmdr. Everett James was as clear in her memory as if he had held her in the cabana bar only the day before. If possible, he drew into sharper focus than he had even in the days she had spent with him in the Keys. When she heard the voices of her children crying for her or for Leslie in the night, or when she saw a Soviet or Chinese military procession on the television, or felt the wind off the Atlantic when she took the trash to the curbside, he would rise up in memory: their feet wet and sandy, his hands on her legs in the bathtub, the Chinese pug watching children's television shows in his hotel room. The thought of him would fill her, and gradually she began to allow herself to believe that what had happened was not simply an episode from the past, not simply a dalliance, but instead a harbinger, an omen, an opening out onto possibility. She would see a tall, fit man in the grocery store picking apples, and for a moment she would allow herself to think it could be him.

She wanted to talk about him, but to whom could she speak of him? Not to Leslie, certainly, nor to the people she knew from his work and their church, the people they called their friends. What would she say, anyway, if she was able? Had she been in love, on Islamorada? And if not love, what then? Was there anything learned, anything that she could take from those days and bring back to her old life?

She thought of her mother when she found herself speaking in vague terms about love, about men and women, about the flash and flower of romance, and Leslie, for his part, took her to mean that she was talking about him and her. She found that he was standing straighter, slumping less often in his chair, speaking more about himself at the dinner table. Perhaps there were things old women knew that young women needed to grow into knowledge of, and perhaps James was right to say that her mother was kind rather than selfish and petty, her lies and her omissions.

One night after a planning meeting for the Angel Tree, she leaned over to Doris Jones, wife of the man who coached the soccer team at Leslie's school—it was late, and they had been joking as coarsely as any of the church women ever joked, about the prisoners and the hunger they must feel for women, and anyway she was tired, and Doris had used the word "dreamy," but only in the abstract, not about any particular prisoner—and Genie said, "If you only could have seen this Navy commander I met in the Keys."

It was as if Doris didn't hear what she said, but of course she heard, because she walked away, briskly, as though a man were following her in a parking lot, and got into her Plymouth Horizon, and started it, and drove away without saying another word.

What if, Genie wondered, I got into my own car and drove away?

He had sent a courier to deliver his letter, a young man in white bell bottoms who stood straight as he did. When she answered the door, the young man said her name, and she answered to it, and he handed her the letter. She said, "What is this?" and the young man said, "I don't know, ma'am," and then he turned and marched toward the street and stepped into a Lincoln Town Car that could not possibly have been his own, and drove away.

Dear Genie, it said, and her blood raced at what came next. He was no longer to sea. He would be stateside, administrative from now on, and he didn't mind. He wanted it. He had asked for it. He wanted her if she wanted him, and here was how. The phone number of a travel agent who could make the arrangements. An airport Hilton in the District of Columbia. His home address, but please, love . . . And of course, when he gave her his address, he meant it as a trust, and of course she would no more visit him there than he would send a letter by post, where Leslie could intercept it. And that word: Love.

She called the travel agent and made the arrangements, and told Leslie about trouble at Budget Travel. The D.C. job that ought to have been hers. "Someone's cousin," she said, "always someone's cousin, or someone who went to school with someone," and this, of course, was how she had come into the assignments she had, too. There was trouble to be straightened out, fact checking, certainly trips to the Library of Congress and the Smithsonian Museum.

"The Hope Diamond," Leslie said. "Friendship Seven. The Lunar Module . . ."

When he said it, some part of her wanted to offer to take him with her. She found that when she thought the words she needed to say to convince him to take a few days away from the school, she could see herself at the museum with him, walking the halls with him, holding his hand as if he were her child, and she could see him rushing ahead, skipping almost, the way he did when they went to see the Atlanta Braves play a Spring Training game against the St. Louis Cardinals at Municipal Stadium, and they were late, and he was afraid he might miss an inning of Jim Kaat. But she also could see him at the Fat Man and Little Boy exhibit, see him lecturing some Japanese tourists about how it was necessary to drop the bombs at Hiroshima and Nagasaki to avoid the land invasion, how it was not just American lives that were saved, but Japanese lives, too, if you considered the projected net casualties.

" . . . the originals," he was saying, "were sure enough carried in the party of Lewis and Clark." And certainly he had vacation days. She could not recall that he had ever used a vacation day. She could go with him and forget about the Navy man, take some of the money she had squirreled away from her work, and, to keep up the appearance of working, slip away here and there on pretense of writing things down . . . And still Leslie was yammering dumbly. She watched him talk and hoped to see something new in him, but everything was the same as it always had been.

On the appointed day, Leslie drove her to the airport at six in the morning, and kissed her on the forehead and said, "Are you all right?" The truth was that there was no way for her to gauge what the truth was, and she said, "Fine," and started out the passenger door.

He grabbed her by the arm—not roughly, but it was still grabbing—and he said, "Something is wrong, Genie. I should see you off at the terminal. Maybe we can talk there. Talk for a few minutes before the flight leaves. Or anything. I want to listen to you."

He let go of her arm and waited. She patted him on the knee. She felt the pillow of air between her tongue and the roof of her mouth. She went out and took her things and did not look back at him before she went through the sliding doors and into the terminal.

James met her at the airport in his dress uniform and greeted her by her last name and carried her bags as though the admiral had sent him, and she looked down at herself, at her pantsuit, and him in his dress uniform, and wondered that any charade were necessary at all, that anyone would look at him and look at her and believe that there could be anything between them, on account of their clothes.

In the Lincoln Town Car, though, he took her face in his hands and kissed her fiercely, and took her directly to the elevator at the airport Hilton, and there in the room he was the lover home from five years at war, and never before had she thought such a thing, and never before had she considered thinking about such a thing—certainly never when she returned home to Leslie.

He presented her with a new dress, charcoal gray, and cut an inch above the knees. It was late in the evening, then, too late for restaurants to be open, and he had arranged for a room in the closed dining room downstairs, and wine and soft lighting and soft music. She had never owned a dress so fine. He poured her a glass of wine, and poured one for himself and drained it quickly, without toasting, and his face flushed, and he poured another. She looked down at herself and the dress, and then across the table from him, and she said, "We are beautiful."

Now he was leaned back in his chair a little, this posture new on her. "You," he said, and now he raised his glass, and she raised hers, and they clinked them together and both of them drank. There were children to think about, and she did think about them.

"My father worked for the railroad," he said. "He would leave for three days and come back with packets of orange marmalade."

She began to cry. He was slow to reach across the table, and then he moved his chair around the table and beside her and held her.

"How?" she said. "How? How?"

Never before had she known options, though she felt like what was left to do had been marked on her before she was born.

In the Devil's Territory

I

East Berlin, September 1961

The first time they took her father, they came in the middle of the night, and when he returned three of his fingers were broken and taped, and he would not speak of what had been done to him.

The second time, they came in the middle of the day, commanded him to stand from the aluminum workbench where he was repairing die of his own making for casting the handles of baby strollers, and made him take the long walk with them past the rows of men he worked alongside. He was gone for four days, and when he returned, his arm was cast and slung in brown nylon, and the right side of his face was swollen blue and purple from chin to forehead. She asked what they had done to him, and this time his silence did not seem willful. It seemed, instead, that the ability to respond had been beaten from him.

The third time, the family had just sat down to dinner. Her father saw the Stasi through the window, and he rose from his chair without saying a word, and walked past her, and past his wife and his wife's sister, who lived with them, and past what pictures remained of the son and daughter he had already lost, and he opened the front door and met the men at the bottom of the steps that he himself had re-poured and leveled after the war ended and they had returned to Berlin. He shook their hands and turned them away from the house and his family and one of the men opened the rear door to the black sedan, and her father slid into the back seat. She watched him go away, watched the back of his head, because he did not turn his head to look back at them.

"Vielleicht kommt er dieses Mal nicht wieder zurück," her mother said. Perhaps this time he will not return to us. Her mother's sister reached across the table and took her mother's hand, and said, "Gerte, der Herr Gott wird ihn beschützen." God will protect him, Gerte.

She—Else Richter—looked at her mother and her aunt. They had lost so much weight, as had her father, and none of them were very big people to begin with.

What was it she felt stirring in her spirit in that moment? Certainly she felt as though she had heard before from the supernatural, though she was not a person to trumpet such things. She was the only person in the house who was not elderly or frail. When her students swam their daily fifty laps, she swam all fifty alongside them, even though she had already risen at four to swim her two hundred before walking the half mile from pool to school.

She had a vision, then, of a place she knew near Humboldthafen, where a canal branched westward off the River Spree toward the west city, and if one could swim unseen past the railway bridge that constituted the border, past the Grepos and their spotlights and rifles, and if one could avoid the patrol boats . . .

Eight days passed. Her father returned wearing the suit he had been wearing when he was taken. It had been cleaned, and he smelled of soap, and his hair was combed. He walked up the steps, past Else and her aunt and mother, and up toward his bedroom without looking at any of them or saying a word. They could hear the sound of the door closing and the latch clicking, and then the sounds of weeping.

It was the sound of her father weeping that cemented the decision for her. They must go. She had never heard him weep before. Not when they reunited after the war. Not at the funeral of his mother. Not when the Jew Hilda sat at their dinner table on her way from London to Tel Aviv and told them she had come to know that God must surely be dead the day she watched an SS officer lift her infant niece into the air by the feet, and then swing her headfirst into a stone column again and again, until all that was left of her was blood, bone, and meat.

Her first thought was to wait until some time had passed. She could come home after her teaching day was over and make stews from the beef stock she knew how to get, despite the shortages. She could kill their two chickens and prepare them and make him eat as much of the flesh as he could, and make soups from the bones and fatten her mother and her aunt on the lards. The vegetables were coming in now, in her small garden plot, and she would not cook out any of the nutrients. She would chop them finely, instead, so that the three of them could eat the vegetables raw without doing damage to their gums or their false teeth.

These thoughts were reasonable to her until she considered how a single night so often brought grave changes no one could have anticipated. Already the barbed wire fencing that had gone up around the city overnight a few weeks ago, was being fortified in stretches of block and mortar. Certainly the Stasi could come for her father again, and each detainment, now, brought with it the possibility that she might never see him again in this lifetime.

Tonight her father was weak, but tonight no one would be watching him. Surely they expected him to spend his evening weeping and sleepless with fear and fatigue beyond fatigue.

She went to bed at eight, as was her custom, but determined that she would wake at midnight, and spend an hour praying for the protection they would certainly need, and then wake her mother first, then her aunt, then her father. They could take nothing with them but the clothes on their back. Anything they took would be ruined with wet, anyway, and she worried that any extra weight would sink them. She would dress them in their bathing suits, then proper street clothing, though there would be no way to avoid rousing suspicion. She could not think of a good answer to give anyone who might see her walking the streets in the middle of the night with three frail old people. She was reminded of the eighth chapter of John, where Christ and his disciples walked miraculously unseen through the crowd that was preparing to stone them to death, and could any such thing be made possible in Berlin?

She lay still for an hour, but she could not sleep. The apartment was not tidy. *The apartment must be tidied.* She rose and put on her light green house gown and went down into the kitchen. She could hear her father tossing above her, snoring and waking but certainly not to consciousness, tossing and crying out, his cries like the braying of a donkey.

She took a dishcloth from the cabinet above the sink and ran it under the water, then wrung it out. Sleep was necessary. She needed the strength, but what if she went back to sleep and then overslept, and what would people say if she left the apartment untidy? They would blame it on her father. They would use it against the people who used to meet in this house and dine together and read the scriptures. Other people would be taken from their houses and beaten and made unable, one way or the other, to speak to their own families.

Yes, this was why she took the wet dishcloth in her hands and knelt and ran it along the baseboards. But oh the pleasure she took, even now, in wiping the bits of dirt and dust from where they lay in secret, and from the blackening of the dishcloth, and then the rinsing of the dishcloth, and the soap in the dishcloth, and the lightening of the black under the water, and then in wiping down the front room, the stairwell, the closet where they kept the linens. She so often wanted for pleasure, only to find that it could be found in these small acts of tidying. With scorn she thought of the untidy students in her class, the ones she was forced to daily badger, to publicly humiliate if necessary, and wasn't this an act of love, to teach a child that their lives need not be cluttered with dross as surely were their parents lives?

On hands and knees she scrubbed the bathtub, the toilet, the sinks. She polished and scrubbed and did not forget the doorknobs or the sills above the door framings. In the dark she made the windows to shine, and she looked through them from various angles, to see that the streetlights were in no way obscured by smear or smudge.

When she was done, she heated the water and set the tea to steeping. Her mother came down the stairs and said, "Else, how will you rise in the morning?"

Her mother's eyes were red-rimmed. Her face sagged, and she no longer kept her posture. It had not been so many years since they would pass an older person on the street, and her mother would say, "Look at how she slouches. She will die of it." Else thought of saying something to her mother, but did not because her mother's slouch did not seem a failure of will. Instead, it seemed to Else that she was weighed down by burdens like lead ballast strapped to each of her shoulders and hanging from the front of her.

Else took two tea cups from the cabinet above the sink and poured tea into the cups and gave one to her mother and took a sip of her own. "I wish you to sleep," she said. "I have things to tell you, but they must wait a few hours, and I want you to gather your strength."

Her father used to talk this way to her mother. She could feel her father receding and herself expanding. Her mother and her aunt needed someone to tell them what to do, and it would be her, now, not her father, who could do it for them.

Her mother sipped her tea, which must have been too hot for her mouth, because she smacked her lips and tongue together and puffed air from her mouth in short bursts. Then she leaned forward in her chair and fixed Else's eyes with her own, with a forcefulness Else had not seen in her mother in many years. "All of us are going to die, Else," she said. "I am not afraid to die. I am only afraid for you."

"I will need you to calm and comfort father," Else said.

Her mother leaned back and blew across the surface of the tea in the cup, then took another sip. "It is not in your nature to accept terrible things," she said.

They finished their tea and put the teacups in the sink, and the teapot, and washed and rinsed and dried them and put them away in the cabinet for the last time, and straightened the dishes in all the cabinets, and the silverware in the drawers, and the pots and the pans beneath the sink. They took the photographs of her dead brother and sister from the walls and took them from their frames, and hid them behind the false wall at the back of the cupboard, where they kept the marks, and her mother reached for the marks. "Leave them," Else commanded, because they could not take them safely across the river, and her mother made an astonished face, but left the marks undisturbed behind the false wall without questioning her.

There was work yet to do. There were no papers left to burn—her father long ago had foresight enough to leave nothing of importance where the Stasi might search and find it—and the passports and identity papers they could leave behind as well, because the West recognized only one Germany, not two, so they were German citizens already, and it was known that they would find help and welcome on the other side of the city, if only they could make it safely there. But there were closets and drawers of clothes to be straightened, and bedside change drawers to be tidied, and she wanted once more to touch everything in the house, and inhale the smell of each room, and run her fingers over the bills and feathers and feet of the ducks her mother had so carefully and skillfully embroidered on the bedsheets.

Her mother laid out her father's brown suit, and his bathing trunks, and his brown socks and brown dress shoes, to which she applied one last brown polish. Else paused to watch and admire her mother. Even now, as she applied the polish, her old frame straightened, and Else imagined what thoughts the work of her hands brought to bear. When was the first time her mother had applied polish to her father's shoes? Would he have been sleeping as her mother worked the polish into the leather, or was he standing behind her, watching her, perhaps guiding her hands, or with his hands on her shoulders? Who were those young people polishing shoes, who did not yet know her, the child they would make who would survive to live an adulthood alongside them, in this place? Perhaps then they were standing somewhere near to where she was now standing, in the stone house that preceded this concrete apartment building, a room or two rooms away from her father's own parents, Else's grandparents, who had lived in that house even as they built it with their hands, and watched it take shape around them.

She went into her room and knelt beside her bed and began to pray, and found that she had no words to say, and was comforted, then, that she could fall back upon the words as Luther laid them: *Unser Vater im Himmel, dein Name werde geheiligt—Our father who art in heaven . . .* —the familiar formulation, and the familiar cadences, and then *Yea though I walk through the valley of the shadow of death, Thou art with me . . .* She made the words with her lips, but soundlessly, and then her mother was beside her, and she did not have to open her eyes and look at her mother to know that her mother was making the shapes of the words with her lips as well. She tried not to think that these daily comforts might be taken from her this very evening, but she did think it, *how could I not think it?*, and lowered herself again into the repetition of the twenty-third Psalm, to the sounds of the German language and the length and flexibility of its sentences and syntax, the comfort of all they could contain within them, and even as her mouth made the shape of Luther's words, she considered the care that had entered into their crafting as they passed from the ancient languages to her own, and she wished to reach across the city with this news, as she often wished to reach across her own classroom with this same news, that beautiful things stood on the other side of rigor and discipline, and though she could not say it aloud for fear she would be misunderstood, she had come to believe that all of it was the language of heaven.

They passed an hour this way, and then it was eleven-thirty, still too early, and she asked her mother to lie down, and her mother said, "Who could sleep now?" and wanted to continue in prayer, but Else was beginning to feel weary in her knees, and the prayer was not restful to her mind, either, not in the way that the cleaning had been, so she left her mother there to pray alone and went into the dark of the front room and looked out onto the stillness and the quiet of the street, and tried to slow her breathing and quiet her mind, and knew that she could, because she was practiced.

In stillness, then, she rehearsed the walk through the city, the four of them arm-in-arm, surely, and smiling with unforced pleasure—the pleasure must be unforced, certainly—and she imagined the four of them walking in the middle of the night through the city, someone calling out to them, and she, giddily, yes, waving to them fondly, as though their calling out was not a challenge but rather a kind greeting, a manner of approval, even, of the freedom of spirit that could take a family of four adults out onto the street at night, arm in arm, and who in these grim times could issue a second challenge when the reply to the first was so completely an affirmation of life?

Immediately she began to make a list of people from her daily life who would challenge her a second time with their voices, and then a third time by calling out, and all of them so close to the false border and the river and the guards with their rifles, and the list was not short, nor was it populated with policemen or Party officials or brainwashed children, but rather with grocers, with restaurant workers, with schoolteachers, with factory workers, with tool-and-die makers.

Again she pushed the thoughts away by patterning her breathing, and raised herself to her full seated height. She fixed upon the stretch of lighted land that led to the river, and caused herself to believe that they would make it safely to the river, and caused herself to believe that she would swim them across.

When it was time, she went upstairs and roused her mother from where she was praying, and her mother went into her father's bedroom and quieted him and helped him into his bathing trunks and his brown suit, and Else went into the room her mother shared with her aunt, and roused her aunt, and whispered to her that the time had come to leave, and her aunt said nothing, just nodded and took off her night clothes and stepped into her bathing suit and put her arms into the straps and slipped her black dress over her head.

Her mother brought her father into the living room, and Else took his chin in her hand and put her face very close to his, and she said, fiercely, "You look very handsome in your suit, father," and she pressed her other palm to his cheek and leaned forward and kissed him on the lips. A light came into his eyes like she had not seen since before he became a target of the Stasi, and he spoke, and he said, "We will join our hands now and pray," and they made a circle—Else, her father, her mother, her aunt—and her father moved his lips but did not make sounds with them, and after he said Amen, they went out through the front door and closed it behind them and did not lock it. Else put her arm through his left arm, and her mother put her arm through his right, and her aunt through her mother's right.

The street was quiet. They began to walk down it, and in two blocks they passed a young father standing in front of his apartment building, bouncing his crying infant, and he did not look up at them as they passed, and Else did not want to allow herself to believe that the miracle she had sought was coming to pass as they walked.

Three more blocks, and they were passed by a black sedan with dark tinted windows, and it did not stop or slow as it passed, nor did it turn around to pass again, but instead continued down the street until it had traveled far enough that she could no longer hear it going by.

Her mother began to laugh, then, not loudly, but with a voice of joy, and then her aunt, too, and though Else did not laugh, she felt her face brighten as though she had been laughing, and the ache in her cheeks. They turned a corner and after another three city blocks, the women still laughing, they passed a policeman on foot patrol, and he looked up at them, and Else's aunt waved at him and Else smiled at him, and she could feel from within herself a warmth toward him, and he smiled and waved back at them. It seemed to Else that he was surprised at himself, smiling and waving at them, and that he did not, then, know what to do with his hands. He put them behind his back and wandered off in a direction that seemed unnatural, and it worried her, a little, the scene they had made. But he had not stopped them to question them, which is the thing anyone in his position would have done.

In this way, they made their path through the city toward Humboldthafen, and as they made their way toward the lights, they could see the Grepos in the distance, pacing by the makeshift sections of wall and the barbed wire. They were children, Else thought, young men not but nine or ten years removed from a classroom like her own. She watched them, their swagger, and reminded herself that it surely masked a fear deeper and abiding than her own fear, which she felt now as a flushing in her face and a growing emptiness in her belly.

They made their way through a clearing and into a thicket of trees from which they could watch, and they waited. She spied the place where they would cross the barbed wire, and then the shallow place by the water, in the dark triangle the two swiveling searchlights did not cover. She would have to leave two of them there vulnerable, her aunt and her mother, while she took the weakest, her father, across first. She worried his body would not bear the shock of the cold water, and what of her own, three times back and forth?

It was not too late to turn back. They could walk back through the city, the way they had come, and it would be less dangerous, heading away from the wall and the river and toward their home. If they were stopped, she could tell them about the pleasure of the late evening walk, and how they had been almost to Humboldthafen, where her father had proposed to her mother on a late night like this one—a lie, but a harmless one—and her mother would know enough to hold to her father's arm more tightly and look up at him adoringly, and then they would be told to be on their way, perhaps told gruffly, and they would make their way back to the apartment and go to their beds shaken but, yes, alive.

Else put the thought out of her mind. Soon the Stasi would come for her father and he would not return to them. Soon her mother would die of grief. Soon they would say to

Else that she was not fit to teach children, on account of her father and whatever wrong thinking she might have absorbed as his daughter, and they would send her to work in a factory somewhere in the hinterlands, and separate her from her aunt, and cause her to live in a place without proper heat, without books, without pen or paper or a radio with which she could listen to broadcasts from the West and keep her hope alive.

Something happened. The Grepos began to run toward the harbor, carrying their rifles in front of them. She did not wait to see why they were running, though she was sure they meant to bring an end to someone attempting escape, as they were. "Quickly," she said, and the four of them began to walk briskly toward the barbed wire. Her father took off his coat and threw it over the wire, and she helped her mother over first, then her aunt, then her father, and then she climbed over. She retrieved her father's coat, and they made their way toward the dark and shallow place, unseen.

They took off their outer layer of clothes and laid them at the wet bottom of the shallow, and she instructed her mother and aunt to crouch down upon them in the wet and the cold. She waded into the muck with her father, and out into the water. He was heavy against her back, and immediately she began to go under. She pushed away from him and helped him to float and hissed at him: "Be buoyant. You know how."

She took him on her back again, and began to swim across the river, toward the canal, a hundred meters away. There was not much weight to him, but what there was nearly took her under when she hit the channel current, and she willed herself not to swim against it, but to let it carry her even as she swam them out of it.

She swam them to the other side, and then into the canal. The railway bridge above—the border—was coming into sight, and she could see the outlines of two patrols sweeping it. "Hold your breath, father," she said, and took them under the cold water. She pushed him off her back under the water, and reached out for his hand, and knew that he was kicking because he was moving forward with her. She opened her eyes under the water to look back at him, but all was black.

She waited until she thought he would no longer be able to hold his breath. She hoped they had put enough distance between themselves and the railway bridge. She pulled on his hand, and they raised up. He came out coughing. She breathed in the cold air. She was shaking with the cold, and she could feel the tremor in his hand. She hoped his coughing would be muted against the sound of the wind.

She pulled him toward the bank of the canal and struggled to push him up onto the marshy grass, and then she pulled herself up after him.

He lay on his side, with his knees pulled up against his bare chest. His teeth were chattering, as were hers, but his body tremored in spasms to match his jaws. She looked around for something to cover him, but there was nothing but the mud and the wet grass. She glanced back at the bridge, but there was no indication that anyone had seen them there, another miracle.

She needed to get back to the other side, to her aunt and mother who were no doubt catching their death in the damp shallows, but she worried, now, that she would be leaving her father to his death here.

She crawled on top of him, then, covered him with her body, covered his back with her front, and put her arms around his abdomen, and her hands over his chest. She could feel the cold of him, not just in the places where his skin touched her skin, but also through the front of her bathing suit. She put her face against his neck, put her mouth to his neck and blew warmth onto it.

His tremors slowed. His teeth were still chattering, but less violently now. They no longer clicked together in the alarming way they had. She breathed on him again. She turned him over, onto his back, and climbed on top of him, and wrapped her arms and legs around him, and she said, "It's all right, father. All is well, father."

She worried that he would be angry with her for entwining her body with his in this way. She thought that she would die in the river and that this would be his last memory of his daughter, her climbing on top of him and wrapping her arms and legs around him, and putting her mouth on his neck and face and breathing moist warmth into his skin.

His body was regulating itself. She could feel the warmth their bodies had trapped between them. She hoped it would be enough to sustain him.

She climbed off him and had him curl around himself in the fetal position again. She leaned down once more to look at his face. He locked onto her eyes, and he said, "Else," and she was moved at the sound of her name on his lips and she could ill afford to be moved.

"Walk west when you are able," she said. She turned away from him and lowered herself into the canal again, and recoiled at the cold, and steeled herself for another dive under the water, and then she dove.

She took a breath as she surfaced, and saw a patrol boat coming down the river. It slowed as she saw it. Had they seen her? She went under but stayed where she was in the water. The bridge was behind her and the patrol boat ahead. Had they seen her aunt and her mother in the shallows?

When she could not hold her breath any longer, she came up again. The patrol boat was drifting slowly, nearly directly ahead of her.

She went under again. She could feel the cold working its way to her lungs, a feeling not unlike the early workings of the pneumonia that had put her months in bed after the war when she was still young. Something lightened in her, and she felt the urge to give in to it, and some part of her imagined it would be better to give in now, before the hail of bullets that were sure to follow her sighting of the patrol boat.

The part of her that she believed to be her true self pushed back against the thought. She surfaced again. The patrol boat was downriver and moving away. She did not look back toward the railway bridge. She tried to keep her head low in the water. She was swimming freestyle now, strongly, the way she was not able to swim when she crossed with her father on her back.

The searchlights were crisscrossing the water again, now, and she timed the pattern of their rotations and went under again, and swam under the water toward the shallows until the bottom rose up to meet her.

She surfaced with caution, only five feet from where her mother and aunt were huddled low in their bathing suits on her father's suit coat and the saturated clothes. Their eyes widened when they saw her, and she could see the fear in them. She avoided their eyes in response, knowing by instinct that the fear might be contagious, and that fear was not far from her, anyway.

It occurred to her that she had not been praying throughout the ordeal, and she dashed off a *Lord, forgive me it*, then pushed it away. She could feel her strength ebbing and did not dare wait for a second wind, which she thought would not come, anyway, on account of the cold and the stopping and the starting.

But the second wind did come a moment back into the river, her aunt on her back, and with it came a boldness, and a strength should could not have predicted. She focused her attention on the canal and then the other shore, and perhaps she let her attention wander too far toward the end, at the expense of the awareness she needed in the moment.

The railway bridge was in sight. She wanted to wait until the last possible moment to take her aunt under. She waited too long. With terrible speed she found herself staring into the eyes of the man—the boy, really—on the bridge. She felt her aunt tense above her, and for a moment she thought her aunt would push her under before they could be shot, but then her aunt returned to herself and relaxed her body again, and all the while—now she was treading water—the boy looked at them, and she hoped she was not mistaken in believing that what his face reported was abject fear, rather than vigilance.

She was aware of the approach of a second man on foot patrol, and she thought for sure that this would break whatever spell of fear or horror had come over the boy, and this would be their end. But at that moment, the boy turned and ran toward the other man and jumped at him playfully, and raised his fists in invitation to a mock fight.

Else did not take her aunt under. She was faintly aware, anyway, that she had lost the strength for it. Instead, she swam them forward, taking care not to make any splash, as the men on the bridge yelled and shouted as boys at play will yell and shout.

When they reached the canal bank and got themselves up and out, she looked for her father, but he was gone, and hope began to rise in her. "Warm yourself by walking briskly," she told her aunt, and lifted her to her feet, and pushed her in the direction her father must have gone.

There was no convergence of coincidences in the world that could possibly account for the things she had now done and seen and witnessed. Surely, she thought, the hand of God had reached down and pressed gentle fingers here and there against the unseen fabric of the universe for the sake of her and her family.

It was then she knew that she and her mother would be safe. She lowered herself again into the canal and toward the river and the east city beyond, and swam long, strong strokes across the water, and went under against the turning of the searchlights, and surfaced again near her mother, in the shallows.

Her mother was shrunken and shivering in the wet and the cold. "Leave me here," she said. "I won't make it across."

"I won't leave you," she said, and she knew, as she put her mother on her back and pushed off into the river for the third time, that they would make it to the other side alive.

Her arms and legs were burning with fatigue. As they reached the channel, she knew she had lost the ability to navigate the current as she had before, and they were pulled farther with the rushing of the waters than she had been pulled when she was carrying her aunt or her father.

Her mother grew heavier against her, now, as she struggled back nearer the bank, swimming against the direction of the river. Yet she pushed, strong in the knowledge that she was being protected. She had fixed in her mind the vision of three angels swimming just above her, where the water met the open air.

They made it to the canal, and she swam them inside. She knew she did not have it in her to anymore go under the water. With vigor, now, she moved them forward, the end in sight. She saw no one up on the railway crossing, and she swam under it knowing that freedom was on the other side, that the patrols could not fire upon them there, because the other side of the bridge was beyond their jurisdiction.

There was shouting from behind them as they emerged from the shadow of the bridge, to the waters belonging to the west. A voice commanded: "You! Stop right there!"

She felt her mother let go of her and push away. Gunfire erupted from behind them. She swam hard for the other bank. Men in uniforms waited there, and some of them began to return fire on the bridge. She felt something sear the top of her head, a great heat, but no pain. She made it to the bank, and hands reached down to pull her up.

A hand was pressing something to her head, and she tried to push it away. She was screaming, "My mother! My mother!" When she looked out onto the water, all she could see was the black. Men were rushing out onto the bridge, now, and the men on her side were pushing her away from the shore, spiriting her away.

She put her hand to her face and it came away bloody. One of the men picked her up and began carrying her, and kept one hand clamped to the top of her head. "Where is my mother?" she said.

"Your father and your aunt are safe," he said. Now he was running, and as the water receded into the distance, she saw a body surface, face down.

"Where is my mother?" she said.

II

West Palm Beach, October 1970

Wayne Adams and three other guys from the Key Club sat up on the benches and watched the Roosevelt girls show the white girls one of the old cheers they weren't allowed to do anymore since the judge made Twin Lakes High School out of Roosevelt and Palm Beach High. They chanted: "I can tell by your eyes you been drinking berry wine, huh! Sardines! And, yeah, and pork and beans! I can tell by your smell that you're on welfare, yeah! Sardines! And, uh, and pork and beans!"

The Palm Beach High girls watched politely, and Wayne and his friends watched them, and one of them, Jim Plank, started chanting along, mocking them—"I can tell by your eyes you been drinking berry wine . . ."—and then Wayne and the others, too, until they got loud enough that the black girls stopped what they were doing and stared at them, hands on hips, and the white girls, too.

It made Wayne feel bad, the cheerleaders looking at them like that, but Jim stood up and yelled, "What are you looking at?"

"Why you gotta do that?" one of the girls fired back, and Jim yelled, "Because this ain't darkest Africa," and then Wayne and the others were hustling him out of there, which he didn't resist any, but he kept yelling, anyway, and Mrs. Raynes, the cheerleading sponsor, was walking their way, and the two black guys sitting on the benches on the other side—boyfriends—stood up, too, and took a couple of steps before their girlfriends went over to tell them to keep cool. Before Mrs. Raynes could reach the Key Club guys, they all piled into Jim's truck and peeled out toward the neighborhood.

Wayne didn't mind mock cheering, but he didn't like Jim escalating things like that. It wasn't safe. Twin Lakes was a powder keg already. Wayne had taken to urinating twice a day in the bushes behind the science labs, because you couldn't go into the bathrooms anymore without three black guys shaking you down at the door—"Piss tax is a dollar"— and flashing brass knuckles and asking you to apologize if you tried to say no. Earlier in the week, on Monday, Wayne's girlfriend Sandra had been sitting in her desk in the third row, listening to old Mr. Sandifer rattle on about differential equations, when the door on the north side of the classroom burst open, and two white guys came jackrabbitting through, three black guys following, one of them slashing at the air with a pocketknife, and everyone yelling and cursing and knocking over desks on their way to out the door on the south side, and there was nothing for Sandra or Sandifer or anyone to do about it, except to get under the desks. Nobody seemed to know how to get it under control, and it seemed like a lot of people didn't want to get it under control, anyway.

Wayne didn't say anything, though, as Jim went on and on from the driver's seat about coloreds this and coloreds that, and then deposited him in front of his mother's house, where he didn't want to go inside, because his brother Davis's Cadillac was parked in the driveway.

"Aren't you glad," his mother said, as soon as the door opened, "that your brother Davis has come for a visit?" and there he was, Davis, in his navy blue blazer with the ridiculous yellow patch on the breast, and his close-cropped insurance salesman haircut and his black loafers with no socks, and what Wayne wanted more than anything was drive off and pick up Sandra and go some place where they could be alone for awhile and talk and kiss some, but he couldn't do it because he didn't have a car, and his father wouldn't lend him any money so he could buy one.

". . . and what I'd like to do is take you on," Davis was saying, and this was nothing new. The arm-twisting had been going on ever since the summer, now that Wayne's graduation was in sight, and the route from here to there was twenty hours a week in Davis's office, plus the daily commute to Florida Atlantic University in Boca Raton, for the business degree Davis would subsidize in exchange for ". . . an easy path, really. You wouldn't have to start from scratch like I did, and after you got a few years under your belt, I'd be glad to call you partner . . ." and everything sounding like a favor Davis was going to do for everyone, and their mother grinned through her pink lipstick, her grin not as fake as it looked, but not any different, either, from the way it looked when she was being fake, which was most of the time she was around anyone who wasn't part of the family.

Davis was still talking, but Davis would keep talking until Wayne gave in, because it was his way, and it was why he was so good at selling insurance, so Wayne interrupted him and said, "I'm thinking it over, Davis," and went down the hallway to his room, and closed the door and turned on the television.

He could hear his mother yammering through the closed door. Last month when he had threatened to burn his draft card, she had taken it from him, and then when he sat down to dinner in the evening, she set it on the table and handed him a pen and told him he wasn't going to eat anything of hers again until he did his duty as a citizen of our nation and signed it, and when he had signed it, she took it from him and mailed it.

He took off his socks and put on a clean pair. His brother's feet must have reeked all the time, sockless like that. It was something he couldn't understand, the socklessness. Wayne liked his feet clean and dry.

He looked out through the bedroom window, and there was old Charlie Yothers across the street, tending to the orange trees in his front yard, and the last few times he had taken five dollars off Charlie to cut and edge his grass, Charlie had told him if he was going to make a life in Palm Beach County, he would be well off learning a trade. Charlie suggested air conditioning, which was Charlie's own trade. "It's hot, and Florida's not going to cool off the rest of your life," Charlie said, which was true enough.

Now, his mother yammering, and his brother in the front room with his socks off, old Charlie Yothers was seeming more and more a reasonable man.

Wayne put his shoes on over his fresh socks, and told his brother it was nice to see him, and made his way out the front door to see Charlie.

The old man put down his pruning shears and wiped his brow with his white handkerchief when Wayne came into his line of view. "What can I do for you, young fella?" he said, and Wayne said he wanted to talk to him about the air conditioning business, about the apprenticeship Charlie had been telling him about, and when could he get started?

Charlie looked him over. "You got to finish school first," he said, nodding his head. "Yes sir, that's the thing to focus on right here. You don't got but the rest of the year left, right?"

"What I was wondering," Wayne said, "was whether there wasn't some kind of part-time apprenticeship, just to get started, to get a leg up."

Charlie seemed to be considering it. "What are your Saturdays like?" he said.

"Free and clear," Wayne said.

"Tell you what," Charlie said. "Saturdays I do side jobs. Trade work with people, work up at the church, things like that. Not every Saturday, but most Saturdays. Keeps me out of trouble.

"I couldn't pay you," Charlie said. "But I could buy you breakfast now and again. Lunch. We usually get started early."

Great, Wayne was saying. Excellent. Superb. Right on.

"Seven a.m.," Charlie said. "Cherry Road Baptist Church."

Wayne told him he'd be there, and shook his hand, and turned toward the house, but his brother's Cadillac was still in the driveway, so he started walking in the direction of Okeechobee Road, and once there he walked up and down the sidewalk, in front of the car dealerships and the car wash and the furniture stores, until it was dark and he knew Davis was gone. Then he walked home in the cool of the evening.

Saturday morning he set the alarm clock for six. He showered and shaved and put bread in the toaster and buttered and ate it. He could hear his mother tossing in her bed. She had been complaining of the change of life for as long as he could remember. When his father was in town, she got up early to make breakfast, but when he was gone with the railroad, she just tossed in the bed in her misery until nine or ten.

It was a ten minute walk to the church if he loafed, which he didn't. It felt good to be up and walking, putting distance between himself and his mother's house, and, even better, taking first steps toward the distance he meant to put between the kind of life his parents and brother would have for him and the kind of life he wanted to make for himself.

Old Charlie was waiting for him in the parking lot, leaned up against the stake truck his service manager had let him borrow for the weekend, sipping coffee. Two massive compressors rested against the far end of the truck bed, up behind the window of the cab, and next to them a hand truck and two refrigerator dollies.

"You want some?" Charlie said. He offered Wayne an empty mug and began to unscrew the lid off his Thermos, but Wayne said no thank you. "Suit yourself," Charlie said.

The old man pointed toward the compressors. "You think a young fella such as yourself could wrangle one of them?"

"Sure," Wayne said, though he couldn't see how one man could do such a job, even with the stake truck's hydraulic lift and the hand trucks and dollies.

"Go on," Charlie said. Wayne jumped up into the truck and pushed on one of the compressors and got the hand truck under it, but he couldn't manage it from there.

"Here," Charlie said, and took a couple of fabric straps out of his pocket and threw them to him. Wayne hooked them to the hand truck and wrapped them around the compressors, one a third from the bottom, and the other a third from the top. He tried again to pull on the hand truck, but he could feel the weight shifting as he pulled backward, and he was afraid that if he pulled back too far, the whole thing—hand truck and compressor—would come over on him and leave him pinned to the truck bed, impaled on the handle of the hand truck.

Charlie laughed at him a little. "I know," Wayne said. "It's a two-man job."

"I don't know about that," Charlie said. He got his old man body up in the truck and put his foot on the axle of the hand truck, and in half a second the compressor was up and balanced on the hand truck perfectly. It didn't seem as though Charlie had even expended any energy.

"You know how to work the lift?" he said, and Wayne did. "I'll get this on it, then you lower us down," Charlie said, and Wayne did as he was told, and on the way down, Charlie said, "The key to the thing is you gotta work smart, not hard. You can't be taking everything on your body. You got to learn the art of nice and easy."

He worked the compressor onto one of the refrigerator dollies, and then repeated the process for the other one, and then they rolled them one at a time into the fellowship hall and out through the side door and down the long hallway toward the education building, and around back, where they were going to be installed.

"Shit," Charlie said, after he set the second compressor against the back wall. "Look at that." He showed Wayne his left palm, which was sliced beneath the knuckles of his four fingers. There was blood on the sharp corner where the compressor had caught him.

"I ought not talk like that," Charlie said. He took the handkerchief from his pocket and wrapped it around his hand.

"You want me to go get you some ice?" Wayne said.

"Naw. Forget it," Charlie said. He leaned his back against the wall, closed his eyes and flexed his hand around the handkerchief. Wayne detected a tremor in the hand. "Yeah, come on," Charlie said.

They went around the front, toward the church office, and Charlie took a ring out of his pocket. It probably held seventy or eighty keys. Wayne didn't know how a key ring that big could've fit in that pocket. Charlie tried two keys in the lock and then the third turned it.

The door opened up to a foyer. The preacher's office door was closed, but there were two voices behind it. "It's Old Charlie," Charlie said, loud enough to be heard clearly through the door, and then came the reply: "Hello Charlie!"

The door opened, and the preacher came out, and there was a large and balding man with him, and the preacher introduced him as Brother Billups. Charlie stuck his cut-up hand in his left pocket and shook with his right. "Brother Charlie, good to meet you," Brother Billups said, "and who we got with you?"

Charlie introduced Wayne—"One of the good ones, I'll tell you," he said, and put his hand on Wayne's shoulder, and it made Wayne feel proud—and Brother Billups said, "I hear tell you fellas are putting in compressors for the school," and Charlie said it was so, and this was news to Wayne, the school. Wasn't this a church?

Brother Billups was clapping the preacher on the back, and he said, "You're lucky, having a man like this for your shepherd."

"Amen," Charlie said. "Amen."

"This is a man," Brother Billups said, "who knows a ministry opportunity when he sees one, and this"—here he gestured toward the walls around them and the ceiling above them—"is just the start. Soon we'll have our own campus. Acres and acres. The Lord is working on it right now. We'll send our young people out into the mission field, and get them serving right here at home, too. Schoolteachers, doctors, nurses, lawyers—Godly lawyers. Yes, sir."

He was steering them—the preacher and Charlie— toward the door, and Wayne followed them. Right now, Brother Billups was saying, the Lord was working on the heart of a Chevrolet dealer out on Okeechobee Boulevard, who lived on five acres of prime real estate in what used to be the outer frontier of Palm Beach County, but which was now the heart of West Palm Beach, not far from what would soon be the geographical population center of the county. "Beautiful, pristine property," Brother Billups said. "Trees imported from all over the place. They got this kind of tree where you pull on the bark and it pulls away like paper." He took a large, thin, folded-up piece of this bark out of his pocket, and unfolded it, and took out a ballpoint pen. "You can write on it," he said, and began to draw a map of the property.

"Over here's the pond he dug," Brother Billups said. "Bamboo shoots growing out of it, and they say a baby alligator lives there among em, though I ain't seen it. If I was him, I'd get it out of there, though, because there's horses in the stables over here." The stables he planned to turn into administrative buildings, offices where the stalls had been. Beside the long row of tall pines, he planned to pave a long circular drive for the school buses. The playground equipment he'd nestle among the Banyan trees, "because they're like little forts in there, and that's what growing boys need at least a couple times a day, to go out there and make like they're cowboys and Indians."

It occurred to Wayne that nobody had noticed or said anything about Charlie's cut hand, and now they were walking the church property, Brother Billups detailing his temporary plans for the rooms in the education building, and how they'd have to make do until the Lord could persuade the car dealer to turn over the land for the right price. As far as Wayne could tell, Brother Billups had it in the bag.

"There's no debate," Brother Billups was saying, "about what kind of education we need to be providing, and that's college preparatory, no argument. But already we got some kind of division in the board members as to whether we need to be offering Latin and German, that sort of thing."

"Latin is a dead language," Old Charlie said, his first words in awhile. The way he said them, and the way he fixed his eyes on Brother Billups, it occurred to Wayne that Old Charlie didn't like Brother Billups. Something flared in Brother Billups's eyes, too, just briefly, and then it was gone, and he was warm again.

"Well, Brother Charlie," Brother Billups said, "that's the same thing I thought at first, but then we got to looking at the days when what was being taught in school was reading and writing and arithmetic, and memorizing from the King James Version, the red letters, all that." He put his hand on Charlie's shoulder and moved his body closer, and Charlie let him do it, even though Wayne was pretty sure Charlie didn't like it. "You know those was the days when there wasn't problems like now, with all the violence and the unrest and so on."

Roosevelt and Palm Beach High, Wayne was thinking, although to a guy like this Brother Billups it was probably long hair, dope, people going to Canada, free love, rock and roll. Twin Lakes, sure, but that other stuff, too.

"You get to looking at how it was back then, the good old days let's call em, and you see there was people could recite the Rime of the Ancient Mariner and knew their *e pluribus unum* from their *habeus corpus*, if you know what I mean."

Now Brother Billups put his other arm on Wayne's shoulder. "Young man like you," he said. "Smart, possibly wise. You know your algebra, I'll bet, maybe your trigonometry even. You got Spanish enough to tell somebody to shut his *boca* if need be. But seems to me you gotta cut through an awful lot of mess to get from here to there. The way I hear it told, that high school over there got classes with three people sitting in the front row taking notes and asking questions and twenty-five other ones their heads down on the desk sleeping. White or colored, it don't make a difference to me, I'm not prejudiced about it, it's people's actions that makes up what kind of person they want to make of themselves. And dope dealing, Mary Jew Wanna, man-children running around there with knives . . ."

Old Charlie excused himself and went through the open door to the bathroom. Wayne could see him leaning over the sink, unwrapping his hand from the handkerchief, could hear him turning on the water, and then the sound of the spray softer against his hand than the washbasin. Now the preacher was asking about declensions—"Greek I had in Bible College. The Koine, like they say. Not enough to read it straight on, but if I got down my lexicon"—and Hebrew letters left to right, and with Latin, it was those declensions, he was saying, you really had to have a certain number of hours in the day to devote to these kinds of things, had Brother Billups considered, since there was the matter of tuition, and the public schools were free.

"Train up a child in the way he should go," Brother Billups said, "and when he is old, he will not depart from it. That's the thing we have to keep first and foremost here. That's what's not negotiable. Latin, Greek, Hebrew, all of that can be worked out one way or the other. Even right now, the board is studying on it . . ." and now his hand was on the preacher's shoulder, and in the bathroom, Charlie was carefully drying his hand with brown paper towels, and waving it in the clean air, and now he was rinsing the handkerchief.

Six o'clock that evening, both compressors installed and fired up—"Purring like a pussycat," Charlie said—they leaned against the tailgate of the stake truck, and Charlie said, "You may have noticed how that Brother Billups is a windbag," and Wayne allowed that he had.

"Two kinds of people in the world," Charlie said. "You got your talkers and you got your doers. I spent most of my life thinking we'd all be better off if we had quite a few less talkers and a whole lot more doers."

Wayne pictured Davis, there on his mother's couch, selling her on insurance.

"You know what, though," Charlie said. "That's a good thing they're doing, with that school."

III

West Palm Beach, 1978

This principal, this Leslie Ratliff, he sat so smug in his chair with the power to give or withhold from her the living she needed to make for herself and her aunt—the last of the money was a month away, or a month and two weeks if she asked for canned goods from the Lutheran pantry, which she was not willing to do, or which she had not been willing to do, and now she was thinking how pride goeth before a fall, but she did not know Hebrew, so she could not know if there were different words for pride in the original language, and here she was thinking about the nobility of her father in his time of death, the way he had told her to refuse the machines when the time came ("The time is soon," he said) and how she wanted him to allow it, how she certainly would have found a way to pay for them if they would have kept him with her a few days longer, and how he simply willed himself out of the bed one last time, and into the wheelchair, and got himself outside in the cold, streetside, and how long had he waited there, and she thought of the Frankfurt cab driver who had presence of mind enough to see him, and to stop, and to call for someone, and to wait with his body there, this cab driver was worried, he said, that someone would steal her father's watch or pick his pocket— and now this Principal Ratliff, this man so young she was amazed he needed to shave, with his seventeen strands of hair combed over his prematurely bald head, she was an intelligent woman, she could count, and surely a young man vain enough to comb seventeen strands over his bald head and pretend they covered his head would be vain enough to count as well, and there they were, between them, these seventeen strands of hair, and all this high-minded talk about the instruction of children, and did not this Principal Ratliff know that she, Else Richter, had certainly taught children now older than he was, in a time and place of real, true danger, where what was threatened was more immediate than the Seven-Day Creation of the Earth, the Seven-Day *ex nihilo* Creation, which, she now told him, she believed in with all her heart, as she did the Bible, inerrant and inspired by God, inerrant, yes, in its original autograph, and here the principal's ears perked up, and he said, "But not inerrant in times subsequent?" and—the child he was!—she had to speak of the Luther Bible and the King James Bible and the ways in which the two were not one hundred percent in accordance word to word, and how could they be?, when one considers that any two languages, even two languages so correspondent as English and German, both of them of the same family of languages—"But the Latinate, you see, has so crept into the English language that only twenty percent of the Germanic words survive, but they are the most important words, the words of being and doing and surviving, your is, are, was, were, be, being, been, and your words for the things of the land and the sky and the Word itself"—but, still, these two languages so much closer one to the other than any European language to the language of the ancient Greeks or the Hebrews, and . . . but now this Ratliff was growing impatient, "I have a master's degree in education from Apalachicola Christian College," he said, "and a four-year degree with an emphasis in Biblical Studies from Bob Jones University, which is, as you know, the foremost"—and here he digressed to talk of the mainline denominations and their descent into the folly of modernism, and of William Jennings Bryan, and of a certain hymn attributed to Martin Luther, and the ways in which, and the harmony of which, and the Spirit's hand upon, and she straightened even more in her chair and tried to remind herself that the reason she was in this office was that, of course, these were the people who were on the side of right, and that they were mostly in agreement, and that what she must do is show the ways in which they agreed rather than picking nits, let the nits lay, and if they hatch the lice, then we shall fumigate later.

"I can see," she said, careful to smile now, "that you are a man under whose authority I could serve."

He relaxed at that, *das Schwein*, all the trinkets on the desk in front of him—the five steel balls suspended from strings that swayed gently with the ventilation draw, and all the pens, and the seven silk ties displayed on the corner nearest her right elbow, their tips hanging like tongues from the oak lip.

"Oh, you wouldn't get the joke," he said, and seemed quite pleased with himself. "The ties," he said, and smiled again that self-pleased smile, and then he reached into the desk and took out seven strips of cardboard, two centimeters by six or so, and handed them to her, one by one, and they were the same colors, and in the same order as the ties: yellow, orange, green, red, light blue, dark blue, and pink.

"Did you have demerits at the schools where you taught before?" he said. "Here we call them tallies. We keep a tally of infractions, you see. We're very strong on this. We find it works for us very nicely."

He handed her a laminated and color-coded Tally Key:
Hullabaloo (yellow)
Out of Order (orange)
Work Late or Incomplete (green)

Intentional Disobedience (red; counts as five tallies)

Attitude Lacking (light blue)
Courtesy Lacking (dark blue)
Talking (pink)

"Spells HOW I ACT, you see," he said.

"What happens," she said, "if a student receives one."

"It varies by the grade," he said. "Fifth grade? Five tallies in one day, you pay a visit to Mrs. Millet, our guidance counselor." He spread his arms wide, to indicate, Else supposed, the girth of Mrs. Millet. "One swat for five, and a phone call to the parents. Two for six. three for seven and the child is sent home."

"The red is five tallies?" she said.

"The red you use sparingly," he said. "The red is the atom bomb. You don't want to overuse the red."

She took the white glove from her right hand and ran her index finger over the laminated card: yellow, orange, green, red, light blue, dark blue, and pink. The colors, perhaps, too distracting. The colors, in any event, out of order, not in keeping with the color wheel, where green did not lie beside red, and yellow came between orange and green. "Did you design the Tally Key?" she asked Ratliff.

"No, no," he said. "It comes to us from Pennsylvania, from a little school in Harrisburg, a good little school we were taken to visit when we started the school." He leaned forward in his chair. "I was the second employee of the school." The first was Thomas Billups, the athletic director and football coach, Ratliff said, and now they were walking the buildings, he was giving her the tour, and in the gymnasium she could smell the bodies of boys even though school would not begin for two weeks, and the school had invested in a 16mm film projector, and there were plans in the works for a yearly trip to Europe for the graduating seniors, and perhaps she would be interested in chaperoning if some year they went to Germany, since she spoke the language, and since she would know people and places. She did not say no, though that would be her answer, certainly. She had left Germany and did not intend to return, and certainly not in some tour group with children. He was rattling off names more quickly than she could remember them or fix them with significance—Mr. Reynolds and Mrs. Marks and Dean somebody. Marti Winget, the fifth grade teacher who had been overheard over the summer taking the Lord's name in vain, Marti Winget the reason they were talking now, her lapse the reason there was a job to be offered so close to the start of school, and: "We take these things very seriously." Then another Billups, this one the chairman of the Board of Trustees, and Else did not have to ask to know that this one would be the father of the football coach, but she did not say anything about this. She had been long enough in the United States to know that this was the way of things, and she remembered her own father's dismay one Sunday morning their first January here, when it was announced that Sunday evening's prayer meeting would be preempted in favor of a Super Bowl party in the church hall, with popcorn and a potluck dinner and a screen projection television. She remembered his talk, then, of the disruption of the graves of the saints, and then of the martyrs—oh, could her father go on!—and Ratliff was saying, "And this will be your classroom," and opened the door to a room bare except for metal frame desks with pressed board desktops, and clean walls freshly painted a matte white, and only then did she realize that she was being given what by now she surely deserved. When they were done, she went to the store and bought what she needed to make a dinner for herself and her aunt—potatoes, sauerkraut, bread rolls, pork.

IV

West Palm Beach, 1986-1987

Their older boy was giving them problems, and he had never given them problems before. This was late September. At home, he had been sullen and quiet, had been locking himself in his room. This had been going on ever since school started. He had been slipping toward the back of the bus, Sandra said, where the high schoolers talked raunchy. He was in the fifth grade. He knew he wasn't supposed to be back there. Sandra wasn't born yesterday, she knew what kinds of things those high schoolers were talking about back there.

"Do you know why your mother drives that school bus?" Wayne said, and the boy shook his head, no, and there was no way to know anymore what it was he was thinking, although Wayne could imagine well enough that the boy, now in the fifth grade, was coming into the knowledge they had kept from him for as long as they could, which was that, especially at a private school, even a Christian one, there was a wide divide separating the children of doctors and lawyers and developers and, yes, insurance salesmen, from the children of heating, ventilating, and air conditioning servicemen. No need to talk about the long tradition of the guilds, of the skilled craftsman, of the genius, really, of machines and the way they worked, and all the things Wayne, anyway, believed less and less the more overtime it took to keep them from getting behind and maybe put a little away for college, or maybe buy a piano, or maybe a used clarinet in a green hardshell case, or maybe some first-rate catcher's gear, even though the boy would outgrow it after a season's use—a chest protector, shin guards with the extra flaps to cover the knees, a good catcher's helmet with a throwaway facemask to facilitate fly ball chasing.

Do you know why your mother drives that school bus? and how could he tell the boy, anyway, about how everything could be changed in the space of one year, from the comfort and the relative peace and security of Palm Beach High, to the snakepit, the nightmare pit of vipers he had been thrown into his senior year of high school.

Their next door neighbor, Raul, who was a Cuban Pentecostal, liked to hunt snakes and chop them into twentysome-odd pieces with his shovel, then scoop the parts up and throw them out onto the empty lot where Sandra parked the school bus. "I hate the snake for who he represents," Raul liked to say, and Wayne would bring his hose over, and they would stand between their houses and spray-wash the blood off the shovelhead—Raul's shovel, usually, but sometimes Wayne's. And how they laughed when they learned that a sprinkling of sulphur in the bushes in front of the house, and some around the perimeter, would keep the snakes away altogether.

That would be important, to talk to the boy about Raul and Raul's family and how Wayne and Sandra admired them. And Wayne *did* admire them, admired almost every Cuban he had ever met. *Those people*, he liked to say, *came over on a raft*, and when he said it, he was speaking not of rattiness, but of a courage and an ingenuity and an intelligence he could hardly imagine possible. Raul was an automobile mechanic for the Palm Beach County Sheriff's Department, but fixing cop cars busted-up from high-speed chases was nothing, really, compared to the feat that had sped him to Miami. Raul and his brothers, the story went, had raised the chassis of a green 1949 Studebaker truck up onto eight buoyant casks, and lashed the casks together with hand-made ropes, and attached an outboard motor to the gas pedal, and a rudder to the steering wheel—had driven a truckboat of their own making across the Atlantic Ocean, so they could make their way to Florida, to the house next door to Wayne's, and paint the brick facade fire engine red, and paint the *faux* grout between the bricks a bright white. Raul's house looked like a fire station, and Raul's paint job would probably cost Wayne seven or eight thousand dollars when it came time to sell his, and yet, he wanted to tell his son, he could forgive it, because Raul was a great man. Look at what Raul had made of his life!

Yes, the story of Raul, and Wayne's admiration for Raul, would be necessary. The boy would need to know it, because now Wayne needed to tell him about how they were zoned for West Riviera Elementary, a half-hour bus ride away, in the poorest neighborhood in the eastern part of Palm Beach County, in, yes, a black neighborhood. "I don't have anything against black people," he heard himself saying, "not all of them," and he knew how it might sound, but he was trying to say how it was a certain kind of black person, somebody who doesn't want to work for a living— "Shucking and jiving is what they call it," and he knew how that might sound, too, but all the same he remembered what it felt like to fear going to school, to witness those knife fights, and, once, to see, close up, a knife plunging into the meat of somebody's leg, so—"Poverty," he was saying, "is a thing it's very hard to escape," and, "Cycles," he was saying, the ways the patterns of people's upbringings are imprinted upon them, and what force of will it must take to change your whole way of acting in the world, or to make choices different from the choices your parents had made . . .

"Your mother drives the school bus," he said, "because it gets us twenty-five percent off your tuition, and that's the only way we can afford to send you to that school."

They were driving, now, up Okeechobee, toward Barney's convenience store near Skees Road, in the white conversion van Wayne used for service calls. The boy was slumped in the front seat, looking out the window.

"Ronny, buddy," Wayne said. "I'm your pal, right?"

More silence.

"We used to talk all the time, you and me," Wayne said. "We used to talk about everything."

Nothing.

They stopped at Barney's, and Wayne parked at pump three, and went inside to get the milk and prepaid eleven dollars and paid for the milk in cash and put the gas on the company card. Outside, he began to pump the gas, and the boy rolled the window down and watched the numbers roll and began to count with the one-tenth gallon meter: "*Eins, zwei, drei, vier, fünf, sechs, sieben, acht, neun, zehn, eins, zwei, drei, vier, fünf, sechs, sieben, acht, neun, zehn, eins, zwei, drei, vier, fünf, sechs, sieben, acht . . .*"

Then the boy began to count faster than the meter was running. He was shouting. The people at the other pumps were looking at them. "Buddy, buddy," Wayne said, his hand still on the pump. "Ronny! Stop!" Wayne shouted. Still, the boy raised his voiced louder and louder, until it began to crack and break. Wayne stopped pumping the gas. He opened the passenger door and grabbed the boy's shoulder with both hands. As soon as he touched the boy, the boy's body slumped toward him, and he began not to cry but to weep. Big, huge, snotty sobs he was weeping, and tears and snot all over the front of Wayne's shirt, and Wayne thought, *This isn't about the school bus.*

❂

The boy was not the problem, Else decided. Ratliff was the problem. The father was a problem, but Ratliff was the bigger problem. The father would go into the office and complain about her, and complain about the calisthenics (as though the boy were not too fleshy; as though the boy did not lose his breath at recess the few times he ran with the other boys rather than prancing about with the girls), and complain that she made them to count in German when they did the calisthenics (typical), and complain about the catechism (as though the boy did not need the moral instruction; as though the boy did not need the mental discipline, the rigor), and complain that she made the boy clean his shoes with the yellow miniature broom and dustpan set (as though the boy would not otherwise track the dirt and the wet and the grass clippings into her classroom.)

The father would complain, and Ratliff would tell him whatever Ratliff told him, and the concessions grew and grew, and now this boy had a laminated permanent blue hall pass with Ratliff's office typed on the line above where it said *Destination*, and Ratliff had told him he could use this blue pass anytime he so desired, and furthermore Ratliff had instructed her to allow the boy to leave her classroom at any time of the day, that if the boy showed her the pass, she was to let him leave her classroom and go visit with Ratliff, and tell him whatever it was that the boy told him.

Now the boy was waving the blue pass in her face again, and she said, "We are reciting the catechism. You will sit down and finish reciting the catechism. You will sit down now."

The boy cried at the drop of a hat. The boy cried at everything. What was wrong with this boy? The boy was saying Mr. Ratliff's name, Mr. Ratliff said, Mr. Ratliff said, and she was aware of the eyes of all the other pupils on her and on the boy, and she knew she should not grab him by the ear like she would have done in Berlin, and like she ought to be able to do now. It would be a gift to the boy, to grab him by the ear and give him the pain of it to think about instead of the crying, the babbling, the scene he was making. If she grabbed him by the ear, the pain of it would dry him up, and then he could follow her outside the classroom with at least some measure of dignity, instead of this melting down that shamed him and shamed his classmates, and she did not want to think about how it right at this moment shamed her, to be in the presence of all this unrestrained emotion and not do the thing that was in her power to do about it, which would be to take the hard cartilage of his outer ear between her gloved thumb and forefinger, and silence him, and pull him silent outside the classroom, and show him the red tally, and ask him if this was what he wanted, another red tally, another trip to Mrs. Millet's, another paddling?

Instead, she took the pass from him. "This is a hall pass," she said, "not a license for poor behavior." She held it up for the rest of the class. "Do you wish for our school days to be disrupted for the sake of a hall pass?" She looked at the boy. "You should hang your head," she said. "You should hang your head low, and you should apologize to the other pupils for disrupting our recitation of the catechism."

She took her good scissors and cut the hall pass in half and dropped the two pieces in the wastebasket beside her desk. "Cease your crying and act like a young man. Sit down in your seat and join the work the rest of us are doing."

The boy went back to his seat. "From the beginning," she said: Who made you? *God made me.* What else did God make? *God made all things.* Why did God make you and all things? *God made me and all things for His own glory.* Who made God? *Nobody made God.* Has God ever had a beginning? *No, God has always been.* Will God ever die? *No, God lives forever.*

There was a rustling. The boy was standing from his seat. "Have a seat, Mr. Adams," she said, but now he was walking toward the door. "Mr. Adams, have a seat this instant!"

His back was to her. He was not crying anymore, but neither was he responding in any way to her command. The other children were watching.

She began to walk toward him. He walked faster toward the door and opened the door, and she had almost caught up to him by time he opened the door. She reached for the door, and he pushed at it, and it slammed against the wall next to the air conditioning compressor. There was a jarring in her stomach that coincided with the slamming of the door against the wall. She felt a heat rise within her. She grabbed the boy by both of his arms and slammed him against the air conditioning compressor. His arms were sticks.

He looked up at her. She could see herself reflected in his glasses. She could see her lipstick and her pearls and the lines in her face. His pupils widened. "Who do you think you are that you might put yourself and your emotions above all the other pupils in our classroom?" she said. "Who raised you to behave in this way?"

The boy parted his lips as if to respond, and she felt her hands tightening around his arms, and pressing him harder against the air conditioning compressor, and she could hear the hum of the compressor and its vibrations through his arms. "I know you," she heard herself saying, as though her voice was coming from outside herself, though she could feel the words forming on her lips, and knew that the words were coming not from outside her, but rather from the deepest, innermost parts of her own self, that she was giving voice to things she had wanted to say to many other boys, in this place and in other places as well, and, yes, to this boy, to this boy especially. This boy brought it out in her like none of the other boys ever had. "I've known you all my life. You are a very stupid boy. You are a very weak boy. And never will you be anything, Ronald Adams. Never, ever.

"Measure my words," she said. "I've lived under the Nazis, and I've lived under the Communists in East Germany, and now I suffer a hundred indignities in the godless West, and still I'm proud to be an American, but not when I see your messy desk, your crayons and pencils and erasers I say in disarray, I say in a state of shame like what you bring me, like what you bring my classroom, your classmates. A state of shame like what you bring yourself.

"You are and never have been any good that I can tell, and surely God does not love a child like you must be."

The high school bell rang, and the classroom doors opened across the grass strip that separated her building from the high school building. She let go her grip on his arms, and the boy slumped forward against her, as though he thought she would catch him. She feared he would fall onto the sidewalk. She was aware that there would be eyes on her, from across the grass. She opened her arms and caught him, and the weight of him was against her as though they were embracing, and he had not properly applied his deodorant, she could tell by the feral smell of him. The grease of his hair touched her cheek.

She pushed against him to stand him up, and she said, quietly, "Go into the classroom and sit down at your desk. We shall finish the catechism now."

Who is God? *God is a spirit and does not have a body like man.* Where is God? *God is everywhere.* Can you see God? *No, I cannot see God, but He always sees me.* Does God know all things? *Yes, nothing can be hidden from God.*

✤

"Do you know what a capon is?" Wayne said. He was standing, now, pacing. The boy was in his bedroom. He had chased Sandra around the house with a butter knife before it occurred to her that he was a very small boy, and that the knife was just a butter knife and she could just grab the dull blade and pull it away from him. Now she was sitting on the couch, looking up at Wayne, letting Wayne lecture, which he knew she didn't like, but he was angry and could not help himself.

"A capon," Wayne said, "is a rooster with his balls cut off. Their heads stop growing, and their tail feathers get long. You can see them preening around in the yard like fairy queens, but they won't fight.

"Leslie Ratliff," Wayne said, "is a capon, a Grade A capon."

"Wayne," Sandra said.

"Do you know what I would do," Wayne said, "if somebody worked for me, and I told them not to do something, and they kept doing it?"

"You'd fire them," Sandra said.

"I'd fire them," Wayne said. "Doggone right I'd fire them. I wouldn't give it a second thought, either." *Shit*, he almost said. He cursed to himself at work sometimes, and once the sheet metal guy they called Catfish heard him and raised an eyebrow, because they all thought Wayne was the last guy to curse, so he had been careful not to curse in front of anyone at work after that, and certainly he wouldn't curse in front of Sandra. He didn't like it when other people cursed, anyway, although he had to hear it all day at the job sites.

✹

Her aunt could not feed herself any longer. The Americans put their old and infirm in homes to suffer a thousand indignities at the hands of strangers. To Else it was reminiscent of the bad days during the war and after, when inconvenient people would disappear. She worried one day she would come home and find her aunt dead in her bed. This was a selfish thought, she knew. To be absent from the body was to be present with God. But Else herself was old, and she would never live with anyone who had loved her after her aunt was gone. Already she sat alone on the third row at the Lutheran church. No one would sit beside her. The younger people dressed differently than she did, and the older people were clannish, did not invite her to their parties.

Not so long ago, there were sweet evenings to be had with her aunt. Else would climb into the bed beside her and read to her from the Psalms, in the old language. Her aunt no longer told her the old family stories, but sitting beside her in the bed, their bodies warm, the space between her aunt's leg and hers warm with the heat the covers conserved, she could imagine her aunt telling again about Klaus, her aunt's grandfather and her own great-grandfather, and how as a very young man he had been swindled into believing that he had an inheritance in Vienna, and how he had traveled there by carriage, and found that there was no one there to receive him, and there was no inheritance, and how a tailor had found him wandering the streets in the evening, and had taken him home. "And there he met your grandmother," her aunt would say, and there would be talk of their courtship in the house, of the morning he woke to find himself sewn into the bed and knew that the tailor had realized the feelings developing between Klaus and his daughter.

This afternoon, Else came home and found her aunt moaning in the bed. There was a rancid smell in the room. She pulled back the bedsheets and found them streaked with excrement. Her aunt was soaked in urine and her gown was brown- and black-stained from the small of her back to the back of her knees.

The neighbor was supposed to check in at ten and two, change her aunt's diaper and give her water. Where was the neighbor?

There would be no touching her aunt without getting covered, herself, in the filth. Else took off her gloves, her pearls, her shoes. Then her hose, her dress, her bra and panties. She put on her swimsuit, it could be washed. She whispered comforting words to her aunt, and pulled off her gown, and undid the diaper. With the clean part of the top-sheet, she did what she could to wipe away some of the filth from her aunt's body, but her aunt was still soilslick when Else lifted her and carried her to the bathtub.

Else stepped into the tub behind her aunt, holding her with one arm beneath both her aunt's armpits. She took down the spray nozzle from where it rested by the showerhead, and turned on the water. She tried to make it warm enough.

✣

After school, Wayne took the boy to McDonald's. "Anything you want, buddy," he said. "You like the onion rings, right? You always liked the onion rings."

After McDonald's, he took him to a four o'clock matinee, *Crocodile Dundee*. Then Baskin Robbins, mint chocolate chip in two waffle cones.

"Sometimes I get angry," Wayne said. "You ever get angry?"

Ronny kept eating his ice cream, but gave a slight nod.

"I'm plenty angry," Wayne said. "I'm angry with your teacher. I'm angry with your principal. Look at me. I'm not angry at you."

The boy looked up at him and kept eating. His eyes were green.

"Never with you. You hear?"

The boy stopped eating. Nodded again.

"I feel, son, like I've been lied to. Your teacher tells your principal things about you that can't possibly be true, and he tells them to me. Ratliff tells me all year to wait, that he's going to work on some things, that things are going to work themselves out. Nothing ever happens. Things are supposed to be getting better. Are things getting better?"

The boy nodded again. "Yes," he said. Wayne had the feeling he was saying what he was supposed to say, and *that pisses me the hell off!* She had broken the boy like a horse, had broken the boy's spirit. His boy. *My boy.*

What he had to say now, he was going to have to be delicate about it. "I don't think it's right to lie. That's what I taught you, right?"

"That's right," the boy said.

"Most of the time it's not right to lie," Wayne said. "Ninety-nine point nine nine percent of the time it's not right."

The boy was very still.

"But here we got a problem," Wayne said, "and I don't know what do about it exactly. We got a problem like they had in the old days, when the saying was an eye for an eye and a tooth for a tooth. We got some people with a lot of fight who aren't willing to have a fair fight, and I'm thinking about the American Indian. Do you know about the American Indian?"

The boy was nodding.

"You got your white man with his muskets," Wayne said. "You got your redcoats, and then you got your regular Americans. They got guns, they got gunpowder. You learn about this in history. Guns and gunpowder, and all the Indians got is bows and arrows, and maybe the British and the regular Americans have cannons, too.

"So what's the smart Indian gonna do? March into battle head-on, with their bow and arrow and get blown away?"

No, the boy was saying.

"No is right. The Indian is smart, or at least he's smart enough to want to stay alive. So he's gotta change the rules of the warfare. He's gotta hide in the bushes, and wait until the white man is passing, and then jump out and brain him with a rock, and then be gone before anybody has presence of mind enough to shoot at him.

"To the white man it's cheating," Wayne said, "but to the Indian it's doing what you have to do to survive. Do you get what I'm saying?"

Yes, the boy was saying.

"So here we are at the end of our rope," Wayne said. "We're at the edge of the cliff with our backs against the wall. So my question for you is this. What is it you could say to Mr. Ratliff that would get her the way she got you? Get her and get her good?"

This was the part he did not want to articulate. What he had in mind was a sexual indiscretion of some sort. The creepy old lady touched me with her white gloves. The creepy old lady invited me out behind the bleachers for some show and tell. Something along those lines. Something horrible. He wondered did the boy have enough experience in the world to know what it was that a child could say and put an end to an adult.

"Do you know," Wayne said, "what thing you could say?"

The boy nodded his head. He did not smile. He nodded up and down and up and down again.

V

March 13, 1987

Ronny's feet had been hurting him. Growing pains, his father said. Natural. You'll get them other places, too.

Yesterday, in Principal Ratliff's office, his feet hurt badly enough that he took off his shoes—his black uniform penny loafers—and rubbed his thumbs into the socked arches of his feet. "Do your feet hurt?" Ratliff said. Yes, Ronny said, more and more.

Ratliff told him he had flat feet. "From my mother's side," he said. "My mother's father. It's a terrible thing. Sometimes"—and here he lowered his voice to a confiding whisper—"when nobody's in the office except for me, I take off my shoes and rub the arches of my feet the same way you're doing. And I have these."

He reached under the desk and pulled off his shoe and lifted it above the desk where Ronny could see it, then reached inside and took out a blue support insert. "Gel," he said. "You want to feel it?"

Yes, Ronny said. Ratliff handed over the shoe insert, and Ronny pressed on the gel. It was pleasingly squishy, gave under his fingers and then pushed back. He squeezed it some more, then handed it back to Ratliff.

"Hold out your hand," the principal said, and took his pump bottle of hand sanitizer and pumped two drops onto Ronny's palm. The drops were cool and smelled like medicine.

Now, Miss Richter counting off the jumping jacks— *Eins, zwei, drei, vier, fünf, sechs, sieben, acht . . .*—the pain began to travel up from the arches of his feet, up through his calves, into his back, his shoulders, his neck. The pain in his feet was the worst of it. The rest was like an electrical storm. Once on television he had seen an airplane flying through black clouds, and when the lightning discharged from cloud to cloud, it struck the airplane, and the plane crashed into the Atlantic Ocean.

He gritted his teeth, to bear it, through the deep knee bends, the toe touches, the high kicks, the reach ups. He tried to roll his foot through the catechism recitation. Ben Brill misspoke toward the end of the plants and animals section, and Miss Richter made him stand up front, facing the class, as they started over from the beginning.

When finally they sat down, Miss Richter began to work through the fractions she had chalked on the board. There was a series of exercises, there were equation worksheets. Two and two cancelled, and two and four cancelled down to one and two. This math appealed to Ronny, but he did not know he could get through the morning without rubbing his feet.

He thought of Mr. Ratliff, kicking off his shoes beneath the desk, when no one was looking. Mrs. Richter's back was to them, her hands on the chalk, her mouth talking.

Ronny slid his feet out of his penny loafers. He put his hand beneath the desk and rubbed his left arch. Then he rubbed his right.

Mrs. Richter took the long wooden pointer she used to compare the distorted Greenland of the Mercator Projection with the right-sized Greenland on the map that looked like a fancy orange peel dissection, and she leaned forward and brought the tip of the pointer to within a few inches of Ronny's big toe.

"Why are your hands beneath your desk, Mr. Adams?" she said.

The class tittered nervously. Ronny would have tittered, too, if it wasn't him being embarrassed.

"Where are your shoes, Mr. Adams?" she said.

Of course she could see his shoes. They were next to his feet.

"Does our classroom seem to you much like your living room, Mr. Adams?" she said.

It did not, but it would not do him good to say so.

"It seems to me, Mr. Adams, that you are Out of Order, and that you are Lacking Courtesy."

What this meant was that he was to rise from his seat and walk over to the bulletin board where the tallies were kept, and to pull out an orange cardboard tally—Out of Order—and a dark blue tally—Courtesy Lacking—and to place them in the construction paper pocket that had his name on it.

He stood up and took a step, but realized that he did not have his shoe on, so he put his toe in his shoe, but he was nervous. She was watching, and the rest of the class was watching. He put his toe in his shoe, but when he slid it in, his toe got twisted around. He overcompensated for the twisting, and he tripped over himself and banged his arm on Jill Lewis's desk beside him, and probably hit her elbow, too, because she said, "Ow!"

He sat down on the floor and put both his shoes on. When he looked up, Miss Richter was smiling down at him meanly. She pointed at her watch. "So far, Mr. Adams," she said, "you have wasted ninety seconds of valuable class time."

He stood up and went over to the Tally Board, and got his orange tally and his dark blue tally and put them in the pocket with his name. Then he walked back to his seat, in front of the rows of his classmates. The Walk of Shame, was how he thought of it.

Miss Richter dug around in the top drawer of her desk, and she pulled out a purple sheet of stickers. She showed them to the class. There were stickers of various body parts—hands, feet, legs, arms, eyes, noses, ears, mouths—as well as stethoscopes, tools for looking into ears and noses, syringes, reflex triangles.

"Which sticker has Mr. Adams earned today?" she asked the class.

Jill Lewis volunteered it was the feet.

"I do think so," Miss Richter said. She took the purple sticker shaped like feet from the sticker sheet, and she affixed the purple feet to the top of Ronny's desk. They were long, skinny, ugly feet. Ronny's feet didn't look like the purple feet.

"We shall leave these feet here for the span of a week," Miss Richter said, "provided you can find a way to keep your shoes on." She turned to the class and smiled again. "For the sake of all of us."

His feet did not hurt any less, but he dared not touch them. He thought of going to see Mr. Ratliff, but it was almost time for lunch, and the afternoon was when it got the worst. Mr. Ratliff had said that more than once a day was probably too often to visit his office.

All through lunch, Ronny thought of the sticker, the purple feet. He saw Miss Richter, one table over, listening to Jill Lewis and Mary Swenson talk, and he saw that Miss Richter's smile was truly pleasant. She never had a smile like that smile for him. She saved those smiles for the girls, and not all the girls, just certain girls.

Across from him, Trey Benioff was mixing chocolate milk into his chicken soup and asking who would like to drink it, who would dare? Across the cafeteria, Mr. Ratliff was chatting with one of the cafeteria ladies. He looked down to see if Mr. Ratliff had taken off his shoes, but he could not see his feet past all the rows of tables and all the fourth, fifth, and sixth graders that sat at them.

After lunch, American history. Presidents. *Blaine, Blaine, James G. Blaine, Continental Liar from the State of Maine,* and, *Ma, Ma, Where's My Pa? Off to the White House, Ha, Ha, Ha.*

The circumstances surrounding all these occurrences, Miss Richter said, were very much in doubt, because politics was an ugly and ungodly business, and fallen man is prone to lying. Ronny was thinking of the catechism: Where is God? *God is everywhere.* Can you see God? *No, I cannot see God, but He always sees me.* Does God know all things? *Yes, nothing can be hidden from God.* And what had got mingled in his head with the catechism, in the voice that delivered it: *Surely God does not love a child like you must be.*

But surely God did. Surely what she had said to him was a lie. At home, he had opened his Bible to a random page, as was his habit, and let God guide his finger to whatever verse God meant for him to hear from. His finger had fallen on Ezekiel 27:26. *Your rowers have brought you out into great and deep waters; the east wind has broken and wrecked you in the heart of the seas.*

This must be the message God had for him about Miss Richter. She was like a boat, and her actions had rowed her out into the middle of the sea, and when she was wrecked there it would be because of the things she had done to others. She was old. She had been doing what she did for a long time.

He worried, though, that he might not have interpreted the verse the right way. Six times a year the high school journalism class came around to sell the school newspaper for twenty-five cents, and almost everyone bought a copy. If he knew it was newspaper day, Ronny would do without ice cream at lunch so he would have his twenty-five cents. And once almost every year, the newspaper would run a front page story about Miss Richter. COLD WAR HERO, the headline would read, or, TEACHER ESCAPED IRON CURTAIN, or, MIRACLE IN OUR MIDST. There would be a map of East Berlin on page four, a picture of the small bald place where a bullet had grazed and scarred her head on page five.

What if Ezekiel's great and deep waters had something to do with Miss Richter swimming that German river? Maybe it meant that it was Ronny who would be wrecked in the middle of the waters. He wasn't sure how it could mean that, but God's ways are not our own, and he had found many parts of the Bible to be confusing when he tried to read it.

"Perhaps you can tell us the answer, Mr. Adams," Miss Richter was saying, but Ronny had not heard the question. The learning had led him inside himself, one thing leading to another thing, each of them farther removed from what was happening outside himself. This happened almost every day.

She sent him to the Tally Board, Courtesy Lacking, because it was not courteous to daydream while the rest of the class was studying. School was for learning. Daydream was a kind of play.

"Count the tallies, Mr. Adams," she said, as he put the dark blue one into the pocket with his name on it. He did not have to count to know that the dark blue tally was his fifth for the day. At her lectern, Miss Richter was already filling out the discipline report and the hall pass to Mrs. Millet's, for swats. She held it out to him. "You will go directly there," she said, "and when you are done, you will come directly back."

He went out the door and counted the air conditioning compressors his father had installed, one for each classroom.

The school maintenance men painted them yellow, the same color as the walls. They looked like giant frogs.

There was a line in Mrs. Millet's office, three sixth graders ahead of him. It smelled of Lysol in the waiting room. The way the smell made him feel was worse than the way the swats would make him feel. The anticipation. Fat Mrs. Millet, and her wall of spanking shoes. "Pick a shoe," she would say. Sometimes when he went to someone's house with his mother and the house smelled like Lysol, he would get the Mrs. Millet feeling, even though she wasn't around.

One of the sixth graders said, "I don't care if she hits me twenty times. It's nothing to me."

From behind the door, Mrs. Millet's voice boomed: "There should be no talking among those children who might be waiting."

The sixth grader went silent. His color flushed.

Ronny waited. He took off his shoes and rubbed his arches through his socks. He listened to the sixth graders get their lectures and their swats. One of them came out crying. Ronny put his fingers inside his socks and rubbed his arches with his bare fingers.

When it was his turn, Mrs. Millet called for him, and he went inside and handed her the discipline report and the hall pass. "Ronny, why do we keep seeing so much of each other?" Mrs. Millet said, not for the first time.

Ronny trembled, and not on purpose. "After you paddle me," he said, "I have something important to tell you."

Mrs. Millet leaned forward. "If it's so important, why wait?" she said.

"I'm scared of what I have to tell you," he said, and this was true.

"Is it the truth?" she said. "Because you don't ever have to be scared of the truth."

"Yes," he said, in a small voice.

She softened her voice, too. "Go ahead and tell me now," she said.

"Miss Richter?" he said. "After lunch? She took the Lord's name in vain."

Mrs. Millet's eyes narrowed. "Are you sure?" she said. "Because this is a very serious charge you're making, Ronny. Do you understand how serious it is, what you're telling me?"

"It was my desk," he said. "I didn't put my pencils away in my zip bag, and I didn't use my broom on my shoes."

"What did she say, Ronny?" Mrs. Millet said. "I need to know exactly what words she said."

"She said G. D.," Ronny said. "I don't want to say it."

"She just said G. D.?" Mrs. Millet said. "Just that word? That's all?"

"She said, 'I grow weary of your mess,'" Ronny said. "'Now straighten this G. D. desk.'"

Mrs. Millet looked him over. "You're sure, Ronny," she said. "You're sure?"

"Please don't make me say it again," Ronny said, and meant it.

VI

Now

For awhile, after I learned to drive, I would see her, or would think I saw her, at stoplights, and once for sure at a railroad crossing. She sat erect in the driver's seat, her white gloves at ten o'clock and two o'clock. She was wearing a white dress that looked for all the world like the white dresses she wore nearly every day when she was my teacher. She still wore the same faux pearl necklace, or maybe the pearls were real pearls.

For many years I would dream about her standing over me, pressing me against the yellow air conditioning compressor, her fingers digging into my arms, those white gloves. My wife Mary, when we were still together, would complain at how often I woke her in the night with my noises and thrashing about, but the truth is that most nights, if I was dreaming, I did not remember my dreams, and the ones I did remember, the bad ones, weren't usually about Miss Else Richter. There was a flattened-out quality to the dreams I had about her, as though the dreams themselves were held away from me by my own long arms.

My father went back to college my junior year of high school—night college, a business degree, business management. He got out of the air conditioning business and into retail construction. He supervised build-outs for a chain of bagel stores. He worked longer hours, and he traveled more. He became as good with people as he had been good with machines, and it seemed to me that he grew into a more fully realized version of himself, although he still carried many things he must have taken on in childhood. When his mother died, he went alone to the funeral and forbade us to join him. When I asked him about what it was like to go to his mother's funeral, he said that he spent most of the time thinking about his brother Davis, and wondering if he still ran around wearing shoes with no socks, and then, at the graveside, Davis knelt down to throw some dirt on the grave, and his pant leg separated a little from his shoes, and, sure enough, he wasn't wearing any socks.

Lately I've been getting into the Internet. You can find anything you like there, if you know where to look. You can find old girlfriends, and you can do a search for your own name and see if you've made enough of a mark on the world that anyone wants to write it down. I have done these things, and the results have disappointed me in many ways. Most of my old girlfriends don't use the Internet, and the ones who do are less attractive and more happily married than I might have expected. No one has written much about me, except at the property records database, in Palm Beach County, Florida, where I still own and rent out the condominium unit in Jupiter where I used to live with Mary, in addition to the house I live in now.

Secrets rise to the surface when you begin to search property records databases. My father, I learned, owns seven rental properties in West Riviera Beach, a part of town he did his darndest to hold as far from our family as possible all the years I was growing up. I imagine him to be an absentee landlord, not one who doesn't fix things, but one who doesn't fix them himself. Surely he knows somebody from the days when he was the person people sent to fix things, somebody honest and good and reliable, and maybe he pays them what he believes to be the fair wage, or maybe he has found a way to trade them for something they want.

Another mystery: My father's brother Davis is entirely absent from the property records, which is curious to me, because I know for a fact he owns large swaths of property in Lake Worth, on Palm Beach, in Boynton Beach, in Manalapan. The addresses for the tracts of land I know him to own are missing from the databases as well.

When I was done searching the names of all the members of my family, my college roommates, our Congressmen and state representatives, the county commissioners and the school board, my favorite columnists at *The Palm Beach Post*, and all the people at work, it occurred to me to type Else Richter's name into the property search. The address it returned was unfamiliar to me, a street name I had never seen or heard before, and a unit number.

It was hard to imagine she could still be alive. She was old, already, when I knew her. By now, she should be in her late eighties, or maybe her nineties.

The street address mapped to a cul-de-sac in Lake Worth, and I was pretty sure, looking at it on the computer screen, that what I was seeing was a nursing home or an assisted care facility of some kind. I wondered who she would have in her life who could pay for it. Certainly my school did not compensate their teachers well in those days, and after she was asked to leave our school, where did she go? What became of her? Did she teach again, and if so, where? Who would hire a woman as old and as freighted as she must have been?

I turned off the computer. I tried not to think about her. Whenever I spoke of her to Mary, I said that she escaped from East Berlin, made her daring rescue, her hero's journey three times across the River Spree, so that she could make her way to West Palm Beach, Florida, and ruin the lives of fifth grade boys. But I did not tell Mary that this was not the whole of the story.

A few times I drove by the building in Lake Worth. It is a nondescript building finished out in stucco, three stories tall, which is quite tall for that part of town, and painted a muted yellow. I saw no sign out front advertising what kind of place it might be, inside.

Finally I screwed up my courage, and parked in an open space near the building, and went through the automatic doors. There was a reception desk directly ahead. A sharply dressed woman said, "Can I help you?"

"I'm here to see Else Richter," I said.

The woman ran her index finger down a list of names. "Unit 234B, if that helps," I said.

"It does help," she said, and turned the page. When her finger found 234B, she looked up and said, "I'm sorry, sir. That unit has been vacant for some time, and it has been privately sold."

"Did she move?" I said. "Did she leave a forwarding address?"

"I'm sorry, sir," the woman said. "That unit has been vacant for some time."

"The woman who was living there," I said. "Else Richter. Did she die?"

"I'm very sorry, sir," the woman said, her voice hardening. "I've told you all I can tell you about that unit."

I searched the paper, but there was no obituary. I searched the property records again, but there was no record of a sale, and the property was still listed under her name. I searched the cemetery rolls, but no one had a record of any Else Richter. I found the name of the company that owned the assisted care facility where she had once owned Unit 234B, and told the woman who answered the phone that I was searching for my beloved aunt, Else Richter, and she said she would call me back, and she did, with apologies: The record was incomplete. The company is very large, multinational, frequent changes of ownership and so on. Mistakes were made long ago. It is someone else's fault. We can't be held responsible, but we are very sorry.

Acknowledgments

Thanks to Doug Watson, Bart Skarzynski, Joe Oestreich, Luke Renner, Joshua Archer, and Okla Elliott, for partnerships in various ongoing crimes.

To Lee Abbott, Michelle Herman, Lee Martin, and Erin McGraw, for teaching me how to build things meant to last.

To Don Pollock, for friendship most of all, and for a thousand kindnesses.

To Steve Gillis and Dan Wickett, for many years of friendship and kind encouragement, and for making this book possible.

To Sonia Pabley, for making many things possible.

To Laura and Pinckney Benedict, for almost daily encouragement, and for abiding friendship. I hope to be like you when I grow up.

To Jane Bradley, Tim Geiger, Rane Arroyo, and Sara Lundquist, colleagues and friends.

To Ben, Paige, Jim, Jessica, Michael, and Ellen, for being family when we didn't have one in our new town.

To Brad, for helping me see that another kind of life was within reach.

To my parents, for indulging two errant and incomprehensible children.

To Andrew Hudgins, David Baker, Kathy Fagan, Bill Roorbach, Will Bowers, Dave Baird, Jon Saari, Gary Brummitt, Angie Estes, Nancy Zafris, L. Spencer Spaulding, Lori Worrell, C. Michael Curtis, Ellen Voight, Willard Reed, and John Edgar Wideman, helpful teachers.

To the memory of Lou Adiano, 12th grade English teacher and patient friend.

To Chris, Ernie, and Slash, lifelong friends.

To Ben Percy, Mike Lohre, Frank Schaeffer, and Chris Coake, heroes.

To David Summers, Kevin Griffith, Alex Steele, Jim Malarkey, Joe Cronin, and Jason Roe, for giving me the comfort of steady work when I needed it most.

To Otto Penzler, George Pelecanos, Matt Kellogg, and Jillian Quint, for helping me find readers.

To Mark Drew, Kim Dana Kupperman, Peter Stitt, Bret Lott, Valerie Vogrin, Allison Funk, Laura van den Berg, Elizabeth Kotin, Mike Czyzniejewski, Karen Craigo, Karen Babine, David Bowen, Phil Deaver, Stephen Elliott, Joshuah Bearman, Joe Mackall, Keith Hood, Molly Westerman, Jennifer Glaser, Megan Fishmann, Jen Town, Molly Westerman, Sheryl Monks, Kevin Morgan Watson, Nicole Walker, Mary Gaitskill, Bill Eichenberger, Kacey Kowars, Kevin Prufer, Chad Simpson, Rodney Jones, Jason Gray, Sonya Huber, Kristin Bullock, Bonita Yinger, Lawrence Weschler, Claudia Curry, Joel Thomas, Jen Hamilton-Emery, Oronte Churm, Bryan Gaines, Scott Cantrell, Dana Eaton, Greg McCaw, Roy Kesey, Steve Davenport, Geoff Schmidt, Deb Martin, Jeff Parker, Jillian Wiese, Lana Santoni, Shari Goldhagen, Rebecca Barry, Chris Higgs, Charlie Metcalf, Colleen Kinder, Danielle Lavaque-Manty, Daniel Menaker, Steven Seighman, Lauren Snyder, Jeff Bruce, John Warner, Mary Beth Ellis, Jess Lacher, Deb Schwartz, Buddy Kite, John Chovan, Clay Housholder, Kim Brauer, Bryan Hurt, Jenny Patton, Alexandra Machinist, Amanda Elgin, Nita Sweeney, Stephanie Pharr, Kristin Watson Heintz, Mike Magnuson, Chris Offutt, Paul Prather, Liz Mandrell, Jennifer Spiegel, Rob and Debbie Cope, Cindy Gaillard, Miriam Berkley, Kate Nitze, Gary Fincke, Kathleen Gagel,

Christopher Griffin, Jon Trick, Kim Thompson, J. Dillon Woods, Katrina Denza, Jason Gray, Pablo Tanguay, Diana Raab, Ron Hogan, Jon McDivitt, Dan Parson (wherever you are), Dean Wilson and the U.S. 2007 crew, the Simmons and Stowe families, Kate Oestreich, Kristi McFarland, Ed Falco, Keith Pait, Thomas Kennedy, Duff Brenna, Rebecca Kanner, Peter Selgin, the Office of the Palm Beach County Clerk of the Court, Zachary Trent, and Mary Huebner, for many varieties of help and kindness during the writing of this book.

To Jenny Conrad, for trailblazing.

To Frederick Taylor, for his book *The Berlin Wall: A World Divided, 1961-1989*, which was of invaluable assistance in bringing verisimilitude to Else Richter's story.

To Letitia Trent, Maureen Traverse, Michelle Burke, Natalie Shapero, Tom Pruiksma, Nick Scorza, Scott Black, Jolie Lewis, Ida Stewart, Jay Cook, and David McGlynn, friends and helpful readers.

To the fond memory of Bill Whittler, my first teacher in the liar's art.

Most of all, to Debbie, Ian, and Dylan, my loves.